The Viscount's Vixen

by

JoMarie DeGioia

PUBLISHED BY:

Bailey Park Publishing

The Viscount's Vixen

Book Two of the
Bridgewater Brides Series

by

JoMarie DeGioia

England 1824

Chapter 1

Michael Reed, Viscount Balsam, stood in the cavernous great hall of his ancestral home in Cornwall. It was late spring and still the walls seemed damp, the rooms cold. He crossed to the massive fireplace set deep into one high stone wall and held his hands out to the welcome warmth issuing from the roaring fire behind the grate.

"My lord?" his butler, Coombs, called from the entryway.

"Yes, Coombs?" Michael asked wearily. "What is it?"

"Several papers have arrived for you, my lord," he answered. "Along with several correspondence."

Michael cursed softly, knowing with absolute certainty the papers could only be from his solicitors in London. It was no doubt bad news.

"Take the papers into my study, Coombs."

"Very well, Lord Balsam."

When he was again alone, he turned back to the fire. Upon his father's passing the previous year, Michael had learned to his great surprise that the man's frugality was due more to necessity than to a quirk of his disposition or his hearty Cornish will.

Although Michael instructed his solicitors to investigate thoroughly the mess his father had left behind him, no additional funds were located save for the stipend paid to him each quarter. While it afforded him a comfortable style of living, he could ill-afford the repairs the great manor sorely needed.

Michael was only twenty-five years, and vastly relieved that he was far from the age to start thinking about getting married. If what he'd learned last week was true, and he had no reason to believe it wasn't or that the papers awaiting him in his study wouldn't bear it out, then he wouldn't be in any position to repair his estate let alone bring some unsuspecting young woman to its damp and drafty rooms for several years to come.

This day he wore black breeches topped by a waistcoat of gray. His shirt and cravat were crisp white, his jacket charcoal. He appeared like the title gentleman he was, as far as his clothing was concerned. He could afford to keep a valet in addition to Coombs and a few other servants. The heels of his fine boots clicked sharply against the stone floor as he reluctantly strode to the study. He raked his fingers through his hair and sighed irritably, finally settling himself behind a massive desk that nearly dominated the space.

Michael opened the folder from the solicitors and quickly

perused the contents. It was as he had fully expected. The men had found nothing of his father's missing fortune. Setting both the folder and the matter aside with a grunt, Michael turned his attention to the waiting missive. He smiled as he opened the letter, most pleased to see it was from his good friend, Philip Wilton.

Baron Wilton wished to expand his line of horses, the letter read, racers and hunters both. Michael was quite gifted at raising and training horses and, as he was at the present time unable to fulfill his own dreams of breeding horses there in Cornwall, he relished the idea of doing so for his friend for both the satisfaction and the profit the partnership could bring himself.

Picking up pen and paper, he wrote a reply to Philip in the positive. He added that, although the Derby in June was a mere six weeks hence, he was most confident he could train a racer currently in Philip's possession to make a decent show in the race. His mind worked as he planned out the details of both his journey into Somersetshire where the estate to which Philip was heir was situated, and his training of what were certain to be magnificent examples of horseflesh.

At the very least the occupation would get him out of his dismal part of Cornwall.

7

***

Lady Elizabeth Bridgewater, third cousin to Philip Wilton, sat in her father's best carriage as it rolled through London. She was enroute to the Derby accompanied by her parents, the Earl of Bridgewater and his wife. Betsy, as she'd been known since she was but a little girl, was eager to see the horse Philip had entered in the race.

Lord, it was good to get out of London proper for the afternoon. Everything that had happened in the time since she first arrived in town two months prior spun through her mind.

Betsy was eighteen and quite dazzled by life in town. It was the height of the Season, her first full one since coming out. She had many suitors among the *ton*. Gentlemen young and old alike vied for her favor. She supposed she was pretty enough, but she was aware her father's wealth and station drew them as well.

She did like her hair, light brown when she was a child and now darkened to a rich chestnut, which she preferred to wear in as loosely-constrained style as her maid could manage. This day, however, she wore it braided into a tight coil at the back of her head, a style more acceptable to her mother. She wore a day dress of white muslin, one of her favorites, which was dotted with tiny blue flowers that matched the wide ribbon on her straw bonnet.

The carriage rolled to a stop at the grounds of the Derby and Betsy felt a tingle of anticipation course through her. She loved horses, both riding about her father's estate in Somersetshire and caring for them in the stables. It was what she missed most about being away from the country for the Season. But horses were not the only draw for her this day. She was certain to see Maggie at the grounds.

Maggie, Philip's wife, was also Betsy's half-sister, although that distinction mattered little. The two young women were extremely close, confidants as well as sisters. Aside from the affection she felt for her sister, Betsy had yet another reason to seek her out this day. She wished to ask Maggie for her advice on a pressing matter. The Earl of Templeton had asked for Betsy's hand, gaining her parents' approval immediately. And while Betsy had admiration for the man, she couldn't help but have more than a few misgivings as well.

Lord Templeton was nearly twenty years her senior and quite an elegant and proper gentleman. Betsy's mother was for the match, stating Betsy's so-called wild nature would do well with a firm hand to restrain it. Though Betsy had all but accepted his proposal, she wasn't certain he was the man for her. If only she could speak to Maggie without her mother's being present.

Betsy and her parents alighted and slowly made their way through the crowded grounds to Maggie and Philip's box. Everyone attended the Derby, the commoners as well as the titled gentry. The grounds were crowded and the weather hot for the beginning of June. Betsy paid all this little mind as her eyes fell on the couple in the box.

"Maggie!" she exclaimed, all but running the last few feet separating them.

Maggie, her beautiful sister with golden hair like their little sister Mary, returned Betsy's embrace with warmth. Betsy turned from her sister and dropped a quick curtsy for Philip, who grinned as he bowed to her.

"How are you faring, Betsy?" he asked, his green eyes sparkling. "Are you quite ready for a day at the races?"

"Oh, yes," Betsy returned with a smile. "I do so miss the horses."

Maggie nodded her agreement. "And what of your betrothal, Betsy? Surely you've set the *ton* on its ear, gaining such a promise in barely a fortnight since coming to Town."

Betsy didn't want to talk about the match her parents so

endorsed. Not today. Unfortunately, as Lord and Lady Bridgewater joined them talk soon became focused on the betrothal and the many plans now necessary to securing the perfect future for Lord Bridgewater's second daughter.

Betsy took her mother's monopolization of the conversation as the opportunity it presented, however. She made her way to the stables to look in on the racehorses. She stepped very carefully over the muddied ground, only absently noticing the glances she received from a few men on the way. When she lifted her skirts clear of mud, all male eyes followed her ankles over the rutted path. *Let them look, then.* They were perfectly ordinary ankles.

Betsy reached the stables and pulled open the door, stepping inside the darkened interior. As she removed her bonnet, she breathed in deeply the combined scents of horses and sweet hay. She closed the door and leaned against it for a moment, reveling in the coolness and relative solitude of the stables. A sigh escaped her lips as she spied Philip's mare. She approached the horse, a smile curving her lips.

"Hello, Gusty," she cooed, placing her hand on the horse's muzzle.

The horse was chestnut with white stockings, a

magnificent specimen. She stroked and petted the horse.

"Have you been a good girl?" she asked the horse. "Are you ready for your big day, sweet?"

She reached into her reticule and withdrew a few cubes of sugar.

"You shouldn't feed the animal such treats before a race," a man said from the shadows.

She gasped and dropped the sugar as the young man stepped forward to throw a saddle over the mare. She ran wide eyes over his splendid form as he adjusted the saddle. The breeches clinging to his long powerful legs were dusty and his shirt was opened at the collar. She glimpsed dark curly hairs at the base of his throat. His black, glossy hair caught the light filtering through the cracks in the wallboards as he turned to face her once more. Lord, he was handsome!

The man leaned on the saddle for a moment, his dark eyes sparkling at her inspection as Betsy struggled to recover her composure.

"Such a trifling won't spoil Gusty's performance," she countered with a tilt of her chin.

He let his eyes slowly run over her in his turn, making her heart race. "And what would you know of it?" he asked, stepping closer to her.

His insolence astounded her. She placed her hands on her hips. "I will have you know, sir, I've ridden this horse many times."

"You?" He scoffed, arching a brow. "You've ridden this horse?"

Betsy took a breath to cool her pique at the handsome rascal's words.

"Yes," she answered. "Do you find that so difficult to believe?"

He tightened the saddle and stood in front of her. His eyes ran over her once more, finally settling on her face.

"She can be a difficult mount," he said, his eyes staring into hers. "One would need a firm hand to master her."

"I...," Betsy stammered, lost in his dark gaze. She swallowed thickly. "I have quite a lot of experience with such things."

He chuckled, leaning closer to her.

"You have experience?" he teased. "Now, that I doubt."

Betsy stared up at him, overwhelmed by his masculinity. His scent. Oh, he smelled like the out of doors, and a bit spicy. She couldn't help but compare him with Lord Templeton. The older gentleman paled considerably by the comparison.

Her eyes fell on his beautiful mouth as he stood so close to her. Would the bold man kiss her? She licked her lips in her nervousness, heat flashing over her face.

He gave a smug nod of his dark head.

"Experienced in mastery, indeed," he intoned.

She recovered herself and glared up at him. "I suppose that had you kissed me, you would think me mastered?"

His eyes roamed over her form once again. He arrogantly arched his brow.

"No." His gaze fell on her lips once more. "Had I kissed you, your training would only have just begun."

A delicious shiver went through her body as she imagined all he would teach her. The Lord knew she had very little experience. Then he chuckled deeply, the rogue.

"I will not be spoken to in such a manner by a common stableman."

Indignant, she stomped from the stables. When that handsome rascal stood so close to her, when he'd nearly kissed her, her pulse had pounded. He was a stableman. That was true. But he was far from common. She'd felt an attraction to him she knew instinctively she would never feel toward Lord Templeton.

Being a lady of virtue, she had no true notion of what she and the strong young man could be to each other. But she knew in her heart that his kisses would set her to flames.

Relief flooded through her as she reached Maggie and Philip's box. She quickly donned her bonnet as Maggie eyed her closely. She schooled her expression, praying that her high color and nervousness wouldn't draw her sister's attention.

"Betsy," Maggie whispered, "What on earth have you been about?"

Betsy was saved from making an excuse for her flustered appearance by the announcement of the second race, the one in which Gusty was entered. Grateful for the diversion, she brushed her hands over her skirts, chagrined to notice her ankles were still in full view. With an impatient flick of her skirts, she quickly remedied that situation.

Her eyes were soon drawn to the track where the horses were taking their places. She spied Gusty immediately, and clasped her hands together in silently prayer for the horse's fine performance.

At the starter pistol's sharp retort, the horses leapt into motion. The rider atop Gusty drew Betsy's notice then. He was much larger than the others, she recognized, but it appeared not

15

to make a noticeable difference. He was bent low over the animal, seemingly at one with the creature. The horses thundered past, causing Betsy's heart to pound anew. Almost too soon for her, the race was finished. Gusty came in second, a fine showing for a previously untried racer. As she cheered happily, Lord and Lady Bridgewater clapped with enthusiasm. Philip gave a loud whoop, grabbing his wife and twirling her about. Thrilled to her toes, Betsy accompanied the younger couple down to the track.

Gusty's rider reined in the animal as the small party approached. Betsy stared up at the rider, dumbstruck as the handsome groom dismounted in one smooth motion to face them. He spared Betsy a telling glance and gave her a cocky grin before he turned from her to receive Philip's hearty handshake.

"Well done, Balsam!" Philip said. "Wonderful showing."

The man patted the horse soundly on her flank. "Thank this magnificent creature, Wilton," he returned in a modest tone decidedly missing from their earlier exchange. "She gave her all, I assure you."

Philip grinned and clapped him on the back. The dark-haired man turned from him to face Betsy and Maggie. He bowed in greeting to Philip's wife and straightened to favor Betsy with another knowing glance. Betsy fidgeted under his

16

gaze as Philip made their introductions.

"Betsy, permit me to introduce someone to you," Philip intoned. "This is my partner and expert trainer, Michael Reed, Viscount Balsam. Balsam, this is Lady Elizabeth Bridgewater, the earl's second daughter."

Michael bowed low to her, his eyes sparkling.

"It's a pleasure to make your acquaintance, Lady Elizabeth."

Betsy stared up at him for a long moment, finally curtsying in greeting. Lord Balsam? Why, she'd called him a common stableman! As he gazed down at her, she allowed herself the luxury of studying his handsome visage in the bright sunshine. Her eyes settled on the masculine curve of his mouth and she suddenly wished that she'd allowed him to kiss her in the stables. No, she amended with a touch of dismay. She now wished she had been the aggressor. She longed to run her fingers through his thick, glossy waves as he teased her with that beautiful mouth. Flushing over the direction her thoughts were taking, she smiled shakily up at him.

"...residing at Bridgewater Park," Philip finished.

Michael smiled and nodded his head.

"What?" Betsy asked in confusion, looking from Philip to

Lord Balsam and back again.

"Lord Balsam will be residing at Bridgewater Park," Philip stated once more. "We plan to establish a strong line of racers and hunters, he and I."

Betsy gazed up at Lord Balsam once more. He was going to *live* at Bridgewater Park? No doubt there would be seemingly endless opportunities to be in his company, then. Surely she could put aside the acute embarrassment she felt over her initial misconception of his station in life.

Nevertheless, she would have to withstand repeated exposure to the gorgeous, gifted man. She hid her smile. What a confoundingly delightful development!

Chapter 2

Michael was surprised by the heat in Lady Elizabeth's big blue eyes, his interest caught as he watched them darken to violet. He desired in that moment to grab her to him, to hold her tightly against himself as he plundered her soft, ripe mouth. Hell, he'd desired her from the moment he'd seen her in the stables. From the moment he'd caught the flowery scent of her. If he had to pinpoint the smell, it was one of wild violets.

She was a slender girl, yet curved in all the right places. Her thick hair was the same rich shade of chestnut as Gusty, and as her graceful hands had stroked over the horse's flesh? He'd wanted them all over himself.

He reined in the inappropriate response. If he stared at her full lips a moment longer, he would do precisely what his body was aching to do.

He was most pleased to learn she would be returning to the estate in Somersetshire at the end of the Season, just a few weeks hence. He wished to learn more of the spirited beauty. Philip's next words dashed his hopes to the rutted track beneath his feet.

"We'll soon have much celebrating to do, if Lord and Lady Bridgewater are to be taken at their word," Philip said.

"Yes," Maggie nodded. "It appears Betsy has attracted the notice of a very eligible gentleman in town, Lord Balsam. She's betrothed to Lord Templeton."

Michael's stomach clenched. How could any man not wish to possess her? Her remarkable beauty was only enhanced by what he sensed was a strong stubborn streak, if their encounter in the stables was any indication. Damn it, he was in no position to make any sort of offer, let alone one that would lead to a betrothal. Now it seemed he wouldn't even be given the chance to get to know her better.

"I hadn't realized all knew of the betrothal," the girl rushed out.

"But all is settled," Maggie said. "Isn't it?"

"Don't you wish for the match, Betsy?" Philip asked.

"I…," Lady Elizabeth began.

Michael stared hard at her, suddenly very keen on hearing her answer. Her smooth cheeks reddened, and her sister seemed to pick up on her discomfort.

"Why don't we rejoin Lord and Lady Bridgewater while Lord Balsam sees to the horse, husband?"

Michael took the escape offered. He bowed once more and led the horse from them. Lady Elizabeth Bridgewater was out of his reach, in more ways than one. The sooner he accepted his momentary infatuation for what it was, the better for all parties concerned.

A fortnight later, Michael put Gusty through her paces at Bridgewater Park. He planned to race her again at Ascot, hoping to best her showing at the Derby. He rode her hard over the grounds, pushing himself as well as the animal. He rode back to the stables. Satisfied, he dismounted with a grin. He patted the horse soundly, generously doling praise on the animal.

As his fingers brushed through the horse's silky mane, his thoughts immediately filled with Lady Elizabeth's image. He remembered her gentle, loving treatment of the horse and smiled. He also recalled her irritated response toward himself. That caused his grin to widen. Her stubbornness was a trait that attracted him as much as her lovely face and pleasing figure. Apparently she spoke her mind, almost to her own misfortune if her expressive features could be believed. She was like a vixen, beautiful but sharp. And even the memory of her drew him as surely as the vixen drew the hounds at a hunt.

When he'd nearly kissed her, he'd seen the heat in her blue eyes. And later, when they'd met on the track? He lost his smile as he recalled the intense desire that flared through him as she had gazed up at him. He'd wanted to pull her to him and kiss her until she could think of nothing else but him.

He'd learned from Philip that she was expected to accept Lord Templeton's offer of marriage before the Season drew to a close. That thought caused him much discomfort. He couldn't bear the thought of her sharing another man's bed, even if that man was her lawful husband. He wanted her for his own. Although he had yet to sample her charms, he knew without a doubt the two of them would be a spectacular match. There was fire smoldering not far beneath her surface. And Lord, it would be his intense pleasure to bring it forth.

Michael turned his thoughts to the coming race at Ascot. Betsy would be in attendance, surely. He was eager to see if the woman truly matched the image he'd carried around in his mind these past weeks. She so plagued his thoughts that he went to sleep on more than one occasion fairly aching with need. Also more than once, he was forced to go into the neighboring town of Bridgewater and see to his needs, pounding out his lust between the legs of a willing and well-paid serving maid. The encounters left him wanting so much more than simple physical release, though.

Irritated at the direction in which his thoughts were

leading, he returned his attentions to the mare.

***

Betsy paced across the fine oriental carpet in the parlor of her parents' townhouse in London. Lord Templeton was sure to call on her that afternoon, and she was quite uncertain of what she would say to him. She had yet to speak to Maggie about her confusion over the prospect of her betrothal. She well knew the reason for her preoccupation. Viscount Balsam. Michael Reed.

Two weeks had passed since the Derby, and in that time she couldn't get the image of him out of her mind. He filled her dreams while she slept and her thoughts upon waking. She'd learned through a series of well-chosen questions put to the proper persons that he didn't attend the functions in London with any regularity, which explained why she'd never made his acquaintance before. She felt tremendous guilt over what she deemed impure thoughts while at the same time wishing he would kiss her until she could think of nothing else.

Her father and mother pressed her for an answer daily, with Lady Bridgewater all but demanding she accept Lord Templeton's offer of marriage. He was quite wealthy, Betsy's mother told her, and considered the catch of the Season. Betsy wasn't quite as certain as her mother was. While she enjoyed the man's company, she felt no physical attraction to him. None of this had plagued her before making the acquaintance of a certain dark-haired gentleman.

She'd always been quite comfortable in Lord Templeton's company before the Derby. She flicked a thick curl over her shoulder in a show of irritation. She wore her hair in a simple but pretty style, upswept to her crown with ample curls trailing down her neck and at her cheeks. She lifted a curl at her cheek and fingered it absently as her mind drifted back to the handsome young viscount. What was he doing at this very moment? The butler's voice broke through her reverie.

"Lord Templeton is calling, my lady," he said with a bow.

Betsy started and turned to the doorway. In walked Lord Templeton, impeccably dressed in formal black.

"Elizabeth, my dear," the man enthused, coming to stand before her. "How lovely you look this day."

"Hello, Lord Templeton," Betsy returned with a friendly smile.

Templeton, a tall and handsome man with brown hair, sat beside her on the settee. He took her hand in his.

"I missed you at the Collins' last evening, my dear," he said, referring to a dinner party to which Betsy had been invited to attend.

She'd avoided attending the function, preferring to ponder her thoughts alone. Her parents had attended of course, as most of the party consisted of their contemporaries.

"I was a bit tired, I'm afraid," she said in half-truth.

He waved his hand. "I enjoyed talking with your parents." His blue eyes sparkled. "It appears you and I have much to discuss."

Betsy felt her heart pound. As if to confirm her fears, he broached the subject she'd been successfully avoiding until now.

"Elizabeth," he said, bringing her hand to his lips. "Would you do me the honor of becoming my wife?"

Betsy stared at him, seeing the affection clear in his eyes. She felt a fondness for him, but no passion. He would be good for her, perhaps. There would be no arguments. No heated longing making her mad. Perhaps it was time for her to calm what her mother termed her wild streak.

"Lord Templeton, I don't know if we suit."

"Elizabeth, I can give you so much. We will travel. We will entertain. We will have the very best of everything. I want to take care of you."

Betsy stared at him, hearing not the words he was saying

but the affection in his tone. She couldn't deny the lure of being cherished. She would be the proper young lady her mother was always instructing her to be, as well. Perhaps then her wicked thoughts would no longer plague her.

"Yes, Lord Templeton," she said softly. "If you wish it."

A dark smile of victory spread across his face, startling her. Just as quickly it was gone, replaced by the benevolent gaze he always seemed to wear in her company.

"Ah, Elizabeth," he said, bringing his lips to hers.

Betsy closed her eyes in anticipation of her first kiss. She froze as he kissed her with dry lips. The kiss was over in an instant and she felt acute disappointment. Perhaps that is what a kiss felt like. Although she imagined Lord Balsam's kisses would be anything but disappointing. Guilt slashed through her at the thought of another man.

Lord Templeton ran his fingers over her hair. "Your hair is lovely, Elizabeth." He frowned slightly. "However, I do believe these loose curls detract from the image I would expect a proper young lady to project."

Betsy's hands flew to her hair, feeling embarrassment at the lustrous curls for the very first time in her life.

"Do not fret, my dear," he said, patting her hand. "We shall remedy such things in the future, yes?"

Betsy nodded, blinking in confusion.

"You are the future Countess of Templeton, my dear," he said. "You must project a certain propriety at all times."

"Yes, Lord Templeton."

He gave a firm nod and stood. "Shall we have tea?"

Betsy set aside the whisper of misgivings and poured the tea.

Two weeks later Betsy readied for the races at Ascot, the familiar tingle of anticipation coursing through her. She so loved the races, but she was certain to see Lord Balsam, too. She chose to ignore the guilt that threatened her at such thoughts. He was merely a friend, wasn't he? Or, he was Philip's friend. And if they had occasion to speak to one another, what was the harm? She was betrothed to another, her mind whispered. She shook her head at her folly and completed her preparations.

When she went downstairs to the parlor, she saw Lord Templeton had arrived. He stood near the mantle in conversation with her parents. Betsy entered the room and stood still, awaiting for his approval at her dress. She wore a beautiful day dress of green silk, the pale color well suited to her fair skin. It was modest in cut, but nonetheless hugged her curves.

She straightened her shoulders and clasped her hands on front of herself. Lord Templeton had told her on numerous occasions since the betrothal that she should carry herself regally. That she shouldn't sway provocatively when she walked or laugh so easily. A small smile and incline of her head was all needed to show she was having a pleasant time, he'd assured her. Keeping all his instructions in mind, she took careful steps into the room.

"Hello, Lord Templeton," she said softly.

"Elizabeth." He bowed to her. "You are the very picture of grace and beauty this day."

She was relieved that he found her appearance acceptable. A tiny voice in her mind told her she was being foolish. That she should dress for her own pleasure and not for his approval. She shook her head and crossed to him, permitting him to take her hand. He brushed cool lips over her skin.

"Are you ready for the excitement of the races, my dear?" he asked her.

"Oh, yes!" She brightened. "I cannot wait to see the magnificent creatures streaking across the track."

He clicked his tongue at her. "My wild one." He shook his head. "Do not say such things at Ascot, my dear."

Betsy's mouth gaped and her gaze flew to her mother's. At Lady Bridgewater's swift nod of approval, she looked to her father. The earl wore a thoughtful look on his face before finally smiling at Betsy.

"Let us be off," her father said, taking her mother's elbow.

Betsy permitted Lord Templeton to lead her to the waiting carriage. By the time they arrived in Ascot, she felt as though she would burst. The strain of saying the correct thing at all times combined with keeping her excitement over the races inside of her had given her a slight headache.

She was most pleased to find the grounds at Ascot far less crowded than those at the Derby had been. The four of them soon joined Philip and Maggie. Philip congratulated the couple on their recent betrothal as Maggie eyed Betsy closely. Betsy sensed her sister's close regard and managed a smile.

"Betsy," Maggie began, "is something troubling you?"

Betsy couldn't put into words the strangeness she was feeling. How could she? She was betrothed to a fine gentleman and yet she couldn't stop thinking of another. She forced her smile to widen as she gazed at Maggie.

"Oh no, Maggie," Betsy said. "I'm quite pleased to be taking in the races with both of you."

Maggie arched a brow at her stilted answer. Philip sensed something in her demeanor as well, judging from his furrowed brow. Betsy turned from them, focusing her attention on the stables visible from their vantage point. Was Lord Balsam inside? She pictured him in her mind's eye as he had been at the Derby: slightly rumpled and wholly enchanting. Lord Templeton's voice reached her, causing her to jump.

"Who is that riding your mare, Wilton?" he asked Philip.

"Lord Balsam," Philip answered. "I've never seen one so gifted in matters of horseflesh, titled or common."

"Balsam," Templeton repeated, his voice low.

Betsy's heart pounded as she watched Lord Balsam take his place beside the others. The starter pistol sounded and they were off and running. Lord Balsam and Gusty streaked past them, causing Betsy to join her voice to the shouts of excitement around her.

"Elizabeth, do calm yourself," Lord Templeton admonished.

Betsy could feel her cheeks flaming at the reprimand and dropped her eyes. When she finally raised them, the race was nearly finished. As she watched, Gusty raced across the finish line. She won! Betsy hugged Maggie and Philip as she cheered without restraint. She caught sight of Lord Templeton's frown then and attempted to rein in her joy, fairly shaking with the effort.

"Come join us in the winner's circle, Betsy!" Maggie cried, tugging on Betsy's hand.

"Oh yes!"

"I think not," Lord Templeton cut in. "Elizabeth has had enough excitement for one afternoon."

Philip and Maggie both stared at the man in obvious disbelief. When Maggie opened her mouth, no doubt to berate the man, Philip grabbed her arm and fairly pulled her from him.

"Come, love," he said. "Betsy will join us later."

Maggie and Philip left to congratulate Lord Balsam on his fabulous win, leaving a wilted Betsy standing beside her betrothed.

***

Michael dismounted and praised Gusty for her performance. He looked up to find Lord and Lady Wilton coming toward him. He quickly searched for Betsy, feeling acute disappointment when he found her absent from the party.

"Balsam, old man!" Philip shouted. "Well done, well done!"

"That was wonderful, Lord Balsam," Maggie said. "We were all so thrilled. Betsy was fairly shaking with excitement."

"Betsy?" Michael rushed out, his eyes scanning the crowd once more. "Lady Elizabeth is here?"

Maggie nodded. "She remains in our box with Lord Templeton and her parents."

Michael heard little of her answer, for his eyes had settled on the girl in question. She looked absolutely lovely. Their eyes met and his breath caught. He flashed her a smile, which she promptly returned with one of her own. All else faded from view as he left the horse to a groom and strode toward the box.

"Lord Balsam, that was wonderful!" Betsy cried when he reached her. "Gusty looked marvelous."

Michael grinned at her enthusiasm. He noticed the older gentleman beside her then and introduced himself.

"Lord Templeton," the older man returned with a nod of his head. "And you would be Wilton's trainer, I presume?"

Michael nodded, his brow furrowed in confusion. This old man was Betsy's intended? Nonsense. When he returned his gaze to Betsy, he noted the change in her immediately. She stood ramrod stiff, her face fixed in a weak smile. He nodded curtly to Lord Templeton and turned to Betsy again, intent on brightening

32

her spirits.

"You enjoyed the race, I take it?" he teased her.

"Very much so," she said, restraint in her voice.

Before Michael could fully break the shell around her, Lord and Lady Bridgewater joined the conversation. Michael noted with disdain that Betsy's gentleman gripped her elbow in an obvious show of possession. He excused himself from them and returned to the stables.

He couldn't stand the sight of the man's hand pressed to her flawless skin.

Chapter 3

Weeks passed, bringing the end of the Season on the twelfth of August. Betsy sat in her parents' carriage as it made its way toward Somersetshire, her mind blessedly freed from tensions of the previous few weeks. Lord Templeton had bade her farewell the previous evening, leaving her with both a kiss and a promise to come to Somersetshire shortly. Guilt threatened even as she reveled in the knowledge she would no longer have to constantly monitor her actions and her dress.

She was fond of Lord Templeton, despite his seemingly constant admonitions to her. But she was unable to rid her mind of the one man whose image caused her heart to flutter. Consequently, the more she thought of Lord Balsam, the more she regretted accepting the earl's proposal.

She'd sought to put the handsome viscount out of her mind as Lord Templeton escorted her to the theater and the like. And when the earl kissed her goodnight, she attempted to feel the passion she believed should be present. It was all to no avail. She straightened suddenly, her eyes widening as Bridgewater Park came into view outside the carriage window. Any further thoughts of her betrothed fled her mind as she spied her family's estate. The glimpse of the magnificent grounds and stables put her in mind of one person: Lord Balsam.

The carriage rolled to a stop on the long drive. Leaving her parents to follow, Betsy alighted the vehicle and fairly flew up the steps to the entryway. She absently greeted the servants in the foyer, ran up to her room, and her maid quickly assisted her into her riding habit. The outfit Betsy chose this day consisted of a light blue skirt topped with a matching spencer. The little jacket reached just to her narrow waist, accentuating her figure. She had little inclination to wear her hair in the manner to which Lord Templeton and her mother dictated.

"One braid today, Ann," Betsy told her maid. "I want to ride and I don't wish to have pins flying."

Ann nodded, happily bowing to her mistress' wishes. Betsy smiled to herself as the girl ran a brush through her hair, pleased to finally have her waves loose from their pins. The maid plaited her hair simply and left her, wishing her a good day. Betsy, humming to herself, hurried down the stairs to find her mother waiting for her outside the parlor.

"Betsy, you are not going riding at this late hour, are you?"

"Oh yes, Mother," she answered. "I'll return in time for tea."

Lady Bridgewater nodded, taking herself into the parlor.

Betsy made her way to the stables, her mind racing with all she wished to say to Lord Balsam. Would he be happy to see her? He had seemed so at Ascot, at least when she'd first seen him. She reached the stables and entered, the familiar smells pleasing her to her toes. She quickly looked into several stalls, and was acutely disappointed when she didn't find the viscount within.

She called out to the groom, thinking that at the very least she could ride about the grounds. The sedate horseback riding she had done in town left her sorely in need of a good hard ride. She wished to smell the clean air and feel the wind rushing through her hair. The groom saddled one of her favorite mounts and she rode out into the late afternoon sunshine.

Not too much later, Betsy turned her mount back toward the stables and reined her in. "Good girl!" she cried, patting the mare's neck.

She reached out for the groom to assist her down, and was surprised as a strong hand gripped hers in a most familiar fashion. She turned to find herself eye to eye with the viscount.

"Lord Balsam!"

His grin sent sparks flying over her skin.

"Hello, Lady Elizabeth." He assisted her down from her mount. "How does this day find you?"

"Very well," she answered, a bit out of breath. "I had a marvelous ride."

He chuckled. "I can see you had a vigorous ride."

Betsy ran her hands over her hair, affecting its appearance little. "Yes, my braid is all but a memory."

"I think you look quite fetching."

"Lord Balsam, you flatter me."

"Please," he said. "Call me Michael."

Betsy's heart gave a happy thump. "Only if you will call me Betsy."

"Betsy, then," he said with a nod. "How have you been?"

"Very well," she said. "I still cannot believe you and Gusty won at Ascot."

"She's a marvelous animal."

His words brought their encounter at the Derby to mind. She looked up at him, one brow arched.

"But she's most difficult, isn't she?"

Michael blinked, then laughed as he apparently caught her jest.

"I believe I have her mastered," he returned with a grin.

Their gazes locked, and his was so warm and welcoming. Suddenly, his expression turned shuttered and he turned his attention to her horse.

"And how did you leave London?" he asked, his tone cool.

"London is fine and will no doubt continue so."

"And your fiancé?" he asked, waving the groom from the stall. "Is the good Earl of Templeton fine as well?"

"Yes." Betsy fidgeted, uncomfortable with the topic. "He is quite well."

Michael focused his attention on the saddle, his capable-looking hands tracing the intricate patterns in the leather.

"Interesting," he muttered, "considering he is such an old gentleman."

"What did you say?" Betsy asked, certain she hadn't heard him correctly.

He raised his head to face her. "I merely stated my pleasure over the man's health."

Betsy stared up at him. "Michael?"

"I believe it's nearly tea time, Betsy," he cut in. "Surely your mother is waiting for you."

"Well, yes," she allowed. "Will you be joining us?"

"No, I'm afraid not," he said curtly. "I have to see to matters here."

Betsy tried to hide her disappointment. She turned to go,

stopping to look back at him over her shoulder.

"Will I see you at dinner?" she asked.

After a long pause he nodded.

***

Michael watched Betsy walk lightly from the stables, allowing himself to revel in the obvious pleasure his answer had given her. Shaking his head, he returned to his tasks.

Dinner proved a trial on Michael's sanity, however. Betsy looked stunning in a gown of ivory. He could hardly drag his eyes from her face though, watching her full lips as she spoke or sipped delicately from her glass of wine. Dessert was served, an assortment of delectable fruit tarts, and Betsy chose one of lemon. She bit into it gingerly, sighing with pleasure. Michael felt himself harden with desire at the provocative sound.

Shifting in his seat, he turned his attention to the earl and his wife. They told him that Philip and Maggie were due to return on the morrow, much to his great relief. With more people at table, he would have an easier time distracting himself from the enchantress.

Afterwards, Betsy very sweetly asked him to escort her to her room. He stared down at her for a long moment. Her big blue eyes beckoned, her lovely mouth curved in a most appealing smile. Cursing himself for a fool, he assented. She paused at the door to her chamber, gazing up at him in anticipation of what, he could well imagine.

"Dinner was most pleasant, was it not?" she asked.

"Yes," he murmured, staring at her mouth.

"I believe I'll go riding tomorrow,"

He raised his eyes to hers. "Perhaps we can ride together?"

"That would be lovely."

He stared at her a moment longer. Unable to resist her lure, he bent toward her, breathing in deeply of her floral fragrance. Betsy gasped in surprise, closing her eyes instinctively. His lips brushed over hers. He cursed softly and pulled back. She gazed up at him, confusion etched on her face.

"Good night, Betsy," Michael said, desire making his voice harsh.

She lowered her eyes. "Good night."

Michael watched her enter her room, and relief flooded through him as she closed the door tight. He turned and strode down the hall to his guestroom, his hands in fists at his side. He'd very nearly kissed her, seized with the longing to taste those perfect lips. But, to what end? She was betrothed to another. The fact that the man was more than twice her age did little to lessen his guilt.

He stripped and stretched out on the big bed, his hands beneath his head. Staring up at the ceiling, he pictured her as she'd looked at dinner. Never a more stunning girl had he seen in his life. She was equally enchanting in the stables, with her hair all but falling free down her back. Lord, he wanted to feel her melt beneath him. To kiss her until all thoughts of her fiancé left her mind. Willing her from his thoughts, he buried his fist in his pillow and prayed for sleep to take him.

Michael was seated at the table in the breakfast room the next morning when Betsy arrived, a plate heaped with eggs and ham set in front of him. He looked up at her, a slow smile curving his lips.

"Good morning, Michael," she said with a shy smile.

"Good morning," he returned with a nod.

Michael eyed her appreciatively as she served herself from the sideboard. Betsy soon joined him at the table.

"You look quite fetching this morning, Betsy."

She accepted his compliment with an incline of her head and poured herself a cup of tea. "I plan to ride Gusty this day."

"Ah." He lifted his own cup to his lips. "That was your ruse all along."

41

She arched a graceful brow at him in question. He set his cup aside and stared at her. "You wish to ride with the trainer to get your delicate hands on the prize mare."

Betsy laughed. "I've ridden her numerous times."

"No more, my lady," he said with a shake of his head. "She's no longer for you."

She shrugged her slight shoulders, smiling as she turned her attention to her meal. He couldn't help but watch her. She was both lovely and quick-witted. An absolute delight. If matters were different with his finances, could he possibly court her?

Michael escorted her to the stables and instructed the groom to saddle their mounts. Betsy chose a spirited filly for her own mount, causing Michael to look at her askance. She must have seen his skepticism for she smiled and mounted her horse with little assistance. She flicked her skirts over her legs and turned to wait for him. He mounted his horse and glanced at her. She sat beautifully. With a wave of his hand, he allowed her to take the lead.

"After you."

Betsy smiled cheekily at him and urged her horse to a canter. As she raced from the stables, he let out an exclamation of surprise. She bent low over her horse, unable to keep from giggling as the animal fairly ate up the ground. Michael caught her easily and the two of them took turns chasing each other over the beautiful grounds. When they returned to the stables, flushed and exhilarated, he assisted her down and bowed low.

"You have my sincere apologies, Betsy," he said, catching his breath. "You are a most accomplished rider."

She nodded vigorously. Michael waved the groom from the stable as he had the day before, seeing to the horses' grooming himself. Betsy sat herself down on a nearby bale of hay. Quite a few strands of hair had come loose from her braid during their vigorous ride, and she attempted to bring them into order. He watched her out of the corner of his eye. She looked absolutely delightful to him with her cheeks rosy and her hair a cloud about her face. Their mood was so comfortable and relaxed that he sought to take the opportunity to learn more of her.

"How long have you been riding, Betsy?"

"Oh, Father likes to say I rode as soon as I could walk," She grinned. "I was quite young."

"And when did you begin to ride sidesaddle?"

Her sudden laughter caused him to raise a brow.

"That is really quite diverting," she began in explanation.

"When Maggie came to live with us after her mother died, she took up my instructions. I admit I was quite a handful."

"I don't doubt that."

She stood and ran her hands over the horse. "I surely got a dose of my own medicine when it was Mary's turn to learn."

"Mary?" he asked. "Your quiet little sister?"

"Oh, she is almost thirteen years old and quite the little lady now," she told him. "But she made the most terrible fuss when I took up her instruction."

Michael chuckled at the image of Betsy dealing with a girl as mutinous as herself.

"Nevertheless," she added with a nod, "I accomplished my goal and the girl rides quite properly now."

He placed the saddles aside for the groom's attention and sat down on the bale of hay she had vacated. He was content for the moment to watch her as she petted the horse, letting her lilting voice wash over him.

"I admit I do sometimes wonder how much better I would ride if I rode astride," she mused aloud.

"But you ride splendidly," he said. "Surely it would make no difference in your performance."

"And yet, I long to ride astride," She sighed. "To truly feel

44

the horse beneath me. To control the animal with both my legs."

Michael's mouth went dry as he suddenly imagined her astride himself, her hair tumbling down over her back as she rode him, crying out his name as her climax took her.

"...Michael?" her voice reached him, snapping him out of his reverie.

He turned his head to find her regarding him closely, an expression of curiosity on her face. He blinked, reddening at the direction his thoughts had taken.

He walked to the other side of the stall. "I've heard Lord Templeton is due to arrive soon,"

"Yes. He should arrive in a few days, I imagine."

Michael sought to learn the nature of their relationship, no matter how distasteful the subject was to him. He studied the wood planking lining the space as he gave voice to his curiosity.

"Does he please you, Betsy?" he had to know. "Are you quite fond of him?"

"I am fond of him, yes," she said. "He's taught me so much. Of the theater, of music and art. We've attended several lovely plays in town."

She spoke of him as she would a favored uncle! Was there no passion in their relationship? Hope filled his breast. He turned to face her again.

"Has he kissed you?" he asked, his voice low.

Betsy blinked rapidly. "Yes."

Her answer displeased him more than he would have imagined. He frowned and stepped closer to her.

"Did you enjoy his kisses?"

She reddened. "They were pleasant."

"Pleasant?" Michael laughed harshly. "Kisses should be a sight more than pleasant."

"I believe I'm capable of judging such matters."

"No," he stated. "You're not."

"W-what?" she asked, her eyes flashing. "How dare you say that?"

"You haven't had a proper kiss," he cut in, standing very close to her.

Betsy shook her head in obvious befuddlement. Suddenly, Michael grabbed her by her waist and pulled her hard against him. She gasped and placed her hands on his chest, her fingers splayed. He stared at her open mouth for a beat, finally crushing his mouth on hers. His kiss was anything but gentle.

She whimpered in pleasure as his tongue stroked hers. Running her fingers through his hair, she pressed herself to him.

Her response thrilled him, causing him to moan low in his throat. She tasted so sweet. Her body felt so right against his. When he finally pulled away, he was pleased to see she was as affected as he. Her eyes were closed and her breath came fast.

"That," he rasped, "was a kiss."

Betsy's eyes fluttered open, darkened to violet. She stared up at him. "Indeed," she whispered. "Kiss me again."

Michael groaned, his eyes on her kiss-swollen lips. He lowered his head once more, his mouth hovering over hers. With an iron will, he pushed her from him.

"No," he answered, his voice harsh. "You belong to another."

Betsy clasped her hand over her mouth, her eyes wide. "Forgive me," she sobbed, shaking her head. "I'm so ashamed."

Michael was alarmed by her upset. She was pale and tears coursed down her face.

"No, Betsy," he said, reaching for her. "You don't understand."

With another heartrending sob, she streaked past him and quit the stable. He watched her go, guilt slashing through him.

"Bloody hell," he cursed, slamming his fist against the wall.

Chapter 4

Betsy kept her eyes downcast through dinner, reluctant to see the anger she'd glimpsed in Michael's eyes that morning. She'd successfully avoided his company until this late hour, keeping to the parlor to work on her needlepoint. Maggie had joined her and rightly sensed her upset. Betsy had maintained her pretense of contentment however, refusing Maggie's offer of a sympathetic ear. After dinner, when the gentlemen and ladies separated, her sister once more made her entreaty. They sat close together on a settee near the fireplace.

"Betsy," Maggie said while Lady Bridgewater rang for the sherry. "Something's troubling you, isn't it?"

Betsy started to shake her head, finally giving a tiny nod.

"Is it something you wish to discuss?" Maggie asked.

"Oh, Maggie," Betsy returned in a whisper. "I'm so frightened."

"Frightened? Of what?"

Betsy leaned closer to her sister. "I'm afraid I've made a terrible mistake," she said tearfully, wringing her hands. "It's my nature."

"Your nature?" Maggie repeated. "What on earth are you talking about?"

Betsy froze as her mother joined them near the fireplace. With a meaningful glance at her sister, she willed her to be silent.

"Lord Templeton arrives two days hence, Betsy," her mother said. "I do hope you will carry yourself like a proper young lady."

"Yes, Mother," Betsy answered softly. "I shall."

"We'll need to speak of the nuptials," her mother went on. "There are many plans to be made."

Betsy nodded, nibbling on her lower lip. She glanced at Maggie again, seeing the concern clear in her eyes.

"Yes, Mother," she said again, her voice flat.

Lady Bridgewater began to enumerate the many things they would need to attend to if the wedding was to take place in a few months' time. Betsy simply nodded her head, letting her mother's voice wash over her.

Betsy looked up as Michael entered the parlor sometime later, and couldn't keep a smile from her lips. He smiled crookedly in return, causing her to drop her gaze to her hands in her lap, but not before she caught Maggie's eye. Her sister wore her enlightenment on her face, causing Betsy to redden. When she finally raised her head again, she found Philip grinning in her direction. She stood suddenly, running her hands over her skirt.

"I believe I'm quite done in," she said lightly. "If you will excuse me, Mother. Father."

"Good night, dear," the earl said with a smile.

Lady Bridgewater bade her good night, swiftly making Maggie the recipient of her recitation of wedding plans. With a curtsy, Betsy turned to leave the room. Michael waylaid her at the door.

"May I escort you to your room, Betsy?" he offered with a bow.

Betsy's eyes widened. Was it really wise to be alone with him again? But after a quick glance around the room convinced her no one was paying them undue attention, she agreed. Grinning, Michael gave her his arm and led her up the stairs.

They paused at the door to her chamber, and Betsy was overwhelmed with all of the feelings she'd been keeping inside this evening. Hot tears spilled over her lashes and she turned to face him fully.

"Betsy, what's wrong?"

"Oh, Michael," she whispered. "I'm so ashamed."

He reached out and brushed away her tears, cupping her

cheek with his hand.

"You have nothing to be ashamed of, Betsy," he assured her. "I take full responsibility for what happened in the stables."

"No," she said, shaking her head. "It's my wild nature. I'm wicked."

"No," he cut in firmly. "You're not wicked. You're a healthy young woman. Passionate."

"My passion is wicked," she whispered. "I'm betrothed to another and I can't stop thinking of you."

"Sometimes what our mind wants and what our body wants are two different things."

She shook her head. "But what my mind wants and what my body wants is the very same thing."

He froze at her words.

"What is it you want?"

She gazed up at him then, her heart pounding. "You."

Michael cupped her face with both hands now, his touch gentle.

"Betsy, love," he murmured, bringing his lips to hers.

Betsy wrapped her arms around him as he kissed her breathless. Her tongue boldly touched his and she moaned as he ran his hands over her, reveling in his caress.

"Ah, Betsy," he rasped, running his lips over her cheek, her neck. "Do you have any notion of how good you smell? How sweet you taste?"

She moaned in answer, letting her head fall back. Michael brought his mouth to the swell of her breast, and her skin tingled. The faraway sound of footsteps on the grand staircase brought him swiftly away from her. He let out a loud sigh.

"Betsy, love," he said, resting his forehead on hers. "I'll put this to rights."

"Michael," she asked softly, "what are you saying?"

He wasn't making an offer, was he? Before she had a sliver of a moment to consider that astounding possibility, he smiled and kissed her lightly.

"Good night, love," he said softly.

Betsy silently agreed to say no more of it, to simply relish the feel of his arms around her as he gently stroked her hair. But she'd heard it in his voice, a promise she didn't dare to think possible.

"Good night, Michael."

He left her then, no doubt bound once more for the parlor. She leaned against her door, watching him as he walked from her. He called her 'love!' She entered her room and readied herself for bed.

She rang for Ann and removed her gown and set it aside, settling herself at her vanity. The maid took her leave and as Betsy ran her brush through her locks, she thought once more of their embrace in the hallway. She set her brush aside and stared hard at her reflection. How could she feel such passion for one man, when she belonged to another? Was Michael truly the man for her?

She lifted her fingers to her face, lightly touching her lips. Closing her eyes, she relished the memory of Michael's mouth on hers. His lips were beautifully made, firm yet sensuously curved. When he kissed her, his lips were soft and warm, his tongue teasing. Betsy ran her fingers over her cheek, her neck. She sighed, wishing in that moment he had not left her, that he was at this very moment with her in her chamber.

Believing herself most wanton, she stood and finished dressing for bed. When she slipped between the linens, clad in her nightgown of lawn, she hugged her pillow tightly. Praying to somehow reconcile her intense feelings for Michael with her betrothal to Lord Templeton, Betsy squeezed her eyes shut and waited for sleep to take her.

***

Michael rejoined the others downstairs. It was best to avoid any suspicion of involvement with Betsy. He'd passed Maggie on the stairs as she went to check on her children in the nursery and had swiftly dropped his eyes, certain she could read the guilt on his face. He'd very nearly taken her sister. If he hadn't remembered himself, he would have opened the door to her chamber and put aside forever any chance she had of marrying the earl. That wasn't the way to manage this mess, however. He'd have to take another course of action to win her from the man.

Philip smiled when Michael entered the parlor, coming to stand beside him. Lord and Lady Bridgewater soon retired for the evening, leaving the two younger gentlemen to speak freely. Michael took the opportunity to glean some information regarding the esteemed Earl of Templeton.

"How well do you know this Templeton fellow, Wilton?" he asked.

Philip shrugged. "Not terribly," he said. "The earl is well-acquainted with him, however."

"Small wonder," Michael grumbled. "He's as old as the earl."

"What?" Philip asked.

"Nothing. How long has he known Betsy?"

"I believe he made her acquaintance this Season."

Michael nodded and crossed the room to stare out at the darkened gardens beyond.

"And so soon he asked her to marry him?"

"It does seem hasty," Philip allowed. "But Betsy is not without her charms."

Michael nodded. "She is perfection."

"There is also her dowry, Balsam," he told Michael, causing him to turn.

"She has a large dowry?"

"Quite substantial, yes."

Michael gave a firm nod. "So that's the old man's motive."

"I don't think so," Philip countered. "Templeton's extremely well-off."

Michael closed his eyes at his friend's words, feeling his heart sink. If money wasn't the man's motive, could Templeton truly care for her? And how could he possibly compete with Templeton? No matter. Betsy would be his and no other's.

He opened his eyes, startled to find Philip smiling crookedly at him.

"Was there more you wished to say, Balsam?"

"No."

"Good night, then."

Michael nodded absently as Philip took his leave, his mind working. He paced the parlor, trying in vain to think of a way to take Betsy from Templeton. The man was wealthy. He could give Betsy all that Michael could not. But, what of passion? It was obvious Betsy wanted him, Michael. She'd very sweetly admitted so, to his great surprise and delight. And Michael had never felt such desire for a woman in his life. Frustrated, he left the study.

The guest chambers were well away from Betsy's room, much to Michael's relief. The thought of her snuggled up in her bed, her lovely chestnut curls spread out around her, caused him to groan. He entered his room and stripped down to his breeches. When he stretched out on the bed, his head fairly ached with his contemplation. He tried to tell himself what he felt for Betsy was simple lust, but before that thought could fully form he knew it was untrue. He admired her spirit. She brought him out of the darkness that had nearly eclipsed him since his father's death and all he had discovered in the months following it. She was like a breath of fresh air, and she didn't belong with a stuffy old man like Templeton.

"Ah, Betsy," he sighed, closing his eyes.

He soon fell asleep, dreaming of his beautiful, spirited enchantress.

Chapter 5

Betsy was disappointed to find Michael absent from the breakfast room the next morning. Maggie was there however, and wearing a cheeky grin.

"Good morning, sweetheart," Maggie greeted Betsy.

"Good morning," Betsy returned with a small smile. Just what was her sister about?

Betsy crossed to the sideboard and served herself a small portion of eggs and bacon. Settling herself across the table from Maggie, Betsy inquired after her parents.

"They've already eaten," Maggie informed her.

Relief washed over her.

"What are you about this day?" Maggie asked her.

"When I awoke, I had thought to go riding," Betsy answered, downhearted. "But I've since changed my mind."

Maggie nodded. "Why don't we retire to the parlor after breakfast to see to our needlework?"

Betsy agreed, happy for the diversion. Her appetite returning, she ate her meal and followed her sister into the parlor.

Mary joined them there, ready to try her hand at some new stitches Betsy had shown her. She was nearly thirteen years old and greatly resembled both her sisters, possessing both Maggie's golden hair and Betsy's big blue eyes. She affected a ladylike pose and settled herself on a settee by the window, her needlework in her lap.

"Mother says Lord Templeton will be here tomorrow," Mary said offhandedly.

Her sisters exchanged a worried glance. Betsy flushed at the suspicion in Maggie's eyes and lowered her own.

"That will be most pleasant, won't it Betsy?" Maggie asked.

"Yes," Betsy said, her eyes still on the square of linen in her lap.

"He's too old," Mary stated.

Betsy raised her head and stared at her little sister. "Why do you say that, Mary?"

"He's nearly Father's age, Betsy," Mary said as if she were simple. "I wouldn't want a husband so old."

Betsy swallowed her own opinion. Her thoughts weren't on Lord Templeton for very long, however. She recalled all that had transpired the previous evening, of Michael's passion that was evident in both his embrace and his words. A warm flush spread through her as her lips curved into a small smile. She finally looked up, her eyes widening as she recognized Maggie's renewed interest in her.

"Betsy," Maggie whispered, her eyes sparkling. "What's going on?"

Betsy quickly shook her head, most relieved as Maggie took her cue and changed the subject. Betsy was grateful for Mary's presence. No doubt Maggie would have pressed her until she admitted she had strong feelings for Michael.

Thankfully the morning passed in a pleasant fashion, the three sisters chatting amiably about the weather and the like. Mary demanded they tell her all about the races, as she was too young to accompany them. She complained for what must have been the hundredth time about spending all her time upstairs in the nursery.

"But I'm vastly relieved to know you are abovestairs with Cecilia and Alexander," Maggie put in, referring to her adorable children.

Mary and Betsy shared a smile then. Cecilia, at age eight, was every bit as obstinate and willful as the other Bridgewater women. Philip indulged her, of course, and she was a handful. Alexander was three years old and the very picture of his father. He was already showing Philip's penchant for getting into mischief as well.

Mary shrugged "I do feel very grown up with those two to look after."

Betsy laughed, dropping a complicated stitch on which she was working. As she pulled on the threads, her head down, Mary stared out the window.

"Ooh, there is Lord Balsam!" the girl cried. "My, he's handsome."

Betsy started, pricking her finger with the needle. She yelped in surprise, putting the finger in her mouth to soothe the injury.

"He's the man Betsy should marry," Mary said.

Betsy shifted nervously in her seat. Maggie must have seen her distress.

"Now, Mary," Maggie said, clicking her tongue. "You're far from knowledgeable of such things."

Mary squared her shoulders. "Maggie, I've seen Betsy with him when they go riding. He likes her very much."

Betsy's heart gave a tiny flutter. "Mary," Betsy began, struggling to keep her voice even. "What makes you think so?"

"He stares at you, Betsy," Mary said. "His eyes get all sparkly like Philip's do when he looks at Maggie."

Maggie laughed gaily and Betsy's flush deepened, but she couldn't keep a smile from curving her lips. She shook her head at Mary, who had already returned her attention to the needlework in her lap. Maggie smiled widely at her sister, biting back her laughter at last.

Soon it was time for Mary's lessons with her tutor, and she left Maggie and Betsy to their own company. Betsy took their seclusion as an opportunity to learn more of Michael.

"Maggie," Betsy began in what she believed was an offhanded manner. "What do you know of Lord Balsam?"

"I know he's very gifted with horses," Maggie said. "Philip was most pleased he agreed to work with him. Their partnership promises to be most advantageous."

"But, why would one titled gentleman work for another?"

Maggie set her work aside and folded her hands in her lap.

"I believe Lord Balsam has had a bit of difficulty since his father passed away last year. There was something of a missing fortune, perhaps? Philip isn't sure of the particulars himself."

"But, his title, his estate. What of those?"

"They remain intact," Maggie answered.

"How confounding." Betsy clicked her tongue. "Poor Michael."

Maggie arched a brow at her familiar use of his given name.

"Betsy, are you in love with him?"

Betsy gasped. "I'm betrothed to another."

"I don't believe that matters," Maggie said simply. "It's obvious you have feelings for Lord Balsam."

Betsy shook her head, but found she couldn't keep up the pretense in front of her sister. She gave a tiny nod.

"I do, Maggie" she admitted in a whisper, wringing her hands. "Oh, what am I going to do?"

Maggie looked quickly to the doorway to ascertain that Betsy's mother wasn't about. Apparently satisfied, she leaned toward Betsy.

"Tell him how you feel," she said softly. "I believe he cares for you."

Betsy shook her head. "I can't," she stated. "I mustn't permit myself to feel such things."

"What things?"

"Passion," Betsy whispered.

Maggie blinked. "Why not?"

"It's wrong."

"Betsy." Maggie took her hand in hers. "What you feel,

what your body and your mind is telling you."

"I know, I know," Betsy cut in. "What my body wants and what my mind wants can be two different things."

"Who told you that?"

"Michael," Betsy said. "He was simply trying to make me feel better, but I know I'm wicked."

"You're not," Maggie said firmly. "Don't say such things."

Betsy sniffled and wiped away her tears.

Betsy held up a hand. She couldn't talk about this any longer. "I will put aside my feelings for Michael and concentrate on readying for Lord Templeton's arrival."

Maggie studied her, her brow knit. Then she seemed to bow to Betsy's wishes. They continued on their tasks in uncomfortable silence.

***

Michael sat in his office behind the tack room that afternoon, brooding. He'd thought long and hard that morning about Betsy and his growing feelings for her. He knew she was merely fond of that old man to whom she was engaged, but that did little to change the fact she belonged to him, not Michael.

He raked his fingers through his hair, once more puzzling over his financial situation. He'd been satisfied when Gusty had placed at the Derby, and doubly pleased when she won at Ascot. His share of the combined purses allowed him to send quite a lot of money to his solicitors. The repairs to Balsam Manor were still a concern, but he pushed the thought of them from his mind. He had but one concern at present: winning Betsy from the Right Honorable Earl of Templeton. His finances were far from adequate to make an offer for her himself.

A flash of blue drew his attention to the office doorway. There stood Betsy, her hands wrapped around the handle of a basket. He couldn't help but smile at the pretty picture she made in her light blue day dress. Her hair was upswept but loose curls framed her beautiful face.

"Betsy." He came to his feet. "To what do I owe this pleasant surprise?"

Betsy blushed prettily, lifting the basket. "You missed the nooning meal, Michael," she said. "I thought you might be hungry, so I had Cook prepare a basket."

"I could eat something," he said with a nod.

Betsy crossed to the desk and rested the basket there. At her insistence, he sat behind the desk once more. She withdrew from the basket an assortment of cold meats, cheeses, and summer fruits. A loaf of crusty bread rounded out the meal.

Although he hadn't realized he missed luncheon, he was suddenly ravenous. He set upon the bounty with relish, consuming a fair amount before returning his attention to the lovely girl perched daintily on the small chair opposite.

He leaned back in his chair and smiled, patting his stomach. "That was a wonderful repast, love."

She'd obviously caught the endearment, but he wouldn't take it back. She was a love. Tempting but sweet. She offered him some grapes from the basket. He popped a few into his mouth and chewed.

"Aren't you eating?" he asked.

"I've eaten."

"You must try these grapes." He stood and leaned across the desk to bring one to her lips. "They're very sweet."

She opened her mouth to him. He rubbed the fruit over the curve of her lower lip before popping it into her mouth. She closed her eyes for a moment and chewed.

"Sweet," she agreed softly.

He stared at her lips for a long moment. He couldn't resist. He skirted the desk and brought his mouth to hers, tracing his tongue over her lips. Betsy parted her lips to him. At her soft welcome, he pulled back quickly, letting out a sigh. She blinked up at him, apparently startled.

"Sorry," he said.

Betsy averted her eyes and busied herself in packing up his leavings. When she was finished with her fidgeting, she set the basket aside and leaned against the desk. "Where do you live, Michael? When you're not here at Bridgewater?"

It wasn't an unusual question, but he did wonder what she might be about.

"My estate is situated in Cornwall."

"Cornwall!" Betsy clasped her hands. "Cornwall is just lovely. So wild and beautiful."

He smiled at that. "Yes. I daresay you would fit in quite well there."

"Oh, I would so love to ride along the cliffs."

"Balsam Manor is quite close to them," he told her. "And nearly as ancient."

"Truly?"

He nodded. "The manor was built more than three centuries ago," he went on. "It has stone parapets and battlements, a large courtyard and an even larger great room. It's quite the medieval castle."

"Hmm. Is there some problem with your family fortune?"

He started. "My father left a bit of unfinished business behind him."

"Yes," Betsy nodded. "The mystery."

"What mystery?"

"Maggie told me of the strange circumstances that took your fortune but left your title and estate intact."

His belly clenched. Why was Betsy was so interested in his estate? He wouldn't speak of it. Not to her. He took a deep breath to calm himself before responding.

"That's no concern of yours," he bit out. "Pray, refrain from commenting on it in the future."

"But, surely there must be something that can be done."

"Do you think I haven't done everything I could?" he challenged, coming swiftly to his feet. "Do you think me a fool?"

"No," she answered, backing away from him. "I merely thought if we put our heads together perhaps we—"

"We?" he cut in, his lip curled. "What on earth could a spoiled little girl like you do to help me?"

Betsy held her hands in fists at her side as she glared up at him. "How dare you speak to me so. I am not spoiled!"

"Aren't you?" he asked, towering over her. "Surely your

main concern is a man's fortune and what it could buy you."

"That's not true."

"Then what reason would you give for selling yourself to a man more than twice your age?"

She raised her hand and delivered a stinging slap to his cheek. Michael brought his hand to his cheek.

"That was uncalled-for," he said evenly. "I merely spoke the truth."

Betsy fairly shook with her anger. "The truth as you see it," she said, her voice low.

He raked his eyes over her.

"Tell me, then," he said. "Tell me why you would consider shackling yourself to that old man when it is most obvious you wish to gift me with that luscious little body of yours."

When she raised her hand once more, Michael reached out and deftly grasped her wrist. He brought his face close to hers.

"I think not," he warned in a growl.

Betsy's breath came fast as she fought to free her arm from the iron grip of his hand. She trembled. He sensed the change in her from anger to fear and he released her.

"My God," he said softly. "I'm sorry, Betsy."

Betsy shook her head frantically and backed away from

him. He quickly closed the gap between them and gently cupped her face with both hands.

"Forgive me, love," he said, brushing her lips with his. "Ah, Betsy."

He kissed her then, tenderly. His tongue delved inside her mouth, teasing her until she returned the kiss. She reached up and ran her fingers through his hair as he pressed even closer to her. He nuzzled her ear, nibbling on the lobe. Betsy leaned her head to the side to give him better access to the sensitive skin.

"Michael," she breathed, running her hands over his back.

Michael placed his hands on her round bottom and held her tightly to him, sending shivers through her body. He was certain she could feel the evidence of his arousal pressed against her. She looked at him in astonishment.

"God, how I want you," he rasped. "Can you feel how much I want you?"

She nodded. He unfastened the few hooks at the back of her dress and tugged at the shoulders. His hand reached into her bodice and cupped her breast. She arched toward him, moaning low in her throat. The little sound set him on fire.

"Do you want me, Betsy?" he whispered, caressing her nipple through her thin chemise.

"Yes." Her voice was soft. Hungry.

"Tell me," he said, reaching beneath her skirts. "Tell me you want me."

"Yes, Michael," she breathed. "I want you."

Michael nodded his satisfaction as he caressed her through her drawers. He could feel the heat of her on his fingers and nearly lost himself. He brought his mouth to her breast. Her nipple puckered beneath him, through her thin chemise.

"Tell me you won't marry that old man," he ordered softly. "Tell me you'll be mine."

"I can't," she whispered.

He lifted his head to stare at her.

"What did you say?" he asked.

She opened her eyes. "I can't break my engagement."

He pulled away from her, leaving her to lean against the wall. They stared at each other for a long moment, both struggling to catch their breath. Michael favored her with a look of utter disgust.

"Why, you mercenary little chit!"

Betsy reached a hand toward him. "You don't understand."

"Oh, I understand perfectly, Lady Elizabeth." He stepped out of her reach. "You wish to have things precisely to your liking."

"No." She shook her head. "My parents, Michael. My mother is pushing for the match."

"No. You wish to have Templeton's fortune and my passion. Well, in this you won't have your way."

Betsy shook her head again, tears gathering on her lashes. Michael fought to steel himself against her, finding the task nearly impossible with both her passion and her vulnerability so clear. He raked his eyes over her, taking in her tousled hair, her kiss-swollen lips. Her dress hung open, giving him a tantalizing glimpse of rosy nipples through her damp gauzy fabric of her chemise.

"Michael," she said softly. "You must understand my position."

Her softly spoken command strengthened his resolve. "Your position? Your position as the promised bride of a wealthy earl, I suppose."

"Michael."

"I suggest you adjust your dress, Lady Elizabeth," he said coldly. "You look like a common trollop."

Betsy sharply drew in a breath. Quiet sobs racked her small frame as she readjusted her clothes, her eyes averted from his.

She slipped past him and exited the office.

Michael watched her leave through hooded eyes. He sat behind his desk, eyeing the basket she had left there. With a growl, he sent both the basket and its few remaining contents spilling to the floor.

Burying his face in his hands, he cursed himself for ever setting eyes on the girl.

Chapter 6

Betsy entered the house and ran up the back stairs. The few servants she encountered appeared to take note of her dress and demeanor but wisely said nothing of it. She reached her chamber and hurried inside. Throwing herself on the bed, she gave in to the tears she'd withheld in Michael's office. She hugged herself and let them come, wetting the coverlet.

"Oh, Michael," she sobbed.

She'd known from the moment his lips touched hers that he was the man she wished to be her forever. He was the one who made her laugh, who made her feel light-hearted and gay. He was also the one who ignited her passion, who made her want things she couldn't even begin to imagine. How on earth could she ever marry Lord Templeton?

But without admitting her sinful behavior, for that was how she viewed her response to Michael's advances, however could she tell her mother she couldn't marry the earl? That thought sobered her. She couldn't shame her parents in such a manner. Not with the engagement already announced. Surely her parents would be mortified were the *ton* ever to learn of her wanton behavior.

She sat up and wiped away her tears. "It's hopeless."

She didn't ring for her maid but shrugged out of her dress, finding her chemise still damp from both her tears and Michael's passionate kisses. He wouldn't want her any longer. His contempt had been clear. Resigning herself to the prospect of married life with the very proper, very restrained Earl of Templeton, she changed into a dressing gown. She had no intentions of taking dinner downstairs with the others. She couldn't bear to see the anger on Michael's beloved face again.

She took dinner in her room that evening, though she pushed the dinner tray aside after barely touching her meal. It wasn't like her to revel in melancholy, but she was unable to rouse her spirits tonight.

She stretched out on her bed, staring at the intricately patterned ceiling of her chamber. Lord Templeton was arriving tomorrow. She'd given her word to both him and her parents, and could see no way out of the mess. She would never again know the passion she'd felt so briefly in Michael's arms. At the very least, marriage to Lord Templeton would afford her protection from her own wildness. She felt no such passion for the older gentleman, only for the man who wanted nothing more to do with her. Irritated at the endless circle in which her mind was traveling, she squeezed her eyes shut and willed herself to sleep.

***

Michael had stayed away from the house as teatime approached, and he wasn't looking forward to sitting through dinner now. Not with Betsy so close. She was forever lost to him. Her resolve concerning her engagement aside, his despicable treatment of her would no doubt divide her from him forever. He groaned as he recalled all the hateful things he had said to her. My God, he'd all but called her a doxy! He'd accused her of selling herself to the highest bidder, damn it all. How on earth would she ever forgive him?

And what of the esteemed earl? His anger threatened to resurface. The man was due to arrive on the morrow, certainly crushing any chance Michael had to win Betsy to him. But, what of her insistence in continuing her engagement? He didn't truly think her mercenary. That horrid accusation certainly stemmed from his own feelings of unworthiness. He didn't believe Betsy was in love with the old man. Surely she cared for him, Michael! How else could one explain the free and open way in which she responded to him?

God, her skin was so soft, so warm when his fingers had stroked her. Sighing irritably, he finished his paperwork and

76

slowly made his way to the mansion to ready for dinner.

When Michael entered the parlor to await the dinner bell, it was with a combination of anticipation and dread. He wished to see Betsy, if only to assure himself that she was all right. On the other hand, he couldn't bear to see the sadness in her eyes. Hell, couldn't bear to see the hurt he himself had cruelly and willfully inflicted.

A quick scan of the room showed him Betsy wasn't within. Relief, and a hearty dose of guilt, washed over him. He nodded to the Earl of Bridgewater and his wife and bowed to Maggie in greeting. He looked over at the settee, picturing Betsy in his mind's eye perched daintily on the cushion. He sighed irritably.

"She's not here," Philip said from behind him.

"What?" Michael started, flushing.

Philip chuckled and simply shook his head.

"Good evening, Lord Balsam," Maggie said.

"Good evening," Michael said.

She smiled at him. "I'm afraid we're one short this evening."

Michael raised a brow, feigning confusion. Lady Bridgewater clicked her tongue.

"Betsy asked to take her meal abovestairs." Lady

Bridgewater said. "I do hope she's not becoming ill. Lord Templeton is due to arrive tomorrow."

At the mention of the name of Betsy's intended, Michael saw red. Taking a breath to cool his ire, he turned to Philip and mentioned a few of the purchases he was planning for the expansion of their horse-raising venture.

Shortly after dinner, Michael bade the others good night and climbed the grand staircase. He paused at the top, fighting the urge to go to Betsy's chamber. No. He had no right to force his advances upon her, or any right to cause her more grief than he had that afternoon.

With a heavy sigh, he turned away from her room and down the hallway toward the guest chambers.

***

Betsy sat at her vanity the next afternoon, readying for tea. Lady Bridgewater had advised Betsy of Lord Templeton's arrival two hours earlier, instructing her to dress with care. She wore a lovely tea gown of deep rose, the color warming her skin tone. Her hair was loosely constrained, which was the norm for her in the afternoons. She stared at her reflection, feeling decidedly downcast.

She'd avoided Michael today, keeping to the house and

well away from the stables. Although Mary had all but begged her to accompany her on a ride, Betsy couldn't bear the thought of seeing Michael for even the smallest moment. His contempt was still so fresh in her mind. Taken with her unrelenting desire for him? She shook her head to rid it of her dark thoughts.

With resignation, she went downstairs to the parlor for tea. As she entered the room, her eyes immediately settled on the dark-haired gentleman leaning against the mantle. Michael took her breath away.

His beautiful eyes sparkled at her as they slowly ran over her. Betsy felt a blush creep up her cheeks and quickly turned her gaze to take note of Lord Templeton. That gentleman wore a benevolent smile as he came forward to take her hand.

"Ah, Elizabeth." He brought her hand to his lips. "How good it is to see you again."

Betsy remembered his past admonitions and merely tilted her head, a small smile on her lips. She had very little difficulty restraining herself, as she felt little joy at his arrival.

"It's nice to see you, Lord Templeton," she said.

Templeton led her to a large chair and bade her to sit. She did so, her eyes once more finding Michael's from across the room. She quickly lowered her lashes, nervously running her hands over her skirt.

"You look lovely this day, Elizabeth," Templeton said. "Although I must say I am disappointed to find you once more wearing your hair in such a manner. I'd thought you understood that I view such a display as quite common."

Maggie gasped audibly at the man's statement, causing her husband to take offense.

"Excuse me, Templeton," Philip cut in. "My wife wears her hair in loose curls, as I prefer it. Are you saying she appears common?"

Templeton sputtered and then recovered, a smooth smile curving his lips. "Why no, of course not, Wilton. She is a married woman, and must bow to her husband's wishes."

Betsy watched the exchange, her eyes round. She stared at her sister, befuddled as Maggie hid a smile behind her hand. She returned her attention to Templeton as he proceeded to regale them with stories of the latest goings-on in town.

"Lady Bridgewater, the *ton* was astounded that your lovely daughter has consented to be my bride."

"We are quite pleased with the match," Betsy's mother said. "Is that not so, Betsy?"

Betsy smiled wanly and inclined her head. She kept her

eyes on her clasped hands in her lap. Time and again she caught Michael staring at her. Did he find fault with her today? No. His eyes were sharp in their intent, but she didn't believe he held Lord Templeton's particular views. Maggie still appeared put out by the older man's comments, but Philip appeared to be grinning in Michael's direction. For his part, Michael turned away to stare out the windows toward the gardens.

Talk soon turned to horses, a change in the conversation that drew Michael's attention as well as her own. Philip spoke of several horses they planned to breed, further expanding his partnership with Michael.

"Balsam and I have quite a venture, to be sure," Philip said with obvious pride. "We'll soon be producing the fastest racers in all England."

"That is an overstatement, husband," Maggie gently chided.

"All right," Philip laughed. "In Somersetshire, then."

Templeton wore his disapproval of Maggie comments to her husband clear on his face. Betsy saw it and was confounded.

"And what of our hunters, Wilton?" Michael put in. "Surely they will be equally impressive?"

"Certainly," Philip nodded. "Templeton, you must ride

while you are here."

Lord Templeton gave a curt nod. "I believe I shall, Wilton," he told Philip. "But one of your more sedate mounts would suit. I would much enjoy it if my lovely Elizabeth were to accompany me."

Betsy jumped at the mention of her name. She'd been gazing longingly at Michael, at the fine figure he cut in his dark brown breeches and jacket. She came swiftly out of her reverie to find all eyes upon her. Her fiancé in particular was staring at her expectantly.

"Forgive me, Lord Templeton," she rushed out. "Did you ask something of me?"

"I merely stated I would very much enjoy riding the estate with you at my side."

She brightened. "Oh, I do so love to ride," she said happily. "To race across the grounds. It is so invigorating."

Lord Templeton's brows shot upward, quickly wrinkling in a frown. "A proper young lady does not ride in such a manner, Elizabeth," he said sternly. "Surely you are jesting with me."

Betsy blinked at his censure, swiftly dropping her eyes to her lap. "Yes," she said in a small voice. "I was jesting."

Michael's brow furrowed as he watched her. What was he

thinking? She knew she had been lively and animated just moments before, describing her great joy in riding. Now she sat still, nearly wilted under the stern gaze of her betrothed. Thankfully he soon spoke of hunting, and Lord Templeton took to the subject. It was obvious that he had long prided himself on being a fine marksman and outdoorsman.

Betsy turned her gaze toward her father. He appeared disturbed by Templeton's admonitions as well as her own odd reaction to them. As for her mother, she didn't seem bothered by them in the least. No, she listened with rapt attention to the earl's descriptions of hunts in which he had recently taken part.

At the conclusion of tea, Betsy was more than relieved to be out of Lord Templeton's company. No doubt she would have her fill of him that evening at dinner. She readied herself for the coming evening and rang for Ann to dress her hair.

As the girl proceeded to pile her locks atop her head, Betsy was suddenly seized with a wicked thought. How pleased would the esteemed Earl of Templeton be were she to wear her hair completely down for dinner? In the end she wore her hair up. But tomorrow was another day, was it not? She did so love to wear a braid when she rode.

She donned a lovely dress of gray, modest in cut. A knock

at her door drew her lady's maid to it. The girl returned to her mistress, a velvet jeweler's box held in her hands.

"What is this?" Betsy asked.

"For you, my lady," Ann said. "It's accompanied by a note."

Betsy took the box from the girl and Ann bowed her head and left the chamber. Betsy opened the box, her eyes growing round. Inside was a delicate necklace of gold supporting an large oval pendant of deepest onyx. She opened the folded note and quickly scanned the contents. As she'd suspected, it was from Lord Templeton. He wished her to wear the necklace, he wrote, as a token of their betrothal.

Unable to think of a reason not to adhere to his wishes, she draped the necklace around her neck, letting the pendant settle against the swell of her breast. She stood and walked to the cheval mirror and admired the stone, dark against her skin. It was nearly the color of Michael's eyes. A sharp pain settled around her heart at that thought.

Sighing, she went downstairs to join the others.

Chapter 7

Michael watched Betsy through hooded eyes as she picked at her meal. He wasn't pleased to see her intended continually touch her, placing his hand possessively on her bare shoulders time and again. Michael's eyes fell on the exquisite necklace encircling her slender neck. Something about it was very familiar to him, although he couldn't begin to fathom the reason. Philip's wife Maggie also took note of the necklace.

"Betsy," she began, "that necklace is lovely."

Betsy's hand flew to the stone as if just remembering its presence. "Thank you, Maggie. Lord Templeton gave it to me."

Michael watched in acute distaste as the earl preened, his chest fairly puffing with pride.

"It is merely a token of my affection, my dear," Templeton said, causing Betsy to redden.

Michael took her blush as one of pleasure. He pulled his gaze from her and kept his eyes fixed on the plate of delicious food before him.

After dinner, the men separated from the ladies and adjourned to the study. Michael studied Templeton as the man conversed with Betsy's father.

"Balsam," Philip began, pouring a brandy for him. "I take

it you're not fond of the earl."

Michael shrugged. "I don't know him," he said. "I don't like the way he speaks to Betsy, however."

"I agree," Philip said in a low voice. "What do you propose to do about your feelings for her?"

"My feelings?" Michael repeated.

Philip chuckled. "You're not a terribly convincing liar, Balsam."

Templeton must have caught Michael watching him, for he soon crossed to where he stood. Michael nodded curtly at the man.

"I was sorry to hear of your father's passing, Balsam," he began. "I do admit I didn't know of your connection to the man at the time of our meeting at Ascot."

"Thank you for your sentiment," Michael said evenly.

"Your father was a pleasant fellow."

That surprised him. "You knew my father?"

"Many years ago, yes. You look a bit like him. When he was of your age."

"So I've been told."

Templeton narrowed his eyes then, his head cocked to one side. "You have a bit of your mother in you, as well."

Before Michael could respond to that strange statement, the earl rejoined Betsy's father. Precisely how did the man know of his mother? She'd died when Michael was very young. He watched Templeton closely until they joined the ladies in the parlor.

Betsy stood when the gentlemen returned, and Michael noticed she appeared anxious. Her sister eyed her closely, as close as Philip had done to Michael. As for Lady Bridgewater, she all but beamed in Lord Templeton's direction whenever he instructed Betsy. Michael's lips thinned. Templeton scolded her really, about everything. Her father wore a look of confusion for nearly the entire evening. Maybe he didn't look as favorably on the match as his wife did.

"I believe I shall retire," Betsy said, coming to her feet. "Good night, everyone."

Michael stood instinctively, and then quickly checked his movement.

"Allow me to escort you, Elizabeth," Lord Templeton said with a bow.

Michael fumed as the man grasped Betsy's elbow and led her from the room.

***

Lord Templeton preceded Betsy up the staircase, as was proper. Betsy was glad for his adherence to propriety, as she knew without a doubt she wore her confusion on her face. How she wished it were Michael accompanying her to her room. No doubt her intended would want to kiss her good night, and how on earth would she permit it without comparing the caress to Michael's?

Lord Templeton smiled down at her when they reached the door to her room. His eyes fell on her hair, on the tendrils curling about her face. He reached out and grasped one thick curl, twining it slowly around his finger.

"You look absolutely ravishing this evening, Elizabeth," he said, bringing his face to hers. "Just as I wish you to be."

Betsy's eyes were open wide as he brushed his lips over hers. He lifted his head and frowned at her.

"I do not doubt your purity, my dear," he said. "But surely you can manage a more enthusiastic welcome to my kisses?"

Before she knew what he was about, he crushed his mouth to hers. His tongue stabbed at her as he groaned softly. Betsy pulled back from him, hitting her head lightly against the wooden panel of her door. Her mouth remained open, her eyes round in shock.

Templeton smiled and touched a finger to her lips. "You do have a lovely mouth, Elizabeth," he whispered.

Betsy lowered her lashes and made an attempt to turn her face from him. He chuckled at what he viewed as her maiden's reticence.

"I will teach you how to please me," he said indulgently, patting her cheek. "Sleep well, my dear."

With that, he turned from her and made his way to the stairs. When he was out of her sight, Betsy wiped her mouth on the back of her hand, feeling utter disgust. She entered her room and turned her attention to readying for bed. Quickly donning her nightgown, she slipped between the covers and hugged her pillow tightly to herself. When Lord Templeton had kissed her, a right he surely possessed as she had agreed to become his wife, she'd felt nothing. And when he'd deepened the kiss? Revulsion had coursed through her. Lord, how she wished Michael had been the one holding her. Kissing her.

She recalled their passion in his office at the stables. The memory of his hands and mouth on her skin. She conveniently omitted from her memory his anger at what he called her mercenary behavior, choosing to focus instead on her memories of the sweet and passionate words he'd uttered before his anger surfaced.

Feeling flush at her recollections, she smiled as she drifted off to sleep.

Less than a week after his arrival to Bridgewater Park, Lord Templeton announced that he had need to go to London to see about some business. Just that morning he'd taken his leave, assuring Betsy that he would return on the morrow. She bade him farewell after taking breakfast with him, more relieved than she would admit that he was gone from her sight.

She'd spent much of the last few days plagued with a variety of discomforts. Her head ached from keeping Lord Templeton's instructions in order. Her stomach ached from continually suppressing her emotions. Her heart ached from Michael's continued avoidance. Whenever she caught Michael's eye when at dinner or the like, a dark look crossed his features and he turned sharply from her. Lord Templeton was a constant companion, darn him. No longer could she imagine them married, for she could barely stand to be in the same room with him. Whenever he found her alone, he pressed his body close to hers, whispering all the things he would do to her after they wed.

"You will be a delightful bed partner, I'd wager," he'd told just the previous night. "I believe I shall not have the need to take a mistress for a year at least."

She'd closed her eyes and suffered his kisses, feeling nothing but revulsion. His pomposity was another plague on her mind. He had told her soon after his arrival at Bridgewater Park that he would not allow such insolence from her as he had witnessed from her sister.

Now that he was gone, she would approach her mother and tell her of her true feelings for her betrothed. She left the breakfast room and located Lady Bridgewater in the parlor. Betsy stood in the doorway for a moment, her resolve strengthening. She cleared her throat to gain her mother's attention. The woman turned at the sound, her eyes running over Betsy. Betsy held her hands in fists at her side.

"Yes, Betsy?" her mother asked, her brow slightly furrowed. "Is something troubling you?"

More than you can imagine, Mother. Betsy came to sit beside her. "I don't believe I can marry Lord Templeton." At her mother's gasp of shock, she added, "So soon."

"Soon?" Lady Bridgewater responded. "Why, the wedding will not take place until January. Do you wish to postpone it?"

Indefinitely. "Yes."

"I promise you we shall accomplish all that's required in

time for the nuptials."

Betsy huffed and tried again. "I don't believe we suit, Mother."

Lady Bridgewater laughed lightly and patted Betsy's hand. "My dear girl, you are simply experiencing a touch of nerves regarding the thought of connecting yourself to such a powerful and commanding gentleman."

Betsy stared at her mother in dismay. Did she truly see the earl is such a light? Lady Bridgewater took her silence as agreement and went on to enumerate the details to which they needed to attend regarding the wedding.

Betsy simply endured her mother's total indifference to her plight until the woman ran out of things to say, her anger simmering.

"Well," she said as her mother paused in her diction. "Thank you for your assistance, Mother."

"Are you feeling better, then?"

Betsy nodded dutifully. "Yes," she lied.

She rose off the settee and left the parlor, maintaining a tenuous rein on her anger until she was well out of her mother's sight. Sputtering a few decidedly unladylike expletives, she hurried up the stairs to her chamber. Only one thing would calm her nerves at this particular moment: a good hard ride over some of the steepest trails on the grounds.

She rang for Ann and wasted no time in changing out of her day dress and into one of her favorite riding habits. The outfit consisted of a light blue skirt trimmed with black velvet cording, topped by a matching spencer. Ann pulled at Betsy's hair with her brush and quickly plaited them into one thick braid. She finished the simple style with a wide ribbon of black velvet. Ann left her chamber then, and Betsy followed suit to hurry toward the stables.

Betsy reining in her horse after a very long ride. She managed a smile for the groom assisting her and dismounted with a sigh.

"I'd hoped our ride would take my mind off of my troubles," she whispered to the horse. "I daresay I should have ridden straight on through to Cornwall."

"Betsy," Michael said softly.

Betsy spun around to face him. "Michael!"

He gave her a crooked grin and leaned against the wooden wall beside him. "I trust you had a pleasant ride, love?"

The tender endearment was all she heard. She rushed toward him and right into his arms. Michael wrapped those arms around her as she sobbed against his chest.

"Betsy, love," he said softly. "What's wrong?"

"Oh, Michael," she sniffed. "I can't marry him. I just can't."

Chapter 8

It was the declaration Michael had hoped for. Her obvious distress wasn't.

"Shh," he soothed, rubbing a hand over her back. "It will be all right."

"No," she sobbed, misunderstanding his meaning. "I can't abide him. He's hateful."

Michael silently agreed with her. He dropped kisses on her hair as he held her closer. "You don't have to marry him, Betsy."

She lifted her head to stare at him, her face set. "I won't," she stated. "I don't know why he wishes me to be his wife. He's tried to change everything about me."

Michael wiped away her tears and shook his head. "Templeton is a fool."

Betsy smiled up at him. She ran her gaze over him and he was reminded of the passionate words he'd spoken the last time he held her this way.

"Tell me you want me, Michael," she softly commanded. "Tell me you want me for myself."

He felt a rush of lust shoot through him. He brushed her hair back from her face with a shaking hand. "How the devil could I not want you?"

Uncertainty clouded her eyes as she gazed up at him. "As I am?"

He held her closer still. "Precisely as you are."

He brought his lips to hers and she opened her mouth to him. Michael moaned softly as his tongue stroked hers, tasting her sweetness. Betsy ran her fingers through his hair as she kissed him back fiercely. He placed his hands on her bottom and lifted her against him. Betsy smiled her surprise and delight. Desire ruled him as he carried her to an unoccupied stall and placed her on her feet in the soft sweet hay.

"Betsy." He cupped her face with both hands and studied her for a long moment. "You're perfect to me, Betsy."

Michael freed her hair from its confinement in the thick braid, letting the velvet ribbon float to the floor. He kept his eyes on her face as his fingers deftly unfastened the black velvet buttons trailing down the front of her short jacket. He spread the material wide open, pushing the jacket off of her shoulders. He dropped his gaze then. Her breasts were nearly visible to him through her chemise.

She brought her hands to his chest and nimbly unbuttoned his shirt. He shrugged off the garment as she ran her hands over his chest.

"You're beautiful, Michael," she said softly.

He let out a strangled laugh. Shaking his head at her, he unfastened the hooks at the back of her skirt and let it drop to the floor. Betsy stepped out of it and stood before him, now clad in only her chemise and petticoat. She placed her hands on his chest again, trailing her fingers over his stomach. She reached the waistband of his breeches and began to unbutton them. But with only two buttons unfastened, Michael gently grasped her hands to still them. She looked up at him in confusion.

"Not yet, love," he said in a rough whisper.

Michael picked up her crumpled skirt and spread it on the hay. He fell to his knees upon it, his hands on her slender waist. She slowly came to her knees in front of him as he ran his mouth over her. She closed her eyes as he caressed her through her thin chemise, arching toward him.

"Oh, Michael," she breathed.

He untied the ribbon holding her chemise closed and set the gauzy material aside. He gazed at her full breasts, at their rosy nipples begging for his touch.

"Perfect," he rasped.

He cupped her breasts in his hands, running his thumbs over her nipples. Betsy trembled at his touch. He lowered her to

The Viscount's Vixen ~ JoMarie DeGioia

the floor, coming down on top of her.

"Ah, sweetheart," he murmured, bringing his lips to her breast.

Betsy closed her eyes as he drew one nipple deep into his mouth. She cradled his head and writhed beneath him.

Michael thrilled at her response and reached under her petticoat to stroke her through her drawers. He could feel her growing dampness through the thin material and struggled to hold onto his control. He removed her drawers and stroked her deeply, finding the tiny nub of her desire.

"Oh, my!" she gasped, pressing herself against his hand.

"Easy, love," he rasped, his pulse pounded in his ears.

When she began to chant his name in a soft pleading voice, he knew he could wait no longer. He unbuttoned his breeches, freeing himself. Never before had he felt such desire. Never before had he been so aroused as to nearly lose himself. He flipped her petticoat up and out of his way. Without waiting a moment longer, he entered her with one deep thrust. He realized his blunder a moment too late, cursing under his breath.

Betsy cried out as the pain assailed her. He held himself still, though the pressure to move was overwhelming. He whispered her name as he brushed the tears from her cheeks. She opened her eyes, pain in their violet depths.

"Michael," she whispered tearfully. "It hurts."

"I know, sweetheart," he said softly. "I'm sorry."

"I don't understand."

"It's your virgin's pain, love," he told her, kissing her cheek. "It will soon cease. Give me your mouth."

She did as he instructed. As she returned his kisses, Michael began to move within her. She gasped, causing him to lift his head and look at her in alarm.

"Have I hurt you again?"

She shook her head, gazing at him through her lashes. "You're inside me."

Michael breathed in sharply. He could only nod, the strain of holding back his pleasure causing his jaw to clench. When he moved again, when she closed her eyes in obvious pleasure, he increased the strength of his thrusts. He was soon driving into her, his control threatening to desert him.

Betsy's nails raked his bare back as she came closer and closer to her release. She tightened around him, moaning. Shouting out his name as her climax took her, she trembled beneath him. Michael gave in to his passion then, coming with a guttural shout. He held her close as his heartbeat slowly returned to its normal rate.

"Betsy," he whispered at last, leaning up on his elbows. "Are you all right?"

Betsy sighed and opened her eyes. Her smile was all the answer he needed. He laughed softly and hugged her to him. He brushed her damp curls back from her face and kissed her tenderly.

"I'll set this to rights, love," he said. "You have my word."

"What do you mean?"

He shook his head. "Know this," he said firmly. "You won't marry that old man. You'll be mine."

Her eyes sparkled up at him. "I'm already yours."

He grinned and kissed her soundly. When he raised his head, it was with regret. He stood and helped her to her feet. As he buttoned his breeches he took in her appearance. Her chestnut waves were in a wild tumble, holding more than a few pieces of straw in their tangles. The straps of her chemise hung off of her creamy shoulders. Her cheeks were flushed, her lips swollen from his kisses, and he was damned if he didn't want her again.

"We need to get you back to the house, love," he said in a low voice.

Betsy blinked in confusion. Michael chuckled deeply and

retrieved her clothes from the floor. She dressed quickly and ran her fingers through her tangled curls, putting them somewhat back in order. He smiled at her delightful appearance and hugged her to him. With a few more tender words, he sent her back to the main house.

He watched her go. What the devil was he to do now? His eyes fell on the velvet ribbon nearly buried in the straw. He deftly plucked it from its hiding place and brought it to his lips. Grinning broadly, he tucked it into his pocket and returned to his office.

***

Betsy entered the mansion and hurried toward the grand staircase, nearly knocking over her little sister Mary in her haste.

"Forgive me, Mary," she rushed out. "I didn't see you there."

Mary furrowed her brow as she looked closely at her.

"What happened to you?" she asked. "Did your horse throw you?"

"Why would you think such a thing?"

Mary placed her hands on her hips. "You look like you've been rolling in the hay."

Betsy bit her lip to keep the laughter from bubbling forth.

She quickly realized that her mother would no doubt soon be joining Mary and would likewise puzzle over her odd appearance. She brushed a few pieces of straw from her skirt and managed a smile.

"I had a bit of trouble seeing to my horse's grooming, Mary. That's all. I'm going to ring for a bath right away."

Mary apparently took Betsy at her word and skipped into the parlor. Betsy breathed a sigh of relief and raced up the stairs. She ordered a bath, caring not a whit it was strange for her to do so at that particular time of day. As she crossed to her dressing room, she caught a glimpse of herself in the cheval mirror. Her color was high, her eyes bright. Her hair was an absolute mess. Smirking at her ludicrous appearance, she donned her wrapper and awaited her bath.

When she was bathed and her hair neatly brushed and styled, she let her mind wander back to all that had happened between Michael and herself. His sweet words and caresses had made her feel like the most beautiful girl in the world. He'd told her he would set things to rights, although what that meant precisely, she was uncertain. Would he offer for her hand? As long as she was rid of the odious Earl of Templeton, she would be most pleased.

Thank goodness he was still in London. She wouldn't have to suffer his barbs that evening. And she could gaze upon Michael as much as she wished to, although she thought it best if she hid her feelings from her relatives until such time as Michael announced his intentions. Humming to herself, she readied for tea.

That evening at dinner—and afterwards, when the men rejoined the ladies—Betsy couldn't keep her eyes from Michael's magnificent form. One glance in his direction brought their passion rushing back to her mind. Her breath came fast as she recalled his body upon hers, the passion etched on his handsome face as he moved above her. Except for her initial pain, it had been the most wonderful experience of her life. No matter what would happen between them in the future, she knew she wouldn't spend another moment agonizing over her betrothal to Lord Templeton.

She knew with absolute certainty there would be no wedding to the esteemed earl, despite her parents' objections to her breaking her engagement. Michael glanced her way in the next moment, his beautiful eyes dark. He would set things to rights, he'd said. How should she approach her parents? Perhaps if she spoke to Maggie first. Her sister would surely understand her feelings, having loved Philip so intensely for so long.

She rose and crossed to where her sister sat. Maggie smiled up at Betsy as she joined her.

"How is your evening, Betsy?"

"Very pleasant, Maggie," Betsy returned, perching next to her on the settee.

Maggie smiled and leaned toward her. "I believe that's due to a certain gentleman's absence?"

Betsy nodded vigorously, her gaze unconsciously returning to where Michael stood with Philip.

Maggie's smile widened. "And also to another gentleman's presence?"

Betsy blushed, unable to keep the smile from her lips. After a quick glance at her mother assured her the woman was paying them little attention, she leaned closer still.

"Maggie, what am I to do?"

"You need to decide for yourself, sister."

Betsy gave a quick nod. "I realize that," she agreed quickly. "But I don't think I can tell my mother."

"Betsy, dear," Lady Bridgewater said, coming to stand before them. "When Lord Templeton returns on the morrow, we'll need to sit down and discuss some particulars."

Betsy and Maggie exchanged a glance. Betsy straightened her slight shoulders and faced her mother.

"Surely we don't have to attend to such matters at this time, Mother."

"Now dear, a wedding takes a great deal of planning. Why, only this morning you asked me if all would be accomplished in time."

Michael watched her closely through narrowed eyes as she reddened. Betsy read his pique and was confounded. Why, just a few moments before he'd been favoring her with those smoldering glances that always made her heartbeat faster. She looked back at her mother and Maggie.

"Mother," she began, "I'd merely asked if we should perhaps postpone the nuptials."

Maggie's brows shot up in surprised approval. Betsy saw it and felt decidedly stronger in her resolve.

"We discussed this earlier, Betsy," her mother said. "I believe we can complete our preparations long before January."

Betsy shook her head as her eyes settled on her father. Lord Bridgewater gazed in wonderment at her.

"Is this true, Betsy?" he asked her. "Do you wish to postpone the wedding?"

Betsy looked from her mother's disapproval to her father's bewilderment and was nonplussed. Taken with Maggie and Philip's speculative glances, she could only wish to divert attention from the topic at hand. She glanced at Michael, further confounded by the mix of emotions evident on his face.

"I only…" She looked back at her father. "I don't think we should discuss this at this moment, Father."

"As you wish it, my dear," he said. "There will be much time to discuss your wedding when Templeton returns."

Betsy smiled not at the thought of her fiancé's return, but at her father's quick dismissal of the topic. When she next glanced at Michael, she saw a look of speculation had replaced that of irritation on his face.

As the evening wore on, Betsy couldn't hide the effects of her tumultuous afternoon, yawning behind her hand.

"Are you tired, Betsy?" Maggie asked her.

"Yes." Her eyes settled on Michael. "I had quite an eventful day, I daresay."

Michael must have heard her comment. He nodded to Philip before coming to stand before her. "Betsy, in light of Lord Templeton's absence, I hope you'll allow me to escort you to your chamber?"

He smiled then, a bright smile that caused her heart to flutter. She nodded and put her hand in his offered one, coming swiftly to her feet.

"That would be lovely," she said with an incline of her head.

She bade good night to her family, barely hiding her own smile.

Chapter 9

Michael stopped before Betsy's door and smiled down at her. He cupped her face and brought his lips to hers, kissing her deeply before pulling back.

"I've wanted to do that all evening." He stroked her cheek. "How are you feeling, love?"

"Feeling?"

He nodded. "Are you tender?"

Her eyes widened. She quickly lowered her lashes, reddening. "I feel fine, Michael."

Relief filled him. He'd watched her all evening for any sign of the unavoidable pain he'd caused that afternoon.

"I'm glad," he said, hugging her to him.

Betsy sighed as she cuddled against him. He dropped a kiss on her hair and held her closer.

"What will you tell Templeton tomorrow, Betsy?"

"I don't know," she said. "I'll make certain, however, that he knows I'm not marrying him."

Damn right.

Betsy toyed with the hairs at the nape of his neck, absently stroking him with her fingers. God, he loved when she did that. He was well aware of her soft body pressed against him, and

108

hardened in response. He moved his lips to Betsy's ear, nuzzling her as she purred against him. When she instinctively cuddled his arousal with her hips, his desire flared. He opened the door to her chamber and urged her inside.

Betsy tilted her face as he brought his lips to hers. She touched her tongue to his, moaning softly in the back of her throat. He ran his lips over her cheek, the side of her neck.

"God, how I want you, Betsy," he murmured.

"Take me, Michael."

He turned and pinned her against the wall, running his hands lovingly over her curves. Despite the fact that their passion in the stables was still fresh in his mind, he tried valiantly to distance himself from her charms. He lifted his head to gaze at her regretfully.

"Ah, love," he rasped. "We shouldn't be doing this."

Her eyes, darkened to violet, pierced him to his soul.

"Love me again, Michael," she argued softly. "Please."

At her whispered plea, his resolution dissolved. He grabbed her to him and lifted her skirts. When he began to unbutton his breeches, he realized the absurdity of their situation and froze. Her bed was merely a few feet from them, she was soft and pliant in his arms, and yet he was moments away from taking her roughly again, there against the wall. The brief flash of sanity brought reality crashing down upon him. He cursed softly and set her from him.

"Michael?" Betsy asked breathlessly. "What's wrong?"

"We can't do this again, Betsy."

"But, why not?"

He had no real answer for her. He wouldn't hurt her again. He couldn't tell her the true reason he wished to separate from her. He didn't feel worthy.

"I shouldn't have taken you this afternoon," he said. "It was a mistake."

She shook her head. "How could you change so quickly?"

"Betsy."

Tears welled up in her eyes as she blinked rapidly. Michael turned from her and looked about the room. He spied the necklace on the vanity then, the onyx she had worn around her neck a few evenings past. He crossed to the vanity and reached out to touch the stone.

"This is quite beautiful," he said.

"Yes it is." She wiped a tear from her eye. "I regret I must return it to Lord Templeton."

Michael turned sharply toward her. "Are jewels so

important to you, then?"

Betsy's eyes widened. "No."

He snorted in disbelief.

"I merely favor the stone because it reminds me of your eyes," she said.

His mouth dropped open. She lifted her chin and opened her door for him.

He stepped toward her. "Betsy, I didn't mean to hurt you."

"Good night, Michael," she said, her voice low.

He winced at the pain visible on her features.

"You don't understand, love. My situation, my fortune."

"And you don't understand me," she whispered. "Good night."

Michael raked his fingers through his hair and stepped past her and into the hallway. He turned to face her again. "If you would let me explain."

"More fool me," she said from behind the panel.

Michael stared long and hard at her door. He still wanted her even as he told himself he never should have taken her. He was pleased she wouldn't marry the earl, but he couldn't make any promise of a future to her. What on earth could he offer her?

"Forgive me, love," he whispered, turning away once

more.

***

When Betsy awoke the next morning, she was quickly reminded of the events of the previous day. She felt a soreness between her legs as she stood beside her bed and groaned softly. How could such pleasure cause such pain? The pain in her heart was far sharper, however. Michael's dismissal of their intimate connection plagued on her mind. Had she imagined his regard for her? No. He'd told her he wished to make her his, after all. That she would belong to none other than himself. Had he been merely reciting the sweet words to take her virtue?

No doubt the Earl of Templeton would be arriving shortly. That thought further darkened her mood. She walked somewhat stiffly into her dressing room and saw to her morning toilette. She rang for her maid and soon donned a pretty day dress of lilac. Ann dressed Betsy's hair in a simple coil at the back of her head, framing her face with fetching curls.

After Ann left, Betsy's eyes fell upon the onyx necklace. Her stomach to clench painfully. She opened the jeweler's box and gingerly placed the necklace inside. After Michael's unreasonable actions of the previous evening, the thought of returning the stone to Lord Templeton no longer caused the slightest regret. Sighing once more, she arose and left her chamber, bound for the breakfast room.

Before she'd finished her breakfast, Lord Templeton called her name from the doorway. He grinned slyly at her, which she found strange, but soon wore an expression of benevolence.

"My dear." He came to sit beside her. "I could not dally another moment in London, knowing you awaited me here at Bridgewater Park."

"Good morning, Lord Templeton," she said softly.

Templeton studied her for a long moment. Betsy shifted uncomfortably under his slow perusal, her cheeks growing hot.

He sat down beside her and leaned toward her. "You look incredibly lovely this day, Elizabeth." He touched her flushed cheek. "I've missed you."

After glancing quickly toward the doorway and seeing no one about, Templeton crushed his mouth to hers. Betsy whimpered as he forced his tongue into her mouth. He withdrew just as quickly, a smile of satisfaction on his face.

"Ah, you taste sweet."

Betsy couldn't keep the disgust from wrinkling her brow. Templeton wrongly interpreted her expression as modesty, apparently. He chuckled deeply.

She held her hands in fists in her lap beneath the table. "I would ask you to refrain from such actions in the future, Lord Templeton."

Templeton pulled back, his hand on his chest.

"You are soon to be mine in every way. Surely you must accustom yourself to such displays of affection. Why, I was most fortunate last evening to find an outlet for the passion the mere thought of you provoked within me. You must not deny me the pleasure of the smallest kiss now that you are once more before me."

He'd taken another woman last evening? His admission caused relief rather than any jealousy. Surely he held no great affection for her, then. She would speak to her father at the next available opportunity.

"I believe I'll see about the fine horses Balsam is training," he said. "Would you care to join me for a ride, my dear?"

Betsy weighed his words carefully. While she longed to see Michael that morning, his actions of last evening caused her to give a quick shake of her head.

"No thank you, Lord Templeton," she answered. "I promised Mary I would assist her in watching the younger children this morning."

It wasn't a lie in her mind at that moment, for suddenly she took great solace in the notion of hiding in the nursery for as long as possible that day. Templeton took her at her word and left her with a jaunty bow.

"Ridiculous man," she muttered the moment she was again alone.

She left the breakfast room then, bound for the nursery abovestairs.

***

Michael had finished his breakfast and was well away from the breakfast room at a very early hour. Betsy had come immediately to his mind upon waking, causing guilt to slash through him afresh. He wouldn't blame her if she kept her betrothal intact. He'd given her nothing but pain over the last twenty-four hours, no doubt causing her to welcome the return of the gallant Earl of Templeton. He cursed loud and long over that thought.

He turned his attentions once more to his troubling finances. Although his horse-breeding venture with Philip would no doubt prove highly profitable in the future, it afforded him no solace this day. He was unable to make an offer for her at present, even if she were to become free. But what of their passion?

What if a child was the result? How the devil would she ever be able to withstand such a scandal? His heart suddenly soared at the thought of a child of theirs. Of a tiny being that would forever tie him to her. He wished for a moment there would be such a consequence from their union, for she would then be his. No. He would never want to force their connection in such a manner. There was nothing else for it. He would never take her again.

"Ah, Betsy," he murmured, shaking his head in regret.

That evening after dinner, Michael was befuddled. It was obvious Betsy hadn't broken her engagement to the odious Lord Templeton, for the man was fairly puffed with pride as he kept his hand on her arm in a show of possession. She, however, looked anything but happy.

Her dejection was obvious to all but Templeton and Lady Bridgewater. Betsy's mother fawned over Templeton as if every word dropped from the man's lips was a pearl of wisdom to be savored. Lord, how he wished to take Betsy in his arms. To declare her as his to all assembled.

He turned his gaze from Betsy's beloved form to find the Earl of Templeton giving him a look of dark speculation. He

116

straightened and scowled at the man, long-tired of hiding his disdain. To his dismay, the earl smiled at him and crossed the room to join him.

"I wished to thank you, Balsam," Templeton said loudly, drawing Betsy's attention as well as that of the others in attendance.

Michael arched a brow. "Thank me, Templeton?" he countered. "Whatever for?"

"I hear you took great care of my Elizabeth in my absence."

Betsy's eyes grew round at the man's words, her hands twisting the skirt of her lovely satin gown. She paled and lowered her eyes to her lap. Michael saw her distress and felt alarm trill in the back of his mind. What was the pompous fool about? Had one of the grooms seen or heard something he shouldn't have yesterday?

"Forgive me, but I don't know to what you are referring."

"Why, my good man," Templeton went on. "You escorted her to her room in my absence, did you not?"

Michael gave a curt nod at the man's words. Why the devil was Templeton goading him? Betsy breathed an audible sigh of relief, her eyes flying beseechingly to Maggie's. Her sister apparently took her cue and turned the topic of conversation to the races to be held in the nearby counties in the coming weeks. Philip warmed to the topic as well, drawing Lord and Lady Bridgewater into the conversation.

Michael added little to the conversation, his mind working. He would win her from the old man. Never again would he see the look of utter shame he'd glimpsed on Betsy's face. No doubt she too had thought the man privy to what had transpired in the stables. Templeton had simply been baiting him, then. But, why?

When Templeton escorted Betsy from the room as the hour grew late, Michael could only hope the man would keep his insinuations to himself and cause her no more distress that evening.

***

The next morning, Betsy awoke with determination in her breast. When Lord Templeton had escorted her to her chamber last evening, he had once more pressed closely to her, and alluded to the marriage bed.

Never again would he say such things to her or touch her in such a familiar fashion. She rang for Ann and dressed quickly. She hurried down to her father's study, most relieved when she found him within.

118

"Betsy," he said with surprise, coming swiftly to his feet. "What on earth could you want with me at this early hour? Have you eaten?"

"No."

Betsy began to wring her hands, causing her father to wrinkle his brow in confusion.

"I believe Lord Templeton is anticipating your joining him in the breakfast room, daughter."

The mere mention of the man's name strengthened her determination. She closed the door and faced her father.

"Father," she said, straightening her shoulders. "I cannot marry Lord Templeton."

Her father's eyes grew round at her declaration. "But, I don't understand. I believed you were pleased with the match. You seemed so in London."

Betsy sighed and sat herself in the chair facing his desk.

"I admit I was content with my decision in London, yes," she said. "I realize now, after spending quite a bit of time in his company, that we will not suit."

Lord Bridgewater rubbed his chin thoughtfully. "Betsy," he said leaning down to take her hand. "Does this have anything to do with a certain young gentleman residing here with us?"

119

Betsy's face flushed hot. She read the enlightenment in her father's countenance and gave a quick shake of her head.

"I assure you, Father, Michael plays no part in my decision this day."

After studying her for a moment longer, her father let the matter drop.

"Pray, tell me precisely why you wish to end your betrothal."

Betsy's composure threatened to desert her. She sniffled, her hands twisting her skirt.

"I cannot abide Lord Templeton, Father," she said tearfully. "He wishes to change me. To make me something I'm not."

"He is much older than you are, child," her father said. "Surely his expectations of marriage would differ from yours."

Her mind raced with Templeton's distasteful comments of the evening past, causing her to cringe.

"His expectations are not what trouble me," she said. "I don't love him."

The earl studied her for a long moment, finally giving her a slow nod.

"If you don't wish to marry him, Betsy, I won't force the

match," he said with a comforting smile.

Betsy flew into his arms in the next moment.

"Oh, Father!" she exclaimed, hugging him tightly. "Thank you!"

He chuckled at her exuberance, and then pulled back to pat her cheek. That matter seen to, another soon pressed into her mind.

"Why are you frowning, daughter?"

"What will Mother say?" she asked in a whisper.

He smiled again. "Leave your mother to me, child," he told her. "I won't have a daughter of mine marry someone she doesn't love."

"I don't even like him," she could not help but add.

Her father laughed, shaking his head at her.

Just before luncheon, a knock came to Betsy's door. She'd just dismissed Ann and was eager to go belowstairs and join her family, certain she would never have to see Lord Templeton again.

"Come in," she called.

Templeton opened her door and entered. "I wish to speak with you, Elizabeth," he said, closing the door.

She turned sharply toward him. "Lord Templeton!"

He ran his eyes over her, finally forcing a condescending smile to curve his mouth.

"I'm sorry if I disturbed you," he said with an incline of his head.

Her heart raced. While she'd suspected she would have to speak to him eventually, she'd hoped to delay their meeting until well after their engagement was broken.

She raised her chin, steeling herself for the distasteful exchange. "It's quite all right. I trust you've spoken to my father?"

"Yes, my dear." He stepped closer. "I'll be leaving the estate directly and wished only to bid you farewell."

Betsy gazed up at him, at the benevolence and good will evident on his face. She consciously chose to put aside all the distasteful comments he'd made to her in the past few weeks and viewed him once more as a favored acquaintance. A small smile curved her lips.

"I hope you aren't upset with me," she said softly.

"Upset?" He clicked his tongue. "I assure you, my dear Elizabeth, I have only your best interests at heart. If you feel we aren't meant to be together," he paused, his voice thick with emotion, "at this particular time," he added, "I shall abide by your wishes."

He reached out to touch the loose tendrils at her cheeks. "I wonder if perhaps you aren't correct in your assumptions, my dear."

Betsy blinked up at him. "I don't understand."

"Perhaps you and I do not suit." He patted her cheek and dropped his hand from her. "I do hope, however, you will still think of me as a friend?"

Betsy breathed a sigh of relief. "Or course."

"I shall be off, then," he said with a nod. "If you are ever in need of anything, Elizabeth, I beseech you to contact me directly."

Betsy couldn't imagine what on earth she would ever need from the man in the future, but thought to ease his mind with an acceptance of his offer. He kissed her hand, bowed gallantly and strode from the room. She closed her eyes, feeling guilt mix with the incredible relief she felt over the matter's smooth resolution.

Chapter 10

Michael stood before the mirror in his guest chamber, readying for dinner. He topped his black breeches with a waistcoat of deep blue, the color immediately bringing Betsy's eyes to his mind. Sighing irritably, he shrugged into his gray jacket and straightened his cravat. He raked his fingers through his hair and studied his reflection.

Despite his having successfully avoided Betsy's company for the day, her image nonetheless plagued him. He had the great misfortune of taking his breakfast with Lord Templeton, barely restraining his ire as the odious man alluded to his "splendid" match with Betsy. Well-matched, indeed? She was his, damn it to hell!

He turned sharply from the mirror and paced about the chamber. How the devil would he ever wrest her from the man?

He ceased his pacing and reached into his pocket. He withdrew Betsy's velvet ribbon, bringing it to his lips. Closing his eyes, he envisioned her as she'd looked in the stables. Tousled and well loved. There was no doubt in his mind Betsy would again be his, body and soul. If that meant dallying with a married woman, so be it. No. Even as the thought entered his mind he knew he could never treat her so abominably. He would simply have to make certain her marriage to Templeton never took place.

The terrible words he'd said to her a few evenings past came back to him. Would she even have him after his horrid behavior? He tucked the piece of velvet into his pocket. Having had his fill of such thoughts at last, he ran his fingers through his hair once more and left the chamber, bound for the parlor to await the dinner bell.

Betsy looked up from where she sat beside Maggie on the settee as he entered. Their eyes met for a brief moment. He nodded curtly at her and strode to the window to join Philip and Lord Bridgewater. Betsy quickly averted her eyes, sighing softly.

"I trust you are well this evening, Betsy?" Lady Bridgewater asked her daughter in a clipped tone.

"Yes, Mother," Betsy answered. "How are you?"

The older woman's lips pursed as she shot a glance at her husband. At Lord Bridgewater's answering scowl, she managed a weak smile in Betsy's direction.

"Very well," she said. "I promised your father I would not berate you this evening, child. But, I wish to speak to you in the morning."

Betsy gazed at her father, gratitude clear on her face. At his benevolent smile, she looked back at her mother.

"Yes, Mother," she said softly. "We'll speak of it in the morning."

The ladies swiftly turned their discussion to more mundane topics, to Betsy's great relief.

Michael listened to the ladies' exchange from his vantage point across the room. Their words' meaning escaped him, but Betsy looked strained, her delicate hands clasped tightly in her lap. He found that surprising, as he'd been quick to take note of the Earl of Templeton's blessed absence. Did she miss the gentleman so acutely? Could it be she now reveled in the man's constant admonitions to her every action? He was grateful when the dinner bell sounded, for once quite pleased to allow the formalities of the evening ritual to occupy his mind.

After dinner, when the gentlemen had separated from the ladies, Michael made mention of Lord Templeton to Philip, able to restrain his curiosity no longer.

"Where is Templeton, Wilton?" he asked, managing to keep his voice even. "I assume the esteemed earl had more business to which to attend?"

Philip looked at him askance. "No." He handed Michael a

glass of brandy. "After the events of this morning, I would have been surprised had he remained at Bridgewater Park."

Michael blinked at him. "What?"

Philip suddenly laughed, drawing the attention of Betsy's father.

"What do you find so amusing, Philip?" the earl asked.

Philip bit back his laughter. Michael scowled at him, anger threatening to replace his confusion.

"Wilton, what are you saying?"

"I never thought you obtuse, Balsam," Philip teased.

Michael looked from him to Lord Bridgewater, confounded.

The earl shook his head. "I assume you are unaware of the events of this morning, Balsam," Lord Bridgewater said. "My daughter's betrothal has been set aside."

Michael's throat tightened at the man's words. It couldn't be. It was his fondest wish. He set his glass aside and faced Betsy's father.

"I," Michael began, his voice thick. He cleared his throat. "I had indeed been unaware of that, sir," he said to the earl. "How is Betsy faring, may I ask?"

He didn't miss the look of speculation exchanged between

127

Philip and the earl, and worried over Betsy's condition.

"Quite well, I believe," the earl said in answer. "It was upon her insistence the engagement was broken."

Michael felt his heart soar at the man's words. She would be his! He sobered in the next moment as the reality of his financial situation struck him. Surely the earl would want another suitor to come forward to offer for Betsy now she was unattached once again. A gentlemen whose financial standing was commensurate to Templeton's, no doubt. He, Michael, was certainly not that. He looked up to find both Philip and the earl staring at him in the strangest manner. He bristled under their close scrutiny.

"If you gentlemen will excuse me," he said coolly. "I have need to see to some matters in the stables."

"Balsam," Philip began. "What's the matter with you?"

"Good night," Michael said with a bow.

He left the study, bound for his office in the stables. He sat behind the desk, his head held in his hands. Betsy's freedom from her entanglement gave him pause. While he took great solace that the Earl of Templeton would never place his hands upon her silken skin again, he couldn't help but feel torn. He wished to go to her directly. To confess his true feelings for her.

What, precisely, were those feelings?

She was a plague on his mind. The angel who haunted his dreams. The clever vixen who challenged him. He couldn't bear the thought of going on without her in his life. She was sweet and kind. Charming and exasperating. He needed her. He might even love her.

He reviewed his comments of a few evenings past and knew them to be false. Regret was the very last emotion he could attribute to their passion in the stables. When he had taken her, when she had sweetly surrendered herself to him, he'd been shaken to the core. Never before had he felt such a connection with a woman. From the moment he'd seen her at the Derby, he'd been drawn to her. And now that she was free from any other attachments, he had little notion of how he could pursue her. He was unworthy of her.

Anger suddenly filled him. If it wasn't for the bloody mess in his father's finances, he would be able to pursue her.

"Bloody hell," he muttered.

***

Betsy stretched out on her bed, her eyes fixed on a small blue flower in the wallpaper adorning the wall opposite. When Philip and her father had rejoined the ladies that evening, she had sorely felt Michael's absence. Was it such a trial upon him to be in her company? No. Surely he loved her. Their passion was certainly the result of such incredible emotions, was it not?

She knew without a doubt that she loved him. She certainly wanted none other but him. She'd set aside her engagement to Lord Templeton, and knew that even if Michael did not offer for her she would wed no other. They were truly made for each other. Was the man so stubborn as to miss what was before him?

"That's of no consequence," she said in quiet determination.

Betsy rose from the bed and quickly donned her wrapper. She belted the ruffled garment tightly about her waist and left her chamber on silent footsteps, bound for the guest chambers.

Before her resolve could desert her, she rapped on his door. She heard rustling from within, and a few moments later the door opened. Oh, he looked incredible. He wore only his breeches, and they were unfastened. Her body flushed as she longed to pressed herself against him.

He blinked at her, running a hand through his tousled waves. "Betsy, what the devil are you doing here?"

Betsy smiled shakily up at him. She stepped into the room and stood still, her hands clasped in front of her.

"I wish to speak with you, Michael," she said softly.

He stared at her for a beat, and then shook his head as if to clear it. "You can't be found here," he said firmly. "You must return to your room."

"I had to see you." She closed the door. "Please don't send me away."

He studied her for a long moment, and then held his arms open wide. Betsy rushed into his embrace, pressing her cheek against his bare chest. Michael held her close, running his hands over her hair, her back. She cuddled closer, reveling in his tender caress.

"Oh, Michael. I love you."

Michael froze at her words. He gently grasped her shoulders and held her from him. "What did you say?"

She gazed up at him. "I love you," she said again.

His mouth gaped open in shock. He looked away, unable to meet her gaze. "You're mistaken," he said, his brow furrowed.

She tried without success to catch his eye, to read his emotions.

"I love you, Michael."

He stared at her then, hard. "We made love, Betsy," he said. "That is passion. Lust."

She shook her head again as tears welled in her eyes. "No!" she cried. "I know that you love me!"

Michael turned from her, apparently unwilling to surrender himself to such an emotion. Betsy ran her eyes over his splendid form. His hands were clenched in fists at his sides, his long legs braced apart. She placed her hands on his rigid back, gently caressing him. She heard a ragged sigh escape his lips as the tension began to leave the taut muscles beneath her fingertips.

"Tell me, Michael," she whispered, placing light kisses on his smooth skin. "Tell me you love me."

He finally turned to face her. She gasped at the confusion and anguish etched on his face.

"Betsy," he whispered, taking her hands in his. "What I feel for you, I can't express."

The tenderness in his dark and beautiful eyes was all the answer she needed.

"You love me," she stated again, her lips curved in a small smile. "Please let me stay here with you?"

Michael reached for the belt of her wrapper, toying with the knot. "You should return to your room, love," he said with little conviction.

At Betsy's insistent shake of her head, he slowly untied the belt. He let the garment fall to the floor, his eyes running hungrily over her. When he gazed upon her face, her knees nearly buckled at the passion in his dark and beautiful eyes.

"My God," he rasped. "You are incredible."

He pulled her to him, placing his lips on hers. Her mouth opened beneath his, silently begging him to deepen the kiss. He obliged her, groaning softly in his throat. His hands roamed over her as she pressed closely to him. His lips left hers to trail over her throat and she let her head fall back, sighing with pleasure.

"Love me, Michael," she breathed, her eyes closed tight.

"Ah, Betsy love," he rasped. "I shall."

Michael caressed her through her thin gown, and then eased it off of her shoulders to join the wrapper on the floor. Sweeping her up into his arms, he carried her to his bed and set her upon it. He straightened, reaching for the waistband of his breeches. She stared at that intriguing part of him and drew in a breath.

"Michael," she gasped.

"Are you frightened, love?"

Betsy gave a quick shake of her head and brought her eyes to his.

"However did you fit inside of me?" she asked. "You're so

133

big and I'm so small."

Michael groaned.

"Yes," he said, his voice low. "You're small. And hot and wet. And when I was inside you I wished to stay forever."

Betsy's heart pounded as much at his words as at the heat in his dark eyes.

"Oh, my!" she whispered.

Michael bridged the gap between them and came down upon her on the bed, kissing her hungrily. Betsy moved beneath him, rubbing her breasts against his chest as pleasure began to pulse through her. He brought his mouth to her breast, flicking his tongue over her taut nipple. She arched upward, silently begging him to end the sweet torment. He gave her what she craved and closed his mouth over her nipple, gently teething the nub as she whimpered softly. His fingers found their way to the curls that shielded her womanhood and she parted her legs for him.

"Betsy, love," he rasped, kissing her once more. "Are you ready for me?"

Betsy could hardly form the words, the intense pleasure of what he was doing to her nearly driving her out of her mind

"Yes," she whimpered.

He gently lifted her hips and entered her. Betsy rose to meet his thrusts, her arms wrapped around his neck as he moved within her. There was no pain this night, thank goodness, and he seemed to fit her perfectly. His big body was poised over her and then he began to move. It was sublime. It was… What had he called her? Incredible.

Michael trembled and made the most beguiling sounds as he thrust harder. At the very moment his climax hit him Betsy joined him in fulfillment, crying out her pleasure into his mouth as his lips found hers.

Michael collapsed on top of her. She could scarcely draw breath, she was so replete with satisfaction.

"Sweetheart," he whispered, kissing her ear. "Have I pleased you?"

She sighed in answer, cuddling closer to him. Her fingers curled in the dark hairs on his chest. He dropped a kiss on her hair and let out a sigh of intense satisfaction.

"What are you thinking, love?" he asked her.

"You and I are so different, Michael," she mused aloud. "How can it be we fit together?"

At her words, he laughed softly. He cupped her cheek with his hand as he looked down at her.

"You were made for my loving, Betsy," he said in answer. "You fit me perfectly."

She smiled lazily and closed her eyes. She ought to return to her room. A yawn took her and she cuddled closer. Lord, it felt so good to be held tight in his arms.

When she next opened her eyes the sun was beginning its ascent, bathing the room with soft pink light through the mullioned windows.

"Good morning, love," Michael said.

"Morning," she said around a yawn.

"You must return to your room, sweetheart," he said, brushing a curl back from her face. "You mustn't be found here."

Betsy hurriedly donned her nightgown and wrapper. Before she left him, they shared a sweet kiss. Betsy stared up at him, waiting for the words she so longed to hear. When no declaration of love came from him, when no offer of marriage spilled from his lips, her heart sank. Perhaps what he had said last evening was true. Perhaps what they shared was merely lust. She accepted another sweet kiss and left his chamber.

Betsy slipped between the covers of her bed and hugged her pillow. It was of no consequence that Michael hadn't professed his feelings. He loved her. It was evident in his beautiful eyes.

Chapter 11

Later that morning Michael reined in his horse and dismounted, patting the animal soundly. He set about the animal's grooming, removing the horse's bridle.

"Balsam," Philip growled from the doorway.

Michael looked up, surprised to find Philip glaring at him.

"Wilton," he said, his brow furrowed. "What the devil is troubling you, man?"

"In your office, Balsam," Philip ground out. "Now."

Perplexed, Michael handed the bridle to a groom and followed Philip into the office. He arched a dark brow at his friend.

"I believe you have me at a disadvantage, friend," Michael said as he closed the door. "You'll spook the horses with that dark look."

"This isn't a matter for jesting, Balsam," Philip said. "What are your intentions?"

Michael blinked rapidly. "Intentions?" he repeated. "I'm certain I don't know what you mean."

"I know you've dallied with her," Philip said curtly.

Michael pulled back. "How do you know that?"

"A servant saw her leaving your room this morning."

Michael closed his eyes as the truth settled on him. "Ah, God." He rubbed his hand over his face. "She'll be disgraced."

"Not necessarily."

Michael opened his eyes and regarded him closely. "What are you saying, Wilton?"

Philip grinned. "I admit I, um, preceded my own wedding night."

"Wedding night?" Michael asked. "I haven't given thought to any such thing."

"You haven't given thought to asking for Betsy's hand?" Philip fisted his hands. "What kind of scoundrel are you?"

Michael splayed a hand on his chest. "You do me grievous injury, Wilton."

Philip took a deep breath. "Tell me, then," he said. "Tell me of your intentions."

"I would marry her tomorrow if I were able."

"What the devil is stopping you?"

Michael paced the floor, raking his fingers through his hair. "My present situation hinders it, Wilton," he said sadly. "Her father will never accept me."

The two men were silent for several moments.

"Do you love her?" Philip asked at last.

139

Michael's brow furrowed in thought. He wanted her like no other. She made him laugh and drove him mad both. Her happiness was most important in his mind. His brows shot up as the truth hit him.

"Yes," he said. "I love her."

Philip clapped his hands together. "It's settled then!"

"But, what of the earl?" Michael asked. "How can you be so certain he'll accept my offer for her?"

"Balsam," Philip began, placing his hand on Michael's shoulder. "Trust me in this. The earl thinks very highly of true love. His views might be considered unconventional by some, but that's the fact of the matter."

Michael nodded absently, his mind focusing on another dilemma.

"I can't give Betsy all she deserves," he said. "If she were to leave me due to my situation, I don't know what I would do."

"She has a very large dowry, Balsam," Philip said. "Surely a man of your talents will no doubt build upon it. And if someday you were to recover your fortune, all the better."

"I will recover it," Michael said firmly.

"Well then, there you have it," Philip said with a smile.

Michael resumed his pacing, determination filling him.

140

"I'll speak to the earl directly," he said with a nod. "He'll accept my offer. I'm certain of it."

Philip clapped him on the back in hearty agreement. "Capital."

Michael smiled in answer, satisfied to have a course of action at last.

After returning to his chamber and dressing with care, Michael went in search of the Earl of Bridgewater. He found Betsy's father to be in his study and rapped determinedly on the door. At the earl's bidding, he opened the door and greeted the man with a nervous smile.

"Lord Bridgewater," he began. "I wish to have a word with you, sir."

The earl furrowed his brow. "Is this a business matter, Balsam?" He came to his feet. "I had thought your partnership with Philip would keep you engaged."

"This isn't a matter of business, sir," Michael rushed out. "It's a personal matter."

"A personal matter?" Lord Bridgewater took his seat once more. "I do hope nothing untoward has happened."

Michael gave a quick shake of his head and sat to face him. He'd given much thought to the many ways to broach the subject of his betrothal, still unsure of the direction he should take. He wished to be diplomatic. To voice his interest and gradually make his ultimate intentions known.

"I wish to ask for your daughter's hand, sir."

The earl blinked in surprise. Michael winced at his own blunder.

"You wish to marry Betsy?" Lord Bridgewater asked.

Michael took a deep breath to steel himself for the possible rebuke as he forged ahead. "Yes, sir. More than anything in this world."

The older gentleman opened his mouth but Michael held up a hand to silence him. At the man's nod, Michael voiced his concerns.

"I know my situation is a bit muddled at present, sir," he said. "I would understand if you had doubts regarding your giving me your consent."

"Balsam," the earl said, his eyes warm. "I know what kind of man you are. Of your fine character. I trust you know of Betsy's substantial dowry?"

Michael nodded. "I do, sir. I assure you that is not my incentive."

Lord Bridgewater laughed lightly. "I should hope not," he

said to Michael. "I know you to be an intelligent and honorable young man. Philip has told me of your fine management of your venture thus far, and of your affinity for handling finances." He looked at Michael with a touch of compassion. "It's a pity your father had not those same talents, eh son?"

"Yes," Michael said. "I regret I cannot offer Betsy all I would wish, sir. But you have my word she will never want for anything."

Lord Bridgewater waved his hand dismissively.

"I must know one thing, son," he said. "One thing that will seal this union."

Michael could hear his pulse pounding in his ears. What would the earl wish to know? He swallowed thickly.

"You may ask me anything, sir."

Lord Bridgewater leaned toward him. "Do you love her?"

"Yes," Michael answered fervently. "More than I ever imagined I could love another."

The earl flashed a bright smile now. "My dear boy," he said, coming to his feet once more. "I could not choose a better man to wed my second daughter."

Michael felt the tension leave his body in that instant. He bounded to his feet, clasping the earl's offered hand with a hearty handshake.

"Thank you, sir," he said with a grin. "You have truly made me the happiest of men."

The earl smiled at him. "We'll settle the marriage contract at another time, Balsam."

"Yes, sir," Michael agreed. "I believe I have need to speak with your daughter directly."

At the earl's nod, Michael left the study and hurried to parlor. He found Maggie working on her needlepoint within and smiled at her. She looked up at him in surprise.

"Lord Balsam," she said with a nod.

"Excuse me, Maggie," he said with a bow. "Have you seen Betsy?"

Maggie shook her head and opened her mouth to answer. Before she could say a word, he bowed again and left the room.

Michael raced up the stairs, intent on finding Betsy in her room. He nearly knocked Mary down in his haste.

"Do forgive me, Mary."

"Hello, Lord Balsam." The girl giggled. "Isn't it a lovely day?"

"What?" he asked, gazing down the hall toward Betsy's chamber. He returned his attention to the girl. "Yes, it is. Have you seen Betsy, Mary?"

"No, I haven't," Mary answered with an adorable pout. "She promised to show me some new stitches this morning but stayed abed until luncheon."

Michael flushed and averted his gaze, knowing full well what had tired Betsy so. He looked back at Mary and soon found the odd speculation in her blue eyes quite disconcerting. He cleared his throat nervously.

"If you will excuse me, Mary," he said with a bow. "I need to speak with your sister."

Mary smiled sweetly up at him. "Are you going to tell her you love her?"

"What?" Michael asked, stunned.

Mary giggled again and dropped a curtsy. "Good day, Lord Balsam," she said, skipping down the staircase.

Michael watched the girl go, his head still spinning at her words. Was he truly the last to know his own feelings?

He shook his head and rapped lightly on Betsy's door. When no answer came from within, he turned and descended the stairs. Where the devil was she? He left the house, bound for his office in the stables.

As he entered the building, a burst of feminine laughter

drew his attention. He turned swiftly, his eyes widening with appreciation as Betsy raced her horse toward the stables. She spied him and smiled brightly, reining in her horse before him.

"Good afternoon, Michael," she said, still out of breath.

"Good afternoon, love," he said in answer, grinning broadly.

He assisted her down from her mount and held his hands on her waist for much longer than was proper. She looked nervously about and shook her head at him.

"Michael," she began in a whisper. "What are you about?"

He grinned wickedly at her. Her eyes widened as he brought his mouth to hers and kissed her ravenously.

"Michael," she quietly admonished. "Someone may see us."

He shrugged. "I care not," he said, lowering his head to kiss her once more.

Betsy pulled back from him. "Do cease this," she gasped, her brow furrowed with worry.

Michael relented and let loose his hold on her. She brushed her hands over her skirt and glanced about once more. He watched her, his grin widening.

"Did you have a pleasant ride, love?" he asked her.

146

"Yes." Betsy regarded him closely. "Whyever are you grinning so?"

He shrugged again. "I can't help myself," he said with a chuckle. "Give me the words again, Betsy love."

"The words?" she repeated in confusion.

He nodded slowly. "Tell me you love me."

She blinked long lashes as she stared up at him. "I love you, Michael," she said softly.

He took his courage from her words, and any apprehensions he had regarding their engagement flew from his mind. He reached out and grasped her hands in his.

"Sweetheart," he began. "Will you marry me?"

He found the surprise evident on her face delightful, her violet eyes were opened wide, her lovely mouth agape.

"What?" she breathed.

"Marry me, Betsy." He smiled, cupping her cheek with his hand. "I wish for you to become my wife."

"But, Michael," she began. "You never said a word of marriage."

"I love you," he rushed out.

She could only stare at him, her eyes huge. "What did you say?"

"I love you, Betsy," he said, drawing her into his arms. "Say you'll be my wife."

She stood there in silence, her face a picture of swirling emotion.

"Don't leave me floundering, love," he said. "Give me your answer."

She smiled brightly up at him, putting his worries to rest.

"Yes!" she squealed, throwing her arms around his neck. "Yes, I'll marry you!"

He let out a whoop and hugged her tightly, twirling around in a circle. He came to a stop and set her back on her feet, smiling his joy. His eyes suddenly darkened as he lost his grin.

"Ah, Betsy," he said, bringing his face to hers. "Sweetheart."

Betsy sighed as his lips touched hers. Their kiss was sweet and tender. When at last he lifted his head, he found her brow wrinkled with worry.

"You don't regret your answer?" he asked.

Betsy laughed sweetly, setting his concerns aside. "Oh, no. I've wanted to marry you for so very long."

He let out a breath he had not been aware he was holding.

"Then what's troubling you, sweetheart?"

"I was simply thinking about my parents. What on earth will I tell them?"

He took her hand and brought it to his lips.

"I've spoken to your father, love." He brushed a kiss on her skin. "He's already gifted me with your lovely hand."

"Truly?"

"How could he deny me?" He couldn't keep a smile from his face. "Once I told him the truth, he knew our match was inevitable."

Her mouth fell open in apparent shock. "Surely you haven't told him of our...trysts."

"No, love," he assured her. "I would never shame you in such a manner."

"Then, what did you say to him?"

"I told him that I love you."

Her eyes sparkled up at him. "You love me."

He stroked his hand over her hair, his eyes dark. "How could I not?"

"Oh, Michael!" she cried, hugging him once more.

He laughed and returned her embrace.

"It's nearly tea time, love," he said at last. "No doubt your father will wish to announce our betrothal this afternoon."

She nodded and the two of them returned to the house to ready for tea, their hands clasped tightly together.

Chapter 12

Betsy stood poised in the hall outside of the parlor. She brushed her hands over the skirt of her violet tea gown and nervously gazed into the room. Her mother sat on a settee, a look of bemusement fixed upon her face. Her father stood beside her, wearing a big grin for his second daughter. Betsy returned his smile, feeling her tension begin to lessen.

Her eyes fell on her sister. Maggie was fairly shaking with excitement as Philip stood smiling beside her. All in all, they appeared as a happy group within.

"Do come in, daughter," Lord Bridgewater instructed.

Betsy smiled at her father once more and began to step into the room. A pair of strong hands suddenly gripped her shoulders, causing her to jump.

"Hello, love," Michael whispered in her ear.

Betsy turned and found him beaming a smile down at her. She was nearly giddy with relief and bit her lower lip to keep a giggle from bubbling out of her.

"Michael."

He took her hand and escorted her further into the room. Her father crossed to the couple and placed his hand on Michael's shoulder.

"Balsam," he began. "I believe I can guess my daughter's answer to your query."

"Yes, sir." Michael nodded. "She has given me her consent."

At his words, Maggie jumped off the settee and wrapped Betsy in a tight embrace. Philip took quick strides to where they stood and clapped Michael on the shoulder.

"Well done, Balsam," he said. "Well done."

Michael, reddening a bit in embarrassment, led Betsy toward her mother and bade her to sit. Betsy did so and clutched her hands in her lap, her nervousness threatening to make its reappearance. She happened a glance at her mother across from her, waiting for the woman to say something, to indicate her feelings on the matter.

"Mother," she began. "You haven't given voice to your thoughts."

Lady Bridgewater took a measuring glance at Michael and nodded curtly. She looked back at Betsy.

"I believe you have your sister's penchant for surprising me," she said with a small smile.

Philip laughed out loud, causing Michael to raise a brow.

"Tell me the story, Wilton."

Lady Bridgewater held up one hand to quiet Philip. She then told Michael of Maggie's previous betrothal, and of her own great surprise when she learned Maggie had accepted Philip's offer of marriage and not that of the man Lady Bridgewater had chosen for her.

"I do hope Mary will take care of her mother's nerves when her time comes," Lady Bridgewater finished with a dramatic sigh.

Betsy bit her lower lip again, quite certain Mary would be as determined in her choice as the earl's other two daughters. Michael sat beside her then, as close as was proper. He reached for her hand, grasping it in his own.

"When will the wedding take place, Lord Balsam?" Maggie asked Michael, drawing Betsy's attention from him at last.

Michael looked to Betsy for an answer and she gave a shrug.

"Perhaps we should have the ceremony in January," Lady Bridgewater suggested.

"No!" Betsy and Michael said at once.

Lady Bridgewater arched a graceful brow at her daughter. Betsy blushed hotly and lowered her eyes to lap. Michael smiled graciously at Lady Bridgewater.

"I cannot bear the thought of waiting for months to make Betsy my wife," he said. "Perhaps you can find it possible to complete the preparations within a fortnight or two?"

Her mother appeared to weigh his words, finally nodding her consent. Betsy clasped her hands.

"But know this, child," her mother went on. "If we're to have the wedding within a month's time, there is much we must see to immediately."

Betsy nodded, barely able to speak. She would be Michael's wife in less than one month's time! When her mother had suggested delaying the wedding until January, her heart and mind had rebelled. However could she keep from touching him until then? From kissing him? She looked up and found her mother and Maggie both watching her expectantly.

"I'll be happy to assist you," Maggie said.

"Oh, that would be wonderful, Maggie. Thank you."

As Lady Bridgewater began to list the matters to which it was necessary to be seen, Michael wore a thoughtful expression.

"I'll instruct my staff at Balsam Manor to make ready for my wife's arrival," he told Lady Bridgewater.

Betsy's mother set her teacup aside and fixed her gaze on

him. "What is the manor's condition, Lord Balsam?"

"The castle is in need of a few repairs," he said. "But be assured, madam, Betsy will live there in comfort."

"Ah, you're in for quite a treat, Betsy," Philip said. "The castle is quite medieval, with coats-of-arms on the most ancient stone walls."

Michael smiled at his friend's words. "I daresay Betsy will find lots of rooms to explore."

"Oh, yes!" Betsy turned to Maggie. "And Michael has told me we can ride along the cliffs, as well."

"You must take several of the best horses to the manor, Balsam," Philip said. "They'll enjoy the rugged countryside as much as your future wife, no doubt."

"Oh, I believe I envy you, Betsy," Maggie said with a smile. "I would so love to ride in Cornwall."

Michael nodded to her, unconsciously draping his arm about Betsy's shoulders. Betsy reveled in the tender gesture, leaning ever so slightly toward him on the settee.

"You and Wilton must visit us at the manor, Maggie," Michael said. "We would welcome your visit, wouldn't we, love?"

Betsy nodded, blushing lightly over his easy use of the

endearment. The four of them discussed the details of their visit, and Michael and Philip would suspend their horse-training venture for the winter months. As Balsam Manor was less than a three-hour ride from Bridgewater Park, Michael assured Philip that he and Betsy would make frequent visits to her family's home to keep their venture solvent.

"At the very least, we'll return for Christmas," he told Betsy's mother.

Betsy could barely concentrate on the animated conversations going on around her, her mind filled with the prospect of having Michael to herself for weeks at a time. She soon turned her thoughts to the manor. What was it truly like? She longed to make use of the many skills she had spent years perfecting on her new home. Her new home! She would be Elizabeth Reed, Lady Balsam.

She gazed lovingly at Michael as he spoke to Philip and her father, her eyes falling to his beautiful mouth. Recalling the incredible feeling of his perfect lips on her skin caused her to flush hotly. Forcing her attention to the various conversations around her, she caught Michael's eye. He stopped in his diction and studied her for a moment. He suddenly favored her with a dazzling smile. She returned the expression, her heart fluttering.

She finally joined the others in their conversation, glancing every so often at her future husband.

The next day began the whirlwind of wedding preparations. Betsy, with help from her mother and older sister, penned the hundreds of invitations. The three ladies sat in the front sitting room chatting as their pens moved over the fine paper, duly excited. Bridgewater Park hadn't hosted such a celebration since Maggie wed Philip nearly eight years earlier. Her mother had planned that event down to the finest detail, as she often reminded Betsy, and this affair would be treated to the same careful attention.

Wedding announcements were to be sent to those not expected to make the trip into Somersetshire. Betsy knew that Lord Templeton must be sent an announcement. She was vastly relieved that propriety didn't dictate inviting him to the celebration at Bridgewater Park. It was certain to be a delightful affair, and she wanted nothing whatsoever to dampen her happiness that day.

Betsy stared out the window at the rolling drive in front of the grand mansion. In her mind's eyes she saw the cobblestone drive lined with the guests' many carriages, and the faces of the delighted partygoers alighting to join the celebration within. A faint smile curved her lips as she imagined twirling about the ballroom, her husband holding her tightly against him as the wedding guests looked on. She swayed slightly in her seat, moving to the music only she could hear.

"Betsy," her mother said, bringing her swiftly out of her reverie.

Betsy stared at her mother blankly. "Yes?"

Her mother clicked her tongue. "This is not the time for woolgathering, child," she said. "The seamstress is due to arrive after luncheon, and I'd hoped to have the bulk of these completed by then."

"Yes, mother," Betsy answered, taking up her pen.

Betsy caught Maggie's eye and saw her smile. Betsy returned the gesture and once more turned her attentions to the task at hand, pausing every now and again to envision the day when she would become Michael's wife.

***

Michael sat in his office at the stables, his mind reeling from his recent meeting with the Earl of Bridgewater. When the earl had told him of Betsy's dowry, he'd been stunned. Sixty thousand pounds! How the devil could he ever accept such an exorbitant sum? My God, he considered himself fortunate to have the privilege of taking Betsy for a wife. Even as his pride nagged at the back of his mind, urging him to reject her fortune, he knew the money could go a long way toward seeing to the repairs to Balsam Manor. As for his own personal horse-raising venture, the money could well provide the means for making his own fortune.

"Sixty thousand pounds," he murmured, shaking his head.

He knew what he must do. He would begin the repairs to the manor, and ready it for occupancy by a woman who deserved to be kept in the lifestyle to which she had become accustomed. With the funds soon to come, he would order the workmen to begin the repairs posthaste. He must return to Cornwall immediately.

He left his office and strode purposefully toward the main house, intent on advising his betrothed of his plans to depart Bridgewater Park. He didn't find Betsy in the parlor so he hurried to her chamber door and rapped sharply. Mary opened the door. She looked up and smiled brightly.

"Hello, Lord Balsam," she said, dropping a quick curtsy.

Michael bowed in return. "Hello, Mary. Is Betsy within?"

Mary bobbed her head in answer, her blond curls bouncing. She turned toward the main chamber, leaving Michael to follow in her wake.

"We've had a busy afternoon," Mary said, looking at him over her shoulders. "There's quite a bit involved with planning a wedding."

"Yes, I would think that's true."

Collective gasps of feminine surprise stopped him in his tracks. He looked from Mary to quickly take in the scene within Betsy's chamber. His eyes widened as he looked from Lady Bridgewater's face to Maggie's, their features clearly showing their shock. The reason became clear to him when his gaze finally settled on Betsy where she stood perched on a stool in the center of the chamber. His mind briefly registered the look of surprise on her face, her beautiful eyes opened wide, her full lips parted, before taking in her remarkable appearance.

Her chestnut waves were pinned loosely upon her head and her slender chemise-clad form was draped in satin of the palest blue. The lengths of fabric did little to hide her incredible figure from his eyes. My God, she looked like Venus emerging from the sea!

He managed to recover himself and reddened. "Excuse me," he choked, spinning on his heel. "I wasn't aware of your, your…"

Shocked silence enveloped the room. Betsy's mother was the first to break the hush.

"Mary," Lady Bridgewater admonished. "Why on earth did you bring Lord Balsam into the chamber?"

Mary shrugged her shoulders. "He wished to see Betsy, Mother," she answered simply.

Her mother clicked her tongue at the child but Betsy and Maggie laughed lightly.

"Did you need to see me, Michael?" Betsy asked, directing her question to his back.

"I," he began, turning toward her. He quickly checked the movement. "I need to speak with you, if you're able," he said. "Perhaps after your fitting we can go riding?"

After a pause, she answered him.

"A ride would be lovely," she said.

Michael let out a breath and nodded his head.

"I'll see you at the stables, then," he offered, fighting to keep his gaze fixed on the wall.

"Certainly," Betsy said.

He glanced over his shoulder and bowed quickly. Hurrying from the room, he closed the door behind him and let out a breath. After a beat, he heard a burst of feminine laughter from within the chamber and smiled in response. Thinking of the folly of finding himself surrounded by the Bridgewater women, taken with the pleasing picture his intended made in her stage of undress, caused his grin to widen.

Whistling, he took himself to his chamber to ready for his ride with Betsy.

Chapter 13

When Betsy reached the stables, she wasn't disappointed at the sight of Michael's beloved form. He stood with his back to her, looking out over the grounds. As she ran toward him she called out his name and he turned, taking her breath away. He cut a fine figure in his impeccable riding clothes. But it was his face that caused her heart to quicken its beat. His eyes were bright, and his smile was dazzling.

"Betsy, love." He held his hands out to her.

"Hello, Michael," she smiled up at him.

He dropped a sweet kiss on her lips. "I've seen to the horses. Shall we ride?"

She nodded and followed him to where the horses awaited. They mounted and raced over the grounds, finally reining them in amid a field of wildflowers. Though it was well into autumn, the flowers were still vibrant.

Michael assisted Betsy down from her horse and took her hand in his, strolling to where a large tree stood among the flowers. He reached down to pluck a bright yellow blossom and held it out to her. Betsy took it, her curiosity finally winning the battle in her mind as she twirled the flower in her fingers.

"You wished to speak with me, Michael?"

163

Michael reached out to stroke her cheek. "I have something to tell you."

Betsy's brow furrowed. "Nothing dreadful, I hope."

"Not at all," he said. "I'm leaving Bridgewater Park on the morrow."

"Leaving?" Betsy blinked. "Why?"

"Don't fret, darling. I'm returning to Cornwall to see to the repairs to the manor. I can't bring my wife home to a crumbling castle."

"It's of no consequence to me, Michael," Betsy shrugged. "As long as we're together."

"Ah, but the rooms are drafty," he said. "They'll be quite cold come the winter." He leaned closer. "Although, I can think of a number of ways to keep warm."

His voice stroked over her like a caress. "I would much enjoy your ways, Michael."

He brought his lips to hers. He pulled her close to him as his tongue slowly stroked hers. Suddenly, he broke off the contact. Betsy looked up at him in confusion.

"Michael, what is it?"

He shook his head in answer, his fingers toying with the buttons of her spencer.

"I believe I favor these little jackets of yours," he said, slowly opening the garment to reveal her thin chemise beneath.

Betsy stared down at his strong fingers as they brushed tantalizingly over her skin.

"What are you about?"

When he cupped her breasts in his hands she closed her eyes and shivered.

"I fear I'm setting myself up for a very uncomfortable ride back to the house," he said.

"I don't understand."

With obvious reluctance, he closed the jacket over her breasts and touched her cheek. "Don't you realize that the mere thought of making love to you causes me to ache to be inside of you?"

She shook her head, placing her hands behind his neck. "Make love to me, Michael."

"I won't take you again, Betsy," he said. "Not until we're wed. I shouldn't have taken you before our wedding. I daresay I suffered from a moment of weakness."

Betsy arched a brow at him and cocked her head to one side.

"Three such moments, Michael?" she teased.

He barked out a laugh and hugged her to him.

"Never mind. We must return to the house, love, before I cast aside all my good intentions."

She smiled sweetly up at him, very pleased he wanted her so. He assisted her up onto her horse and the two of them returned to the main house to dress for tea.

Michael left Somersetshire the next morning. Betsy accompanied him to the drive in front of the house, where his carriage stood waiting. They were alone for the moment, and took advantage of the relative privacy to share a sweet kiss of farewell. She was suddenly seized with melancholy.

He touched his finger to her chin and gently lifted her face to his. "What's troubling you, Betsy?"

"I don't want you to go, Michael."

"We discussed this, love," he gently reminded her. "Although I'm most pleased your reluctance to part matches my own."

She managed to smile at his words.

"I promise you this," he went on. "I'll endeavor to return to Somersetshire before a fortnight has passed."

"Give me your word." She lifted her chin. "Promise me you'll return to Bridgewater Park within two weeks."

"If not sooner," he said. "And will you make a promise to me?"

She gazed up into his dark eyes.

"Anything," she breathed in answer.

He took her hand in his. "Write me letters," he said, dropping a kiss on the back of her hand. "Long, flowery missives written in your delicate hand."

"I will."

"And I'll keep them close to my heart, love." He reached into his pocket and withdrew the velvet ribbon tucked within. "Along with this token," he said, bringing the ribbon to his lips.

Recognition dawned on Betsy as she spied the familiar hair ribbon, bringing their encounter in the stables rushing back to her. The romantic gesture and sweet words made her heart race.

"Oh, Michael," she cried, throwing her arms around his neck.

He hugged her tightly to him. "Ah, how I'll miss you."

He placed her on her feet and kissed her soundly. After a few more sweet words of farewell were exchanged between them, he climbed aboard his carriage. Betsy watched as the vehicle rolled down the drive, her eyes intently following it until it was but a speck on the horizon. She felt the tears welling in her eyes and squared her slumping shoulders.

She returned to the house, more intent than ever upon seeing to the wedding plans. The sooner the tasks were completed, the sooner she could concentrate all her thoughts on the delightful prospect of becoming Michael's bride.

***

Michael's head was filled with the tasks awaiting him at Balsam Manor as the carriage rolled on toward Cornwall. He stopped to take his nooning meal at an inn familiar to him, in Devonshire. One of the serving maids, a dark-haired girl whose ample charms he had enjoyed on more than one occasion, served him. She smiled widely as she set a platter of cold meats and cheeses before him.

"Lord Balsam," the girl said cheekily. "How nice to see you once again."

"How are you, Molly?"

Molly sighed dramatically, placing her hands on her hips.

"Quite disheartened, milord," she said. "It's been too long I saw you."

"I've been in Somersetshire, Molly." He took a long sip of his ale. "I'm sure you've kept yourself busy."

Molly nodded enthusiastically. After a quick glance at her

employer, a stout man standing guard beside the bar, she pulled out a chair for herself and sat very close to Michael.

"I've missed your visits, milord," she said huskily. "Have you been much in need?"

Michael nearly choked on his ale. He set the tankard down on the table and wiped his mouth. Shaking his head, he turned to face her.

"I have not."

Molly laughed out loud. "I find that difficult to believe, milord." She brought her lips to his ear. "Who knows of your great need more than I?"

He shook his head again.

"Molly, don't speak of such matters, pray. I'll be bringing a wife to Cornwall when next I pass through here."

"A wife?"

"Yes," he answered. "And I'd hoped my nuptials would not put an end to my taking meals here."

Molly smiled slyly. "I grasp your meaning."

Michael blinked at her in confusion.

"My meaning?"

She placed her hand on his thigh, slowly stroking him. He placed his hand on hers to still its movement.

"No. I'll be faithful to my wife."

Molly studied him. "I believe you're sincere."

"Very," he said. "Now would you be so kind as to refill my ale? Our conversation has left me a bit thirsty."

After giving his leg another quick squeeze, Molly rose to see to his request. Michael sat there, watching her hips sway as she saw to the task. In the past, his body would have hardened with desire at the sight of her ample endowments. Now, however? He only wanted his beloved Betsy. He loved her beautiful face and figure. Adored her free spirit and kind heart. He even loved her cunning mind and stubborn insistence.

When he finished his meal, he bade Molly farewell and once more boarded his carriage. Putting their conversation aside, his mind turned once more to the repairs in need at the manor.

He arrived in Cornwall and alighted, filled with determination. Balsam Manor was ancient and majestic, and its setting was rugged but beautiful. The gray stone walls seemed to rise to meet the cloudy sky above. The sea could be heard from below the great cliffs, crashing against the rocky shore.

Michael stopped and stared up at his home, breathing deeply of the salty air. Pride swelled in his breast. In his mind's eye he saw the manor as he wished it to be, with smooth stone walls and well-tended grounds befitting its stately setting. Reality soon crashed down upon him, as harshly as the waves upon the rocks below.

The walls were crumbled in sections and the grounds in dire need of tending. The huge wooden door of the entry was sagging to the point of its barely managing to clear the stone floor. Out of habit, he leaned against the door and made his way into the manor.

Michael called out to Coombs, the Reed family butler. The man came rushing over the polished stone floor of the entryway.

"Greetings, my lord." Coombs bowed. "It's wonderful to have you back at the manor."

"Thank you, Coombs. Have the stone workers arrived?"

"Yes. I've seen them settled into the servants' quarters."

"Very good. Surely we'll need them for some time. What of the other tasks? Have those been seen to as well?"

Coombs nodded. "As you instructed, my lord."

Michael nodded and strode into the great room, seeing evidence of the truthfulness in the servant's words. He'd instructed Coombs to scour the vacant rooms abovestairs for additional pieces of furniture to fill the cavernous space. The added pieces did little to make the room appear any more comfortable than previously, however. Michael looked up at the beamed ceiling, far overhead.

"Why the devil must this place be so bloody immense?" he wondered aloud.

"My lord?"

"Never mind," Michael said. "The room will be vastly improved upon by the presence of my lovely bride."

His eyes were downcast as he made his way toward the fireplace, closely studying the slightly worn but nonetheless high quality carpets covering the cold floors.

"The carpets are a welcome addition, Coombs," he said. "They do lend the room a certain warmth, thank God. Well done."

Coombs followed Michael as he walked from room to room. The library met with Michael's approval, as did the front parlor. Those particular rooms had walls of plaster, a remnant of the time before his mother died, when the late viscount had thought to renovate the house and bring it into the nineteenth century. Michael should follow his father's lead, and reinforce the outer walls of the castle while seeing to the warming of the interior. He reached the dining hall and peered within, quickly making note of the maids busily polishing the silver and seeing to the china closets. He arched a brow at Coombs, who wore a small smile.

"I've set the maids upon readying the dining hall, my lord," he said with a nod. "I daresay you and Lady Balsam will be entertaining."

"You're a wonder, Coombs," Michael said. "I believe the future Lady Balsam will learn to rely greatly upon you."

"Thank you, my lord."

Michael walked over to the outer wall of the room and ran his hand over it, frowning as the mortar crumbled beneath his fingers.

"Tell the stone workers' foreman I wish to speak with him directly," he said. "Much repair is needed before the house is deemed inhabitable."

The butler nodded and left his master to continue his inspections on his own. By the time Michael reached his chambers abovestairs, he was downhearted. Upon closer examination, he found many of the outer walls would need to be reinforced, if only to keep the dampness from giving Betsy an inflammation of the lungs. The ridiculously dark thought caused him to smile for, although Betsy was slight, he knew of no woman with a stronger spirit. She would never allow such a thing.

He opened the door to the outer chamber, pleased that this room was sound. It was a sitting room, and much larger than his guest chamber at Bridgewater Park. A fire burned in the fireplace, and the addition of several pieces of upholstered furniture had been made. "Good man, that Coombs."

Crossing through the large space, he strode through the open double doors leading to the sleeping chamber. The heavy draperies on the deeply mullioned windows had been replaced with those of satin, matching the muted carpets in tone. The room was decorated in dark blues as before, but now it was accented with ivory, following the new color scheme he'd noticed in the sitting room. While the sleeping chamber was still stately in manner, it no longer seemed as dark and intimidating as before.

He eyed the huge four-poster within, set on a platform in the center of the chamber. It too now sported the ivory satin, and appeared very inviting. He suddenly envisioned Betsy upon the magnificent bed, the dark blue of her eyes, the creaminess of her skin well matching the coverlet and draperies. Fierce wanting shot through him, causing his breath to catch. Ah, the things they would share in that bed.. His mood considerably lighter, he changed his clothes and went downstairs to his study to await the foreman.

Chapter 14

Michael stood in the courtyard, overseeing the work's progress. He'd joined the men in the clearing of the property and seeing to the laying out of the new stone blocks. The work was exhausting, but he welcomed the physical demands he placed upon himself. He missed Betsy, and climbing into his bed after a day of physical exertion allowed him the luxury of falling into slumber quickly. She haunted his dreams however, and his arms ached to hold her when he woke every morning.

The work on the manor was progressing, though more slowly than he wished. The plasterers were to start work on the interior of the castle by the end of the week. Several of the outer walls had been reinforced to Michael's satisfaction. He was confident the dining and breakfast rooms would see sound new walls by the end of a fortnight.

As per Michael's request, Coombs had seen to the hiring of several men to work the grounds, to return some of the beauty to the barren stretch of land. Floral plantings would be added, along with the trimming of the overgrown brambles that seemed to flourish everywhere. Michael's memory of the long-ago condition of the grounds was cloudy at best, so he relied heavily on Coombs's recollections in that regard. The butler assured him that the new Lady Balsam would like the changes. The courtyard would soon boast rose bushes in the formal section of the gardens, as well.

Michael crossed through the archway into the courtyard, and his eyes fell upon the crumbling outer walls of the garden. He recalled the smooth stone walls enclosing the gardens at Bridgewater Park and frowned. Would his home ever approach the grandness of Betsy's father's estate?

"My lord," Coombs called from the entryway.

"Yes, Coombs?"

"A letter arrived for you."

Was this yet another disappointing missive from his solicitors? What the devil was the matter now?

"It's from London, I presume?" he asked the butler.

"No, my lord," Coombs assured him. "It is from a different origin entirely. From Somersetshire."

Michael took the letter from the servant's hand. The paper was sealed with the Bridgewater crest. Turning the letter over in his hands, he smiled as he recognized Betsy's elegant hand in the address.

"Thank you, Coombs." Michael grinned. "I'll be in my study."

He turned and strode into the manor, leaving the butler wearing a similar expression of pleasure.

Michael entered his study, opened the letter and began to read.

Dearest Michael,

How did you find Cornwall? The wedding preparations are proceeding quite to my mother's satisfaction, and she assures me Bridgewater Park is ready to host our nuptials. I can scarcely believe we will be married within a fortnight!

I miss you terribly, Michael. I cannot stop thinking about you, about your kisses. I fear you will think me wanton, but I must make this confession. I wish you were here with me this very moment, as I pen this letter in my chamber! Oh, do return to Somersetshire and soon. To be unable to see you, to touch you... I cannot bear it! You promised me you would soon return, and I shall hold you to your word. I love you, Michael. I remain...

Forever Yours,
Betsy

Michael was grinning broadly as he finished Betsy's letter.

Her bold words pleased him. He saw her in his mind's eye as she penned the letter, a pretty pink blush staining her cheeks as she made her confession. He knew what he must do. Unable to resist, he read the sweet words again and placed the letter in his pocket. He walked to the study door and pulled it open, calling out to Coombs.

"Yes, my lord?"

"Please advise my driver we leave for Somersetshire on the morrow," Michael said, striding toward the wide staircase. "I trust you will oversee the improvements in my absence?"

"May I ask what causes you to act with such haste?"

Michael stopped on the steps and turned to him.

"My future bride has requested the honor of my presence, Coombs," he said with a grin. "And I find I can't refuse her."

By lunch time the next day, he was back at Bridgewater Park. He found Betsy in the gardens, a thoughtful expression on her face.

"Hello, love," he called.

Betsy turned fully, and then her eyes went round.

"Michael!" she squealed, throwing her arms around his neck.

Michael chuckled and caught her up in his arms, twirling

her in a circle. He placed her on her feet once more, his hands on her waist. He smiled at the bewilderment on her face.

"What are you doing here?" she asked. "Why, I wrote you only yesterday."

Michael feigned confusion. "You wrote me? Hmm. Perhaps you can tell me the contents of your letter."

Betsy lowered her lashes and moved out of his arms. She brushed her hands over her skirt, her cheeks pink.

"I merely…"

He laughed then, loudly. She cocked her head to the side, her hands on her hips.

"I received your letter, darling."

Betsy gave a nod. "I can scarcely believe I put such things in writing. What must you think of me?"

He placed his hands on her shoulders and turned her to face him. "Betsy, my opinion of you hasn't altered in the least."

She stared up at him for a moment. "But my words were most improper."

"No. Your letter pleased me, love," he said. "You've missed me nearly as much as I've missed you."

"I have missed you, Michael. So much."

"Ah, Betsy," he answered, bringing his lips to hers.

He kissed her, first tracing her lips with the tip of his tongue until she opened beneath him. Betsy sighed, pressing herself against him as their tongues touched. When at last he pulled away, she leaned her head against his chest with her eyes closed. He stroked her hair as she cuddled against him.

He draped his arm over her shoulders as they began to stroll. "And how are the plans progressing, love?"

"Very well. My dress is complete, along with my trousseau."

"Ah, the dress." He smiled. "A luscious confection of blue, if my memory is accurate."

She swatted him on the arm. "You weren't supposed to see it, Michael. You were in my chamber!"

"If I hadn't been, I would have been denied the most alluring sight I've ever encountered. That lovely satin." He paused to wink. "That lovely figure. You were a vision."

"And you are incorrigible," she returned with a tilt of her chin.

He laughed and kissed her again. She could not help but smile as they made their way back into the house for luncheon.

"What of the repairs to the manor, Michael?" she asked as they were served.

"The work is progressing, love." He shrugged and set upon his meal. "It will more than likely continue after we take up residence, I'm afraid."

Betsy waved her hand. "If you insist upon the repairs, then they must be needed."

"Indeed they are," he returned with mock-severity. "And quite costly. It's most fortunate I'm marrying a woman of means."

She laughed at his words.

"The gardens are being restored as well," he said. "I believe you'll find them enchanting."

Betsy sighed. "I can imagine the heath and wild roses fairly covering the space."

"Hardly," he said. "I've seen the place arranged more like the gardens here at Bridgewater Park."

"That will be lovely as well, I supposed," she said. "Although I believe I would much prefer the wild flowers."

"Why does that not surprise me?" he teased.

***

Betsy wore a smile on her face as Ann dressed her hair that evening, her mind on Michael. She hadn't missed the heat in his gaze before he left for the stables that afternoon. She'd wished

The Viscount's Vixen ~ JoMarie DeGioia

they were alone in that moment. She closed her eyes and sighed.

"Was there anything else you required this evening, my lady?"

Betsy started. "No, thank you."

When she was alone again, she allowed her thoughts to return to her intended. She studied her dress in the mirror, thinking of his response to the daring gown. Her eyes widened as an absolutely delicious thought came to her.

"No, I dare not." She giggled then, nodding her head in acceptance. "Yes, I will!"

She ran into her dressing room, making the certain change to her dress she'd contemplated.

Michael wasn't in the parlor, to her acute disappointment. He joined her just as she was entering the dining room, however. When he arrived downstairs at last, he reached her side and took her elbow, sending sparks through her. It felt so scandalous, keeping such a provocative secret.

"Betsy," he began softly. "Whatever are you—?"

She shook her head and made her way to the table, pausing only long enough to allow him to hold the chair out for her. She sat then, brushing her hands over her skirt. Dinner passed, and after a brief separation of the sexes they all sat in the parlor.

183

Betsy interpreted the heat in his dark eyes and a tingle coursed through her. She lowered her lashes. Whatever would his reaction be to her delicious secret? She hid a smile at his expression of curiosity.

Michael escorted her to her room a bit later, and her heart raced at what was surely to come.

"I'll say good night, love," he said, stepping back from her.

"Michael, don't go."

"Betsy, we've spoken of this. You're making it difficult for me to stand by my convictions."

She did smile then, and brought her lips close to his.

He stiffened, and then crushed his mouth to hers as he lifted her in his arms. His tongue stroked hers, and he somehow managed to open the door to her chamber and urge her inside. Betsy pressed herself to him, slamming his broad shoulders against the door and shutting it tightly. Michael's hands ran freely over her, loosening her hair and cupping her bottom.

"Ah, Betsy," he rasped, running his lips over her cheek, her neck.

"Michael," she whispered, pushing his jacket from his shoulders.

He raised her skirts as he had so desired earlier, running his

184

fingers over her legs, her thighs. He suddenly froze as his hands reached her bottom. He lifted his head, his eyes opened wide.

"Betsy, you're not wearing any drawers!"

She smiled up at him. "Do you think me wanton?"

He blinked rapidly. A wicked grin suddenly split his face.

"I think I'm the luckiest man alive."

Their remaining articles of clothing soon littered the floor of the chamber as he proceeded to make her feel like the luckiest woman.

Chapter 15

Michael left Bridgewater Park the next morning, but Betsy had little time to miss him. Her mother had lists of last minute preparations for the wedding, and she was besieged with the details. Almost before she was aware, the most-anticipated day arrived. She sat at her vanity and stared at her reflection. Maggie and her mother would surely join her any moment.

Ann dressed her hair in a most becoming fashion, twining thin satin ribbons of the palest shade of blue through her hair piled elegantly upon her head. Several long tendrils framed her face and brushed her shoulders. Betsy had dismissed the lady's maid mere moments before and now she relished her short-lived solitude.

Glancing quickly at her closed door, she pulled open the center draw of the vanity and withdrew several folded pieces of paper. She had written several missives to Michael during their second separation, missives she viewed as nearly as scandalous as her first. She trusted he enjoyed them, if these responses of his were any indication. More than one mention was made of the revelation of her delicious secret on their last night together. He'd taken obvious delight in her boldness, and stated as much in his letters. Such heated words!

A knock sounded at the door, startling her out of her reverie. She rose and hurried to the door. When she opened it, she was surprised to find a servant standing there. He handed her a letter, bowing to her.

"For you, my lady," the man said before taking his leave.

Betsy smiled as she closed the door, certain the note was from Michael. She was stunned to recognize the proper handwriting of Lord Templeton! She sat at her vanity once more and opened the letter with more curiosity than enthusiasm.

My dearest Elizabeth,

Please allow me to extend my very best wishes to you on the day of your wedding. Although the announcement you so graciously sent caused me much surprise, I nonetheless trust you are quite fond of Balsam and your parents are for the match despite the disparity in your respective stations.

I am wintering with friends in Yorkshire but shall return to town soon after the New Year. Please do not hesitate to call upon me should the need arise within you for assistance of any kind. I remain...

Your faithful servant,

The Earl of Templeton

Pompous fool! How dare he make mention of Michael's station? Michael was a titled gentleman, and carried himself as such. If there was some sort of mystery regarding his fortune, surely Lord Templeton had no cause to speak of it. And he wished her to contact him for assistance when in town?

"Not bloody likely," she muttered aloud.

"Betsy!" Lady Bridgewater said with censure.

Betsy spun toward the doorway, surprised to see her mother. The paper in her hand fluttered noiselessly to the floor.

"Mother."

Her mother waved her hand. "I've rung for Ann, child. It's time to change for the ceremony. Lord Balsam awaits."

"Yes, Mother."

No doubt Michael looked sinfully handsome in his formal black. His long legs, his broad shoulders.

"Betsy!" Lady Bridgewater urged once more.

Flushing, Betsy arose from her seat in response to her mother's rebuke. She turned as Ann exited the dressing room with the wedding gown held in her hands. Betsy stepped into the gorgeous blue silk dress. Her mother ran a critical eye over her, at last giving a nod of approval. Betsy beamed a smile at her mother, who suddenly appeared thoughtful.

"Mother, is something troubling you?"

"You do love him, don't you child?"

Betsy smiled her happiness once more. "Oh yes, Mother. Very much so."

Lady Bridgewater nodded once more, returning Betsy's smile. Her father then knocked on the chamber door, anxious to escort Betsy to the parlor for the commencement of the ceremony. The pair, linked arm in arm, exited the chamber with her mother following in their wake.

Mary grinned at Betsy from where she stood at the entrance of the parlor. She was clad in a lovely dress of light rose, and wore her golden curls atop her head as Maggie did. Both of her sisters hugged Betsy and they were soon set to begin.

Mary stepped through into the room first and Maggie followed. Maggie entered the parlor in the next moment, a smile on her face for Betsy's groom. She glided across the room to join Philip, who smiled down at her.

Betsy and her father paused in the doorway. Then she ran her eyes over her beloved, finding more to please her than she had imagined. His glossy waves fell across his brow, and his shoulders looked impossibly wide in his formal black. But the way his eyes darkened as they ran slowly over her was what thrilled her. Lord, she was a lucky woman!

As if in a dream, Betsy felt herself drawn to Michael's side. She barely took note of her father's hand leaving hers yet was well aware of Michael's fingers when they touched her. He smiled then, a dazzling smile that made her heart flutter. The ceremony was a cloudy memory by the time she recovered herself. She smiled up at her husband as he leaned his face close to hers.

"Michael," she whispered.

When he said nothing, merely widening his grin, she cocked her head in question.

"A kiss, wife," he whispered back.

Betsy blinked and brought her lips to his.

Maggie was the first to embrace her when at last the newlyweds separated. Philip beamed a bright smile at the couple, giving Michael a hearty handshake and Betsy a warm hug.

The newlyweds shared but one champagne toast before preparing to depart for Balsam Manor, wishing to take their wedding supper in solitude at the estate in Cornwall. They gave all the party guests a perfunctory greeting and left them to revel in their absence.

Betsy settled herself close to Michael as the carriage rolled away from Bridgewater Park. She was a married woman! Married to Michael, the most handsome, most passionate man she had ever known. He never told her to hush, or scolded her for being silly or unladylike when she spoke with enthusiasm. He was the most gallant of men.

***

Michael turned to face Betsy. Her traveling dress, a light confection of pale yellow, hugged her slight figure and caressed her curves. Even in the dimmed interior of the carriage her skin glowed a blushing pink. If he'd believed himself the luckiest of men when he'd seen her on her father's arm, she somehow managed to surpass his dreams in her less formal attire.

He wished in that moment to slip his hand into the demure neckline of the frock and feel her silken flesh with his fingers.

"Michael, what are you thinking?"

The grin he gave her made her visibly tremble.

"Ah, wife," he said, letting the word roll off of his tongue. "I believe you can guess my intentions."

She grasped his meaning with absolutely certainty and smiled brightly at him. Surely he was jesting with her, she thought.

"Oh, Michael," she laughed. "You would never attempt such an assignation here in this bouncing carriage."

He nodded. "I would," he said. "The bouncing would add an interesting element. However, I want our first time together as husband and wife to be in our big, soft bed at the manor. You'll find it most comfortable, I promise."

She nodded absently, her mind obviously on something else he had said.

"Betsy, love," he began. "May I ask what has you so captivated?"

She flushed, gazing at him out of the corner of her eye. "This 'bouncing,' Michael," she said softly. "Precisely how interesting would it be?"

A surprised laugh rumbled out of him as he grabbed her and held her close. He held her on his lap as the carriage bounced along, kissing and cuddling her until they were nearly ready to expire from the titillation.

They soon crossed over into Cornwall and the driver called out to signal as much. Betsy slid off of Michael's lap, brushing her curls back from her face.

"When will we arrive at Balsam Manor, Michael?" she asked, peering out the small window.

Michael took a breath to cool his blood and ran his fingers through his hair.

"We have to ride nearly to the cliffs, love. Another thirty minutes, perhaps."

She smiled back at him. "I believe I can smell the sea air."

He smiled at the delight on her face. The brisk scent of the ocean was sea was indeed carried on the stiff autumn breeze. The afternoon was waning, and with the fading sun went the day's warmth. Michael saw her shiver slightly and reached across the carriage to pick up her spencer where it had laid since leaving Somersetshire. He placed it on her shoulders, giving her a squeeze. She nodded her thanks and accepting a sweet kiss on her cheek. He suddenly straightened from her.

"There, love," he said, pointing toward the horizon. "Balsam Manor lies there."

Betsy smiled, but that expression was soon eclipsed by one of surprised delight. The manor stood proudly upon the rise, the red and gold of a glorious sunset framing the towers and walls. Michael watched Betsy's eyes widen as the carriage drew closer.

"What do you think, Betsy?"

"Oh, Michael." Her gaze was fastened on the edifice. "It's positively marvelous."

He wished he could see his ancestral home through her eyes. Instead he could see where the east wall was patched with skill by the stone layers, where the grounds were still bare from all but the wildest growth. Surely she deserved to live in an house as grand as Bridgewater Park. Not a mausoleum with drafty corridors and damp walls.

"Michael?" Betsy asked, drawing his attention.

Michael found her wearing a look of befuddlement on her features and forced a smile. He was saved from making an excuse for his odd behavior when the carriage rocked to a stop in front of the manor. He helped Betsy into her jacket and assisted her down from the carriage, grasping her elbow as they approached the massive entry.

"Balsam Manor is remarkable," she said.

"It remains in need of quite a bit of work, wife," he gently pointed out.

She waved her hand dismissively, delight still widening her eyes and curving her lips.

He allowed a bit of her enthusiasm to wear away at his

doubts. "What say you, Lady Balsam?" he asked her. "Can you turn this mausoleum into a stately manor?"

She nodded. "Oh, we must go inside!"

Michael scooped her up into his arms. She laughed gaily as he took long strides over the grounds sloping up toward the entry, her hands clutching his shoulders tightly. A smiling Coombs pulled open the massive wooden door, which no longer sagged against the stone steps.

"Welcome home, my lord." He bowed at Betsy. "And this must be Lady Balsam."

Betsy nodded as Michael deftly set her on her feel to face the butler. Michael held her hand in his as he made the introductions.

"I'm pleased to meet you, Coombs," Betsy said with a pretty smile.

"A pleasure to make your acquaintance, my lady."

He advised them of the dinner hour and left them. Betsy took small steps further into the manor, and Michael waited for her to say something, anything, to give him an indication of her opinion regarding the appearance of the great hall.

The walls were plastered a cool ivory in the entry, but here in the hall the walls were rough stone. Taken with the high, heavily-beamed ceilings, the place seemed positively medieval. The polished stone floor beneath reflected the light from the many candles in the huge iron chandelier hanging from heavy chains over the center of the space. The deeply set windows with their many leaded panes reflected the candles' light as well, along with that of the fire blazing within the massive fireplace. Did she like it?

She walked slowly over to the hearth, her steps whisper quiet due to the warm carpet now beneath her feet, her eyes following the stone wall all the way up to the ceiling. She turned to face Michael at last.

"Oh, Michael," she breathed. "The manor is simply wonderful."

Michael blinked, surprised at the pleasure shining in her eyes. "It's our home, wife," he said, staring down at her. "Are you quite certain you find it to your liking?"

Betsy smiled widely. "It's the most magnificent home I've ever seen."

Michael let out a sigh of relief and bent his head to hers. The sound of the dinner bell stopped him in mid-motion. He gently grasped her elbow.

"Dinner awaits, Lady Balsam," he said with a bow.

Betsy dropped a quick curtsy, an easy laugh spilling from her lips.

Chapter 16

Betsy was delighted to find the dining room decorated in the same fashion as the great hall. The chandelier hanging above the fine cherry dining table was of polished brass, however, lending its own elegance to the fine crystal and china set upon the table. Betsy found the contrast between the rough walls and the refined furnishings quite pleasing to her eye, and told Michael as much.

"I'm glad this room pleases you, love," he said, holding her chair out for her to sit.

She sat and he followed suit, commencing with their wedding supper. Several courses were served, including soup, roasted vegetables and tender leg of lamb. After they'd consumed their fill of the fare, Michael waved the maids away from the room. He leaned toward Betsy then.

"What say you, wife," he began, "if we were to take our dessert abovestairs in our chambers?"

"That would be delightful."

He nodded and stood. "After a while, that is," he added with a sparkle in his eye.

"Oh yes," Betsy agreed, her heart giving a little flip.

He led her from the room and toward the curving staircase

leading to the second floor. At the top of the grand staircase, Michael directed her along the hallway. It was open to the floor below, giving a nice perspective of the great hall. She followed him further down the hall to the door to their chambers. He opened it with a flourish and stepped aside, bidding her to enter. She did so, looking into the sitting room with clear interest.

The room's ivory and deep blue décor pleased her, and the fire ablaze in the hearth set between two wing chairs was inviting. A glimpse through the wide doorway into the bedchamber caused her to gasp. The magnificent bed sitting upon its platform made her heart race. He would make love to her on that bed. She jumped as Michael's hands gently gripped her shoulders.

"What are you thinking, Betsy?" he asked, his voice low.

She turned and smiled shyly up at him. "I'm thinking about that bed, Michael," she said. "I daresay I've never seen another like it."

"My grandfather had it made to his specifications, love," he told her. "He was as large a man as myself."

"Was he as handsome?" she asked, tilting her head to one side.

Michael laughed. "That, I don't know."

199

"Are there no portraits of him here at the manor?"

"No."

"Whyever not?"

"I never gave the matter much thought. Why don't you ready for bed, wife?"

She nodded, permitting him to lead her toward a door set to one side of the massive bed. She opened the door and found a large dressing room within, and it was clear that Ann had already seen to her personal effects. A nightgown of the finest lawn was laid out for her, accompanied by a matching wrapper. Betsy changed into the gown, letting the soft fabric drape over her. The bodice dipped low over her breasts, tied with satin ribbons of pale blue. The wrapper was a froth of ruffles, trimmed with more of the blue satin ribbons. She didn't need to ring for her maid to dress her hair tonight. She simply loosened it and let it settle about her shoulders. She tied the belt of the wrapper and stepped out of the dressing room and into the bedchamber.

Michael was waiting for her beside the bed, an elegant dressing gown of deep blue satin draped over his form. She crossed to him, placing her hands into his outstretched ones.

"You look quite the lord of the manor, Michael."

"And you, love, look absolutely delicious."

Betsy blushed at his provocative statement. Michael reached out and cupped her cheek with his hand, bringing his face close to hers.

"Ah, sweetheart."

His mouth rubbed against hers gently at first, his tongue tracing over her lips. She opened beneath him, letting out a soft whimper as his tongue slipped inside. Her hands stole inside his dressing gown, running lovingly over his hair-roughened chest. Michael brought his lips to her ear, nibbling gently at the lobe.

"Delicious," he rasped, letting the tip of his tongue trace the shell of her ear.

"Michael," she said with a shiver, gripping the lapels of his robe in her hands.

His lips and tongue ran over her neck, into the bodice of her wrapper. The garment fell to the floor with a whisper, forgotten by the two of them as he swept her into his arms and laid her on the bed. There his mouth became ever more bold, capturing her lips in a hot, wild kiss.

Betsy ran her fingers through his hair as she returned the kiss in full measure. He lowered his head to her nightgown's bodice and gripped one satin ribbon in his teeth, growling softly as he pulled the ribbon free. She gasped as the garment fell open, then sighed as he fastened his mouth on one nipple. She cradled his head as he teethed the sensitive nub, her eyes closed in bliss.

Before she was aware, he had divested her of the nightgown completely. His mouth moved lower, licking and kissing her belly. He parted her legs and placed a kiss on the curls at the juncture of her thighs. Her eyes snapped open.

"Michael!"

He stroked her gently with his fingers. "I must taste you."

His tongue flicked into the damp curls and she shivered.

As he lowered his head again, she glanced down at him. The sight of his dark head nestled between her thighs caused passion to flare through her. She closed her eyes and surrendered.

At her submission his caresses became bolder, his tongue and lips running wildly over her tender flesh. When she arched against his mouth he grasped her bottom and held her there, bringing her swiftly to orgasm. Her screams of delight barely registered as her heartbeat hammered in her ears. He lifted his head at last, coming up to hold her in his arms.

"What think you of that, love?" he asked softly.

Betsy opened her eyes at last, gazing up at him as if through a haze. "Oh, my," was all she could utter.

He gave a strangled laugh and brought his lips to hers. At his urging, she parted her legs again for him, taking him deep inside of her. He thrust into her again and again, swiftly arousing her passion to match his. She tightened around him and came with a shout, bringing her with him.

After his big body quieted against her heated skin, she wrapped her arms around his neck.

"I love you, Michael," she said softly.

He smiled lazily down at her and held her close.

After several minutes, they donned their nightclothes once more and Michael rang for their dessert. He rose to see to its delivery in the sitting room. Betsy watched him as he strode from the bedchamber, admiring his blatantly masculine form. Sighing, she settled herself against big fluffy pillows on the bed.

When he returned, he carried a large silver tray of delectable pastries. He set it upon the bed and fetched a bottle of sherry and two glasses. He poured the sweet wine and offered her a glass. She smiled and took it from him, sipping delicately from it. He drank some of his own and settled down beside her, reaching for the pastries. Betsy watched him consume quite a few of the little sweets. She drank a bit more of her sherry and chose one pastry for herself, a tart filled to overflowing with rich berries. She bit into the tart and sighed with pleasure. Michael looked sharply at her, and then a wide smile spread over his face.

"What has you grinning so, husband?" she asked, reaching for another treat.

"I love it when you make that sound."

"These tarts are positively delectable."

"They don't taste nearly as sweet as you do."

Betsy stared at him for a moment. She suddenly grasped his meaning, blushing hotly at his reference to the deeds he'd performed on her person that evening.

She gave him a quick nod and drank deeply of her sherry as she thought back to the incredible feeling of his mouth on her most private place. Would he be pleased if she performed such a deed on him? Her eyes ran over him, reclining as he was on the bed leaning up on one elbow. His dressing gown was open at the neck, showing her quite a bit of his muscular chest. Her eyes fell to the expanse of satin below the belt of the dressing gown. Michael's voice broke through her reverie.

"What are you thinking, love?" he asked, bringing his glass to his lips.

"What do you taste like, Michael?"

***

He nearly choked on his wine. Sputtering, he set his glass on the bedstand.

"I daresay I have no notion," he managed to answer.

He was intrigued as a look of contemplation came into his new wife's eyes. She set the silver tray on the floor and leaned toward him.

"May I find out?" she asked in a soft voice.

Michael drew in a breath as hot desire flared through him.

"Betsy, you don't have to."

"I wish to taste you, Michael," she quietly insisted.

He swore softly and took her glass from her hands. Cupping her cheek with his hand, he brought his lips to hers. She kissed him with ever-increasing ardor, pushing him down upon the bed. He happily gave in to her gentle insistence, letting his arms fall to his sides.

She ran her lips over his chest, dropping little kisses over him. When she flicked the tip of her tongue over his nipple, he moaned softly. He moaned again as her fingers reached beneath the satin to gently grasp him.

"God, love," he murmured.

He watched her in anticipation as she lowered her head, thinking that he might die from what she was doing. Although many an experienced woman had performed such a deed upon him in the past, the tentative touch of his wife's perfect mouth upon him had him rock hard in moments. Her lips caressed him, her tongue teased him. She closed her lips over the very tip and he began to move against her. He ran his fingers through his hair in an effort to retain some semblance of control.

"Ride me, love," he groaned, arching off the bed. "Ah, God! Please ride me."

Michael opened his eyes and saw the befuddlement in her expression. Her hands still grasped him gently, her moist lips were parted. With a shout of intense longing, he grabbed her and pinned her beneath him. He drove into her, painfully close to his release. He braced his arms on either side of her, his thrusts deep and hard. Betsy held on tightly to his arms, her body bowing back as her climax shot through her.

Michael came then, holding himself deep inside of her as his body shook. With his release his mind began to work, the intensity of his passion stamped on his memory. He hadn't taken the time to learn if she was ready for him. His thrusts had all but sent her through the bed. He kissed her cheeks reverently.

"My God," he rasped. "Have I hurt you, Betsy?"

Betsy gave a quick shake of her head, opening her eyes to

stare up at him. To his acute relief, she smiled lazily up at him.

"Not at all," she answered softly.

"When you put your lovely mouth on me, you nearly drove me out of my mind."

"That's a good thing, isn't it?"

He nodded, hugging her close. They settled beneath the coverlet, their arms entwined.

"Michael?" she began, her hand gently stroking his chest.

"Yes?" he returned with a yawn.

"I like the way you taste," she whispered.

He chuckled deeply, dropping a kiss on her tangled chestnut locks. They snuggled together under the satin coverlet, their sighs of satisfaction soon lengthening to the deep even breathing of slumber.

Chapter 17

Betsy awoke early the next morning, a bit disoriented to find herself in the handsome blue and ivory room. A quick glance at the man occupying a large portion of the bed beside her brought her mind sharply into focus. Her lips curving into a smile, she yawned inelegantly and draped her arm over his broad chest. Michael mumbled in his sleep, drawing her deeper into his embrace.

"Good morning, Michael," Betsy whispered in his ear.

"Hmm," he returned sleepily. "Morning."

His eyes suddenly snapped open. She smiled as the confusion on his face was slowly replaced with a heart-stopping grin.

"Betsy," he said, kissing her gently. "Did you sleep well?"

She nodded, resting her head against his chest. Michael stroked her hair, her arm. She sighed and dropped a kiss on his chest, resting her chin upon him and gazing up at him.

"What do you wish to do today?" she asked him.

He smiled and brushed a wayward curl away from her eyes. "I daresay if we acted on the notion in my mind at this moment, we would scarcely make it out of this bed before noon."

Betsy lowered her lashes. "It is a very comfortable bed."

He chuckled and kissed her lightly. "Never mind," he said. "There's much I must see to today, if this manor is to be made suitable."

"It's very suitable, Michael."

Michael waved his hand and stood beside the bed. He donned his dressing gown belted it tightly about his waist.

"Do you wish me to order a bath for you, love?" he offered.

Betsy thought it was a marvelous notion and told him as much. He leaned down and kissed her once more. After ordering her bath, he took himself into his dressing room to see to his own morning toilette. He emerged shortly thereafter, dressed suitably for a day of work about the manor grounds. Betsy sat up in the bed, running her eyes appreciatively over the fine figure he cut in his rugged clothes.

"You look most fit, Michael," she said with a smile.

He chuckled and picked up her wrapper from the floor and handed it to her. "I'll see you downstairs in the breakfast room, love."

After taking a bath in the largest tub she'd ever seen, she dressed with her maid's assistance and went in search of her husband. She found him apparently waiting for her in the great hall.

"Hello, Michael."

"I believe you take quite a long time to ready yourself," he teased, taking her hand in his. His eyes ran over her from head to foot. "Although I must say the results are well worth the wait."

She was pleased, as she'd chosen one of her favorite day dresses in a pale green. As he led her from the hall, her gaze was drawn to the high stonewall above the hearth. They entered the breakfast room, which was smaller than the dining room but very elegantly-appointed. It sported plaster walls and fine furnishings, and its sideboard was laden with a selection of breakfast foods. Betsy made her choice, arching a brow at her husband as he piled several pieces of ham upon his own plate.

"I would have thought you ate already, Michael," she said, taking her seat.

"I did, but I must keep up my strength. My wife is quite demanding."

Betsy giggled and set upon her meal of eggs and sweet rolls. As she sipped at her tea, she thought once more of the blank stonewall of the great hall.

"Michael," she began, setting her cup aside. "What do you

think of hanging a large tapestry above the fireplace in the great hall?"

Michael shrugged. "You may decorate our home in any manner you choose, love," he said. "I trust you have many pieces of needlework and such?"

"Yes," she allowed. "I'll write my mother directly and have her send several of them." She smirked. "The largest of them, I daresay."

"But above the fireplace," she went on. "I believe a tapestry depicting your family crest would be most fitting, don't you think?"

He was quiet for a moment, a thoughtful expression on his face. "I believe there was such a tapestry there at one time, Betsy," he said. "Long ago. I don't believe I've seen it since my mother's passing."

"Oh," she said dejectedly.

"Coombs has been here since before my father's time," he went on. "I'm certain he'll be able to assist you in discovering its whereabouts. I wouldn't hold much hope of its present condition."

Betsy nodded, her mind working. Why would a gentleman of such a long-standing and ancient title have the depiction of such removed? Could it be tied in some manner to the missing fortune?

"Another mystery," she mused aloud.

Michael lifted his head to stare hard at her. "What did you say?"

Betsy blinked at the intensity in his eyes. She was reminded of his cold anger the last time she spoke of such things, on that long ago afternoon at Bridgewater Park when he'd called her a spoiled little girl. She wouldn't broach the subject again, not when they were basking in newly-wedded bliss.

"Nothing of import," she said lightly. "Do you truly believe it will be possible to locate the item?"

He wiped his mouth on his napkin and set it aside.

"I believe so." He came to his feet. "I'll send Coombs in to you directly."

Betsy tilted her face to him as he brushed a kiss on her lips. She watched him go, nearly biting her tongue clear through to keep her thoughts to herself. No matter. She was quite certain she would soon learn precisely what was at the center of the mystery surrounding her proud husband's family fortune.

The butler soon stood in the doorway of the breakfast

room. "You wish for my assistance, my lady?"

"Yes, Coombs." She came to her feet. "Lord Balsam assured me you can direct me to a storage room of sorts here at the manor."

Coombs nodded, a look of curiosity on his distinguished features. "Several, my lady," he said. "May I inquire as to what items in particular you are seeking?"

"Tapestries and such, Coombs. Don't you think these austere stone walls would benefit nicely from such fripperies?"

Coombs smiled in response. He led her up the wide steps and down the hallway to a section of the manor far from the living areas, to a room set in what he referred to as the east tower. They stopped before a door of thick wood, unadorned and quite ancient.

"I believe you'll find several interesting artifacts here, my lady, along with any number of fripperies."

Betsy smiled and reached for the door. Coombs stilled her, quickly retrieving a branch of candles from a table set in the hall.

"It's quite a dark room, Lady Balsam."

The door creaked open on iron hinges, giving them access to the dim area within. Coombs lit the candles and preceded her into the room.

213

"Do you need my help, my lady?"

Betsy waved her hand in the dusty air.

"No thank you, Coombs," she said. "I'll call for you should the need arise."

"Very good."

He left the room, closing the door behind him. Betsy felt the darkness press in upon her. Squaring her shoulders, she took small steps further into the room. While the light from the candles managed to illuminate the room a bit it did little to expel the gloom of the place. She couldn't even ascertain its dimensions. She set the candles down upon the stone floor and placed her hands on her hips. A sliver of light from the far wall caught her attention and she approached it, her hand outstretched. She recoiled as her fingers brushed over animal fur of some kind. The flap of fur moved then, showing her it was covering a small window. She held it aside and looked at the window. It was narrow and, taken with the thick stone wall in which it was set, afforded little view of the grounds below. She located an iron hook set into the wall beside the window and set the flap on it.

"How utterly medieval," she said to herself.

She turned and regarded the room once more. A gasp

escaped her lips. It was a tall space, and nearly twenty feet in diameter. But that was not was caused her surprise. In the gloom she could make out the outlines of several massive trunks set against the curved walls. A glance around the room showed her more trunks filled the space, along with what appeared to be large panels and frames. Delighted curiosity filled her and she rubbed her hands together.

She picked up the branch of candles and knelt beside the trunk nearest her. "Oh, what mysteries await?"

She set upon her task with relish, humming to herself to dispel a bit of the gloom in the space. She knelt on the floor before one large trunk. It was latched but unlocked, so with merely a soft grunt of exertion she lifted the lid. She peered inside the felt a trill of happy surprise. Inside were numerous banners and such, carefully rolled up into tidy bundles. She reached into the trunk and withdrew the first one her fingers touched. Placing it on the floor, she carefully unrolled it.

A beautiful tapestry was revealed, one with an intricate floral design which showed both the skill of the creator as well as the love in which they had created it. The year embroidered in one corner assured Betsy only Michael's mother could have worked the fine piece of needlework. She trailed her fingers lightly over the silken roses and vines, her mind on the woman she would never know. What had she been like? Would she approve of her proud and handsome son's choice of a wife? A bit melancholy, she carefully rolled up the tapestry and set it aside.

She found many more pieces of needlework within the trunk, pieces depicting such motifs as animals and wild plantings as well as the formal flowers she'd seen in the first tapestry. They all seemed to have been made by the gifted hands of Michael's mother. She gave a nod. It was only right that the previous Lady Balsam's work be displayed throughout the manor, along with the pieces Betsy's mother would be sending directly. Surely such lovely pieces of work, those of the past and present ladies of the manor, would warm the stark castle.

At the bottom of the trunk she found a very large parcel. It was much thicker than the others, and quite heavy as well. With a bit more effort than she had expended thus far, she heaved the rolled parcel out of the trunk and laid it on the floor. Its width was nearly equal to her height! She set the candles further aside and untied three thin strips of fabric binding the bundle. Taking much care, she unrolled the treasure.

Even in the dimness of the chamber Betsy could see the

brilliant colors of the intricately wrought tapestry. It was a sea of ivory embellished with deep midnight blue and gold. The pointed bottom of a shield became visible as she unrolled the piece fully, along with the crest emblazoned upon it. It was Michael's family crest! Her excitement dimmed as she unrolled the tapestry fully.

An angry tear marred the piece, beginning at the top and continuing on the diagonal through the crest. The massive tree emblazoned on the crest was nearly torn in half. Betsy ran her fingers gingerly over the awful rent. The harshness of the tear, taken with the otherwise fine condition of the tapestry itself, seemed to indicate that the piece had been damaged deliberately.

"Who would perpetrate such a horrid deed?" she murmured.

No matter. Both her mother and Maggie had taught Betsy all she needed to know of needlework. She would repair the fine crest. She would carefully mend the awful rent and see the tapestry hung over the fireplace in the great hall. She bound the tapestry once more and set it beside the others.

Closing the lid of the trunk at last, she stood and stretched. As she turned from the trunk, the corner of a gilded frame caught her eye. She placed the branch of candles atop the trunk and crouched down behind it. There she saw many frames of various sizes leaning against the curved wall. Several portraits became visible to her, many of persons bearing very familiar features. The unknown gentry staring dispassionately at her were clearly Michael's ancestors. Betsy's breath caught as one portrait in particular became visible to her. It was of a most beautiful woman, a woman whose beauty the artist had obviously taken much care in capturing. Betsy knew without a doubt upon whose portrait she was gazing. Even without the evidence of a particular dress or hairstyle to date the portrait, there was no mistaking the woman's identity. Dominating her exquisite face were eyes of deep onyx, seemingly fathomless. Michael's eyes!

She studied the portrait, sorely wishing she could know the woman gazing back at her. Why weren't these portraits hanging in the great hall? Her eyes fell upon the necklace encircling the woman's slender neck. The thin gold chain hung down to the swell of her breast, nearly to the neckline of her formal ball gown. Betsy squinted as she sought to view the pendant more clearly. It appeared to be a dark stone, but she couldn't ascertain its shape due to the angle of the portrait.

"I think I've seen that before," she said to herself.

"Betsy?" Michael called from outside the chamber,

drawing her attention from the portrait. "Where are you, love?"

She stood and glanced down at her skirts. Chagrined, she saw dust and grime soiled her green dress as well as her hands. She quickly brushed her hair back from her face, no doubt leaving dirt there as well.

"There you are," he said as he opened the door.

She smiled in return and tilted her face toward his. He kissed her lightly and took her hands in his.

He ran his gaze over her, and then brushed his thumbs over her cheeks. "You're covered with dust."

Betsy reddened slightly and stepped back from him.

"I'm sorry you have seen me like this," she stated.

"Nonsense," he returned, stepping closer. "The grime does little to mask your beauty, I assure you." He looked about the cluttered space. "What discoveries have you made, love?"

Betsy clasped her hands. "Oh, Michael," she began. "There are so many tapestries here. I believe your mother created most of them."

"Is that so?"

"We must see them hung about the manor," she said. "They'll look simply marvelous."

"But what of your own handiwork?"

"I believe the manor can more than accommodate all of them and more."

He nodded his agreement and led her from the room. They soon entered their chamber to ready for luncheon. Betsy pulled her hand gently from his grasp and rang for her lady's maid. She turned to find Michael regarding her in a most intriguing fashion, his dark eyes nearly devouring her. Her own eyes ran slowly over him. He had loosened his cravat at some point, she noted, and discarded his jacket. His sleeves were rolled up and she could see his muscles work as he crossed his arms and leaned against the wall. Ann's arrival brought her back to herself. She took a breath and gave a small shake of her head.

"Oh, Ann."

"Your mistress has no need for you at this time, Ann," Michael said.

"But, Michael," Betsy began as she turned toward him. "I need to change out of these soiled clothes."

Michael smiled wickedly then, setting her pulse racing.

"I'm well aware of that."

Without sparing a glance at Ann, Betsy dismissed her. The maid giggled behind her hand, dropped a quick curtsy and took her leave.

Michael assisted Betsy out of her dusty garments and into his arms. He carried her to their bed, satisfying their passion and making them rather late for luncheon.

***

"Your mother was quite gifted with the needle, Michael," she said at dinner that night, taking a dainty bite of the fine roast beef on her plate. "And quite beautiful, as well."

"And how would you know this?"

"I've seen her portrait," she said. "There are many portraits in the storage chamber. We must see them arranged about the manor."

"I suppose we can create a gallery adjacent to the great hall." He swallowed past the lump in his throat. "You saw my mother's portrait?"

Betsy nodded as she sipped delicately at her wine. "She was most beautiful."

Michael lowered his eyes to the table, his fingers toying with the stem of his glass. "I scarcely remember her."

He gave a shake of his head to clear it. "What of the crest, love?" he asked. "Did you find such a tapestry abovestairs?"

Betsy blinked at the abrupt change in subject but apparently caught his reticence and spoke no more of his mother's portrait. She began to describe the tapestry she had uncovered, the brilliance of the threads forming the Balsam crest.

"It's quite remarkable, Michael," she told him. "And quite beautifully wrought. Although it has a horrible tear nearly renting it in half."

"It's been in storage for years. Surely more than a little damage was bound to occur."

Betsy shook her head. "Oh, no. The rest of the piece is unsullied. I'm afraid the tear had to have been deliberate. Do you know anything about it?"

A hazy memory sprang to the front of his mind. He was but a child in his recollection, huddled in the hallway abovestairs in the manor. Angry male voices came from the great hall below. He shuddered, the memory of fear strong even in the present.

"Michael?" Betsy asked. "Is something troubling you?"

He looked up to find worry visible in her gaze.

"No, no," he assured her with a small smile. "It's nothing."

Betsy's brow furrowed, but she finally returned his small smile with hers. "Shall we take our dessert in the great hall?"

Michael concurred with relief, taking her elbow and leading her from the dining room. As they shared their dessert of tea and lemon cakes, Betsy spoke of anything but the ruined tapestry or the portraits she had discovered. Michael didn't mention his brief and cloudy memory. The coldness, the fear, had felt very real to him in that moment. He wouldn't worry over its importance now.

He'd puzzle over it in solitude, when he could face the truth of what must truly be horrible to evoke such iciness within him.

Chapter 18

"The tapestry is coming along," Betsy remarked as they entered their chamber to ready for bed a fortnight later. "I tell you, I was very pleased to finally change colors and thread something other than deep blue on the needle."

Michael nodded absently. He hadn't given much thought to the hazy memory Betsy's mention of the ripped tapestry had provoked two weeks earlier, choosing instead to occupy his mind with the many tasks needing to be accomplished at the manor. But tonight the memory came back to him. Intent to somehow keep the fact from her, he strode into his dressing room and shut the door, leaning against it as he took deep breaths to calm his racing heart.

In his mind he was once more that tiny child huddled in the hallway, his arms hugging his knees to his chest as he listened to the men arguing in the great hall below.

"You are a bloody fool, Balsam," a man taunted. "You now have nothing but your worthless title to pass down to that puling little brat of yours."

"You bastard!" Michael heard his father retort. "How can you live with yourself?"

The unseen man laughed, an ugly sound that sent a shiver

through the little boy.

"I shall live quite well, I imagine," he answered. "As for you, you can take comfort in the knowledge that your lovely wife isn't here to witness your disgrace."

A scuffle was heard from below, followed by the sound of his father's assailant laughing once more.

"At the very least you have that ridiculous crest of yours," the man jeered. "Perhaps it will keep you warm on those long cold nights in this mausoleum."

The sound of boot heels clicking upon the floor signaled the man's swift exit. A brief silence enveloped the manor, soon broken by a guttural shout of intense grief and rage. A loud tearing sound was heard, punctuated by several crashing noises. As his father's cries of outrage were replaced by heart-wrenching sobs, the tiny boy in Michael's recollection squeezed his eyes shut.

"No, Papa," the little boy sobbed. "No...."

"No," Michael said to himself, his voice shocking him out of his reverie.

He opened his eyes to find himself in his dressing room. As he covered his eyes with one hand a soft knocking came from the other side of the door.

"Michael, is everything all right?"

He took a deep breath, shaking his head to rid it of any lingering memories of that long-ago night. Were these true recollections or simply the recurrence of a terrible nightmare that had plagued him as a child? He forced his attention to the present.

"I'm fine, love," he called through the closed door. "I'll be out in a moment."

True to his word, he stripped down to his breeches and rejoined her in the main bedchamber. She was tucked cozily into their bed, her hair arranged becomingly about her shoulders.

"Were you growing impatient, wife?" he teased, stretching out beside her.

A blush crept up her cheeks as she gave a tiny nod. A laugh rumbled from deep in his chest as he gathered her into his arms. He proceeded to show her without words just how much her silent admission pleased him.

The next afternoon, Michael sat in his office down in the stables. His desk was littered nearly to the point of obscuring its top. There were papers listing the items he needed to order to fortify the tack room, lists of the repairs yet to be completed to the remainder of the stables, and a tentative schedule of training and breeding sessions he would see to in the spring. Several items from the tack room were also set upon the desk, and he was taking time of his own to repair them. He fiddled with a broken stirrup as his mind made its way unerringly back to his dreamlike recollection of the previous night.

The fierce argument all those years ago must mean something. The anger and despair in his father's voice had been as clear to Michael in that moment in his dressing room as if his father had stood before him. And who was the man taunting him? He had yet to examine the tapestry of his family's crest, and he realized he repeatedly left the breakfast room as soon as his wife made preparations to set upon her daily task.

"Coward," he muttered. Cursing softly, he set the broken stirrup aside and sighed.

"Good afternoon, Michael," Betsy called from the open doorway.

Michael looked up and quickly took in her fetching appearance in her pretty pink day dress. She wore an expression of mild irritation.

"Hello, love," he said, coming to his feet. "What brings you down here?"

"I believe my husband has no desire for my company at

long last," she stated, rolling her eyes heavenward.

He chuckled as he came to stand before her, taking her hands in his.

"Not likely." A quick glance at the clock upon the wall showed him teatime was long since passed. "I've missed tea, haven't I?"

"Yes. I'm afraid I consumed too many biscuits in your absence. If such behavior on your part continues, I daresay I'll grow quite stout."

He placed his hands on her slender waist, his fingers nearly touching. "While I have no fear in that direction, it wouldn't detract from your appeal."

He returned to his chair behind the desk, taking her with him to sit in his lap. She ran her fingers over his fine lawn shirt. He's set his jacket and waistcoat on a chair nearby.

"Are you nearly finished with your work here?" she asked, toying with his shirt buttons.

He nodded. "And what of yours?"

She shrugged. "There's still much work to be done on the tapestry. What a horrible tear."

Michael stiffened beneath her, his hands clutching at the arms of his chair as the room seemed to spin.

"Michael, what's wrong?"

Michael's eyes snapped into focus, a great breath escaping his lips.

"What?" he murmured. "What did you say?"

She placed her hands on his face, dropping little kisses on his brow. "You seemed so very frightened just then," she said in a quiet voice. "And so very far away."

He laughed shakily at her words, unwilling to tell her just how fearful his fleeting memory made him. He would not share such recollections with her. Surely she would insist on learning all about his childhood memories and he wasn't yet prepared to delve into his past.

"I wasn't frightened, Betsy. I was simply lost in thought for a moment, that's all."

Betsy didn't seem to believe him for a moment. She placed her hands on her hips and frowned. "You'll tell me what you were thinking."

"Hush," he urged, bringing his lips to her ear. "I have no desire to discuss anything so mundane as my thoughts of a moment ago when the thoughts currently occupying my mind are so much more interesting."

She closed her eyes for a moment, purring in response to

the sensations he was causing with his lips and his tongue. Suddenly she straightened in his lap.

"But, Michael," she insisted. "I want to."

"Yes," he cut in, turning her in his lap so she straddled him in the chair. "I want to, as well."

She gasped as his hands closed on her bottom, pressing her tightly to him. His growing arousal was evident to her even through their layers of clothing. She gazed at him, finally closing her eyes as he brought his lips to hers. His tongue traced her lips, delving inside to taste her. Their tongues touched and he caught her sigh in his mouth.

He murmured her name as he made quick work of unhooking the back of her dress, tugging down her sleeves to reveal the thin chemise barely covering her breasts.

"How can anything else occupy my mind," he rasped, his mouth on her plump flesh, "when you're such an enticing package here in my arms?"

Her drawers give with a soft tearing sound as Michael swiftly removed them. He touched her then, gently and then with more insistence.

"Oh!" she cried, her body arching toward him as she spread her legs further apart.

She was lost in sensations as he teethed her nipple, as first one then two strong fingers drove her unerringly toward her peak. When his thumb found her most sensitive spot, she came with an intensity that left her stunned. He felt her release almost as if it were his own, his own breath harsh in his ears.

"Ah, love," he whispered when she had calmed, cradling her in his arms.

Her eyes slowly opened as she caught her breath. She ran her eyes over him.

"Michael, come inside me."

He started to bend her over the desk, suddenly letting out a curse. He sorely wished in that moment he was in his study at the manor, at his large desk with its neatly placed accessories allowing an expanse of smooth desktop on which to lay out his wife's lovely form. He stood with her in his arms then, causing a startled gasp to escape Betsy's lips.

"The stable, wife," he said in answer to her unasked question.

Before she could utter a word of protest, they were cozily tucked into one clean unoccupied stalls. Michael grabbed a large blanket and spread it quickly upon the soft, clean hay.

"What if someone hears us?" she whispered as she sat

beside him on the blanket.

He arched a brow. "I don't recall your worrying over that when last we found ourselves in such a situation."

She had no argument for that statement. Smiling, she removed her dress. He began to unbutton his shirt and she took over the task for him, pushing him down upon his back as she spread the material wide. His hands tangled in her hair as she ran her lips teasingly over his chest, his stomach. He was prone beneath her ministrations and he thought in that moment there was no other place he'd rather be.

"Betsy," he rasped as she unbuttoned his breeches.

"Yes?" she whispered as her lips came tantalizingly close to his arousal.

"Ride me."

Biting her lower lip in apparent concentration, she lifted her petticoat and straddled him. As she lowered herself onto his arousal she let out a cry of surprised delight. He grasped her hips and began to thrust upward. Grabbing on to his wrists for support, she rode him as he drove up into her. Her hair cascaded down her back as she arched above him, pleasure clear on her beautiful face. The highly erotic sight was nearly his undoing.

He squeezed his eyes shut as he sought to hold onto his

control, determined to let her find her second release before he gave in to his own. When she tightened around him, when she began to sob his name, he pulled her tightly against him and drove higher still. She cried out her release, causing him to do likewise as he poured himself into her. She collapsed upon his chest, her breath hot against his skin.

"My God," he rasped as regained his wits.

"Mmm," she murmured in answer, rubbing her cheek against him.

He stroked her hair as his breathing slowed.

"That was better than I'd imagined it would be," he said. When she lifted her head to gaze at him in question. "Do you know for how long I've wanted to love you in this manner?"

Betsy nodded, lowering her lashes.

"Since our wedding night," she said with certainty. "I'm afraid I didn't understand you."

He shook his head. "I wished for this after our first ride together at Bridgewater Park."

She blinked in surprise. "But how can that be?" she asked. "How could you have wanted me so soon after we met?"

He traced his fingers lightly over her cheek, tilting her face up to him. "I wanted you from the very moment you lifted this determined little chin at me at the Derby, insisting you knew what was best for Gusty."

She laughed sweetly and turned her head, kissing his fingers.

"I still believe a few cubes of sugar wouldn't ruin a horse's performance."

He shook his head at her again, and hugged her tightly. Losing himself in his beautiful wife was vastly preferable to worrying over a long-ago fright from his childhood.

Chapter 19

Betsy hummed to herself as she donned her heavy woolen cloak, knotting the laces beneath her chin. The weather had grown quite chilly in the past weeks, and the Christmas holiday was now nearly upon them. She left their chamber with determination, bound for the stables. She had need to see her husband directly, and wouldn't wait for him to enter the great hall of his own accord or when it pleased him to do so. She'd made a certain addition to the hall and wanted him to view it immediately. What would his reaction be? He must be pleased or all her work would have been for naught.

Taking purposeful strides, she entered the stables and did not stop walking until she stood in the doorway of his office. Michael looked up at her in surprise before smiling.

"Betsy, I see you're once again here in the stables. Can it be you wish a repeat of our tryst of several weeks past?"

His smile widened as her cheeks, already pink from the cold, surely turned rosy red.

"Perhaps another time, Michael," she said. "I'm here to request your appearance in the great hall."

Michael came to his feet and took her hands in his. "You shouldn't have ventured out of the manor in this cold. I won't

235

have you catching your death. Your father would never forgive me."

"I won't. I promise you."

"Then tell me what requires my attention in the hall at this precise moment."

Betsy simply shook her head at him, a secret smile curving her lips.

"Indulge me."

He nodded and donned his great coat. "Always."

He led her from the stables and into the manor. As they neared the great hall Betsy grabbed onto his hand, all but dragging him along with her.

"Betsy," he began with a laugh, "what has you in such a hurry?"

He stopped in his tracks as he gazed upon the wall above the fireplace. The banner bearing his regal crest hung in the place of honor, its colors magnificent in the light given off by many candles and the fire burning in the hearth itself.

"My God, what a sight!" He took her hands in his and drew her closer. She saw that his eyes didn't leave the crest. "Your handiwork is exceptional, Betsy. I can't discern any tear in the piece whatsoever."

Relief threatened to swamp her. "You're pleased then, Michael?" she had to know.

She studied his face closely for a long moment, waiting for his answer. The smile that curved his beautiful mouth was all the proof she needed that dark thoughts weren't plaguing him at the moment.

"You're pleased?" she asked again.

He spared another long glance at the tapestry and faced her at last, hugging her to him.

"It's wonderful, love." He lifted her hands to his lips. "Your hands are quite gifted, and at more matters than pleasing your husband."

She pulled one hand free to swat him on the arm.

"Never mind." She removed her cloak. "I'll await you down here while you ready for dinner."

Michael glanced at the clock set on the mantle and turned back to her, one black brow arched.

"It's not the dinner hour yet," he said. "And why are you in such a hurry this evening? And dressed so magnificently, I might add?"

Betsy smiled as she handed her cloak to a waiting servant. She turned to her husband and brushed her hands over the skirt of her sapphire blue gown.

"Tomorrow is Christmas Eve, Michael," she pointed out to him. "We leave for Bridgewater Park on the morrow and I so wished to celebrate our holiday at bit early, here at the manor."

He ran his eyes over her in blatant appreciation.

"'Celebrate our holiday' is it?" He chuckled. "Surely that can wait until we are abovestairs."

She clicked her tongue. "I've instructed the staff that we'll be taking our Christmas meal a bit before the day. This way, we get two holidays."

"As you wish, love," he said. He rubbed his hands together. "Ah, the thought of goose and plum pudding does set my mouth to watering."

She sighed in mild exasperation and placed her hands on her hips.

"Then do ready for dinner, Michael," she urged. "I'll await you here."

He kissed her lips to ease their pouting and took himself up the grand staircase to their chambers. When he joined her in the great hall once more, dressed as splendidly for dinner as she could have wished, he held a velvet jeweler's box in his hand. She rose from the settee on which she had been awaiting him and smiled. Her eyes widened as she spied the box.

"Michael, what do you have there?"

He grinned and held it out to her, bowing slightly.

"For you, my lady," he said. "A Christmas gift from your husband."

"Oh!" She squealed as she reached for the box. She suddenly checked her movement to clasp her hands together. "But it's not yet the day."

"No matter," he said with a shrug. "You yourself said you wish to celebrate our holiday early."

She smiled brightly at him and watched as he opened the box. Inside rested a pendant of deepest blue, the sapphire cut into an oval. It was not an exceptionally large jewel but it was flawless and sparkled prettily in the candlelight.

She reached out to stroke the gem. "Michael, it's beautiful."

"It's not as large as the pendant Templeton gave you," he said softly. "But the color reminded me of your beautiful eyes."

She looked up at him for a moment. Surely he doesn't still think of Lord Templeton. She never gave a thought to the man. She ran her gaze over her husband's beloved face.

"It's perfect," she said simply.

She turned her back to him and lowered her chin. He lifted the necklace out of its satin bed and draped it over her. He fastened it, letting his hands rest on her shoulders for a moment. She touched the stone again.

"Thank you, Michael," she said as she looked at him over her shoulder.

"There are earrings to match," he told her.

She took up the pair of them and quickly fastened them to her lobes, then looked at him expectantly.

"Beautiful," he said, drawing her into his arms.

He kissed her thoroughly as she pressed herself against him. When the dinner bell sounded he lifted his mouth from hers, leaving her with more than a touch of regret.

"Our Christmas feast awaits," he said to her unasked question.

She nodded and took a breath to regain her wits and they retired to the dining room.

A while later they were abovestairs in their chambers, readying for bed. Michael sighed in obvious contentment and patted his flat belly.

"That meal rivals anything your cook at Bridgewater Park can prepare, I wager." he said, shrugging off his jacket.

"Mmm," Betsy agreed, admiring the breadth and strength of his back as he turned to enter his dressing room.

"No, wait a moment," she said.

He turned to face her, unbuttoning his waistcoat as he did so.

"Yes?"

"I haven't given you your present as yet."

He ran his eyes over her as he had in the great hall.

"I have no doubt you will, love," he teased. "And more than once tonight."

She blushed at his meaning.

"Yes, well," she began, her eyes lowered to the floor. "Your gift is in my dressing room, if you would but wait a moment."

She hurried into the dressing room, her skirts swirling about her. She returned in the next minute, a large flat box held in her hands. A wide ribbon of red satin wrapped the box, the effect quite festive despite the simplicity.

"Your present," she said, holding the box out to him.

He took the offering and slipped the ribbon from the box. Moving aside the tissue within, he found a waistcoat the likes of which she'd never seen outside of the finest houses in London. It was of a deep blue satin, nearly black it was so dark. She'd embroidered it with an intricate pattern of vines and leaves, the decoration worked in a fine thread barely two shades lighter than the waistcoat itself.

"This is your handiwork, is it not?" he asked with surprise. "I'm speechless."

Betsy smiled widely at him and bade him to don the garment right then, in that very moment. He laughingly obliged her, fastening the pearly buttons and striking a pose.

"What do you think?"

"You look splendid," she answered. "I hadn't been certain when I was working the design, but now I see my instincts were correct. What do you think, Michael?"

He turned to gaze into the cheval mirror, a crooked grin on his face.

"I believe your cousin will be green with envy when he sees me in such finery."

"Philip certainly would never be so."

"Ah, believe me, wife," he said, taking her hands in his. "Wilton will no doubt make great sport of my handsome self and my fancy waistcoat."

She smiled as she agreed with him, thinking him the most

handsome and elegant man she'd ever seen and marveling he was hers. He carefully removed the waistcoat and set it aside for his valet and turned to her once more.

"Now," he drawled, pulling her closer. "What of the other present, Betsy love?"

She smiled up at him in sweet innocence, letting her beautiful blue dress fall to the floor around her feet.

"As you will, husband," she whispered.

He quickly divested himself of his remaining articles of clothing. With her help he stripped her bare of all but the sapphire necklace and earrings and lifted her in his arms. He carried her to the massive bed and stretched out upon it, holding her above him. As she kissed him and caressed him, bringing him high and deep inside of her, she marveled at the great fortune that had brought him into her life on that day at the Derby.

She lost all thought as she took her pleasure from him, and then brought him to a shattering climax.

"Happy Christmas, Betsy love," he whispered, holding her close.

She sighed and cuddled closer.

***

They left for Bridgewater Park early the next day, soon after breakfast. Michael knew Betsy was eager to see her family and share the Christmas holiday with all of them. She'd been in correspondence with both of her sisters but surely she missed the opportunity to converse freely and frequently.

He settled back beside her as the carriage rolled away from Balsam Manor. As he faced her he found the look in her eyes very interesting.

"May I ask, what is in that cunning mind of yours at this particular moment?"

Betsy smiled, and heat suffused him. "I'm thinking of nothing of much import."

He eyed her closely, correctly interpreting the heat in her pretty violet eyes.

"I believe," he began, leaning back and assuming an air of supreme relaxation, "you're thinking of me at this moment. Don't shake your head, love. You're thinking of having your way with your poor husband."

"Michael," she breathed.

"Yes, you're considering using my body as you will for your own wicked pleasures."

She shook her head. "I am not."

He held up a hand. "You're wishing at this precise moment to sit upon my lap, to lift your skirts and feel me deep inside of you."

Her mouth was an O of astonishment.

"Michael!" she said again with much more force. "Such words are quite scandalous!"

He chuckled, bringing his lips to her ear.

"Ah, Betsy love," he rasped. "Such words are quite effective at evoking an image." He nuzzled her neck. She sighed and leaned against him. "Yes. Quite effective."

"I remember your comments on our trip from Bridgewater Park after our wedding," she said softly.

He drew back to gaze at her with growing interest. "And what were those comments?" he asked with a crooked grin.

She turned fully toward him, nearly sitting on his lap.

"I believe you told me that the rocking of the carriage would add an interesting element."

He blinked at her then laughed.

"I did say that, didn't I?"

"I believe I would like some proof of your words," she said, kissing him on his chin.

Michael kissed her deeply, finally pulling back to curse

softly. Betsy blinked at him in surprise.

"Now is not the time or place, love," he told her with regret.

She arched a graceful brow at him.

"But Michael," she purred. "Surely you jest with me."

He shook his head.

"Even if I could somehow manage to work my way through all these layers of clothes, darling," he began, kissing her nose. "It still wouldn't change the fact it's quite frigid. I won't have you exposed to the cold weather."

"But you could keep me warm."

He quickly drew in a breath. He saw her smile widen as her words had the desired effect.

"Never mind, vixen," he said with a playful growl. He held her fully on his lap, arranging her cloak and skirts to well cover her. "I'll make you this promise," he went on, kissing her ear. "I'll take great pleasure in letting you have your way with me at the very first opportunity after our arrival at Bridgewater Park."

"Ooh, I wonder what guest chamber we'll be given."

"Perhaps I would like to take you in your former bedchamber," he said. "Yes," he went on, pleased by the interest evident in her lovely eyes. "I believe such feminine quarters would be well suited for our purposes. I will press you against those little blue flowers that adorn the walls and finally give you what you have been so desiring this day."

Betsy breathed through parted lips. "You inside of me?"

"Such scandalous words, wife," he teased.

Chapter 20

Michael and Betsy soon arrived at Bridgewater Park and promptly proceeded to spend a very pleasant holiday. That evening after dinner, a feast that was even more sumptuous than the one Betsy and Michael had shared at Balsam Manor, the gentlemen took themselves into Lord Bridgewater's study for the leisurely consumption of some of the earl's fine brandy. Michael swirled the liquor in his glass, staring absently into its amber depths. He lifted his head and brought the glass to his lips, surprised to find Philip regarding him in an odd fashion. His friend's green eyes held both interest and amusement, a confounding combination.

"Wilton," Michael began after sipping from his glass. "Pray, what has you so earnest?"

"I wondered if you were aware of a certain gentleman's recent visit to Bridgewater Park."

Michael looked at Betsy's father, who nodded in his direction. Clarity struck.

"Don't tell me the Right Honorable Earl of Templeton graced the park with his presence?" he asked, managing to keep his tone even.

Philip apparently wasn't fooled by his nonchalance.

"Balsam, surely you wish to know the occasion of the gentleman's visit?"

Michael looked at Philip pointedly to cease his verbal teasing and state his meaning.

"Apparently the earl is concerned over Betsy's well-being," Philip said. "He managed to evoke the very image of the concerned benefactor."

"Why that pompous old man," Michael muttered.

"Now, Balsam," the earl put in. "Lord Templeton did seem genuinely interested in my second daughter's welfare."

Michael set his glass down on a side table and took a breath to calm himself. "Excuse me, sir," he said to Betsy's father in a controlled voice. "Do you have any misgivings regarding your daughter's well-being?"

"Certainly not," the earl answered swiftly to Michael's great relief. "I've never seen my daughter so content in her life."

"Then why would Templeton come here and allude to such a thing?" Michael asked of both the earl and Philip.

Philip shrugged and drained his brandy glass.

"He claimed to possess some worry over the living conditions of your home in Cornwall, Balsam," he said. "Apparently he believes the place to be fairly falling down around your ears."

Michael once more felt anger surge through him.

"I assure you both that the manor has had extensive renovations. I would never expose Betsy to any hardship or discomfort."

"We're well aware of that, my boy," Lord Bridgewater said. "I was quite confounded by both Templeton's visit as well as his words."

Michael was quiet for a moment. He knew precisely what the man's goal was. The pompous ass wished to discredit him in the eyes of Betsy's family. But why?

"How could Templeton have any notion of the manor's condition, Lord Bridgewater? When could he have been there?"

Philip shrugged again. "Didn't he profess to know your father? Perhaps he paid him a visit at some time ago."

Michael nodded absently, brooding over that possibility. Philip's next comment brought him swiftly back to himself.

"Now," he began with a laugh. "Let's talk about that waistcoat."

Michael chuckled and ran his fingers lightly over the intricate design adorning the rich satin.

"My dear wife worked this design with her own delicate

hands."

"Betsy is quite gifted with the needle, my boy," the Earl of Bridgewater said.

"Yes," Philip said. "Maggie told me of her work on the tapestry bearing your crest. I believe it was quite done in?"

Michael stood still. While the thought of the restored tapestry caused him no discomfort, the mention of its past destruction apparently still did.

"Yes, the banner has been restored to its former glory," he said.

If Philip sensed something odd in Michael's tome he didn't mention it. He once more ran his eyes over the waistcoat.

"You simply must bring that waistcoat when you visit London," he teased. "I daresay you'll rival the fanciest dandies in town."

Lord Bridgewater's laughter joined Philip's. Michael regained his good humor.

Long after dinner, Michael accompanied Betsy to the large guest chamber set aside for their use. It was decorated in gold and ivory, and referred to by all as the Gold Room. Betsy had been tickled when she discovered they would have the room, but Michael took little note of it as he went into the dressing room.

His mind was filled not only with Templeton's unwanted visit but also with his own strange reaction to Philip's innocent question regarding the tapestry's destruction. Why the devil would such matters continue to plague him?

Betsy soon blotted out any lingering thoughts of the tapestry. When he reentered the chamber, clad in his dressing gown, his eyes were drawn to his wife. She remained at the vanity, her brush slowing running through her chestnut waves. He quickly noted, although she wore a lovely wrapper over her nightgown, it wasn't belted tightly about her waist or clasped closely together at her neck. His eyes went to the fire burning brightly in the fireplace, and then to the smooth plaster walls and well-glazed windows. He noted the room was warm, not damp or drafty as were their chambers at Balsam Manor. Did she feel discomfort in the rooms they shared there? Did she now revel in the immense comfort and luxury of her family home?

Betsy looked up at last, her eyes finding his in the mirror. She smiled and set her brush down on the vanity's surface and turned to face him.

"Michael," she said in soft greeting.

His lips thinned as he noted not a trace of a shiver from a draft nor one goose bump marring her silken skin.

"Templeton paid a call on your parents," he said, walking toward her.

Betsy nodded. "Maggie told me." She came to her feet. "I find that strange."

"Do you?" he could not help asking. "You were unaware of his visit prior to this evening?"

"How on earth would I be aware of the man's comings and goings?" she countered, her bewilderment slowly turning to pique. "What, precisely, are you intimating?"

Did she know of his visit? he wanted to ask. Did she write him about the deplorable conditions in which her husband keeps her?

"Nothing." He slowly took in a breath. "I'm tired."

She stepped closer. "Michael, what's troubling you?"

"Never mind," he said, forcing a smile. "Come to bed, wife."

She came into his arms and he finally began to relax.

"Forgive my odd ramblings, pray. As I said, I'm tired."

"I do hope you are not too tired, husband," she softly teased. "I'm reminded of a promise you made to me on our journey here."

At her words he felt any lingering tension leave his body,

253

replaced instantly with desire.

"Ah yes," he said softly, brushing his fingers through her silken waves. "But there are no feminine frills in this room, wife. No tiny flowers."

"No." She lifted her head to smile prettily up at him.

"I suppose we must make do with that ridiculous golden bed."

She giggled then, placing a hand in the center of his chest. "I suppose."

He quickly divested her of her nightgown and wrapper, kissing her skin until her laughter grew into gasps of pleasure until they both fell into satisfied slumber.

In his dreams Michael was once again that scared little boy, alone in the hallway of Balsam Manor. He stiffened as a hand grasped his shoulder.

"Why are you here, young master?" a familiar voice asked him.

He blinked up into the butler's face.

"Coombs," he whispered both in his mind and aloud, though he was unaware of it. "The man hurt Papa, Coombs."

"Hush now," Coombs said, lifting Michael to his feet. "You should be abed."

The boy rubbed his eyes as he shook his head firmly. He tried to pull away from the butler, digging in his heels.

"Where's Papa? Is he all right?"

"His lordship is in his chamber, young master. Fast asleep as you should be."

Michael stood firm, his small feet refusing to take a step from his hiding place.

"Who was that bad man, Coombs?"

"Never mind," Coombs said. "Now let's go to the nursery. Nanny will be put out to find you absent."

He nodded and followed the butler to the nursery.

Michael awoke with a start, the dream still clinging to him. He found Betsy staring at him, worry furrowing her brow.

"Michael," she asked softly. "What's wrong?"

He blinked, a bit befuddled.

"Nothing's wrong." He looked about and saw the sheets in a tangled around his lower body. "Let's go back to sleep."

Betsy nodded after a long moment, finally laying her head against his bare chest. His heart had ceased its pounding, and he closed his eyes and sought to join his wife in slumber.

***

The next morning Betsy woke before Michael.

"Michael," she whispered.

He said nothing, just flashed her a wicked grin as he placed his hand full on her breast. The thin sheet was the only barrier between his palm and her flesh. She gasped at the contact, her nipple puckering.

"Good morning, wife," he said, kissing her brow.

He began to squeeze her breast gently, teasingly. She smiled sleepily and stretched beneath him.

"Michael," she said, placing her hands behind his neck. "What was the matter last night?"

Michael stiffened, his eyes flying to hers.

"Your dream, Michael," she continued, running the fingers of one hand through his tousled waves. "Was it about the tapestry?"

He pulled back. "What?"

Betsy blinked at the wariness in his dark eyes. She sat up, holding the sheet to her bosom.

"You seemed far away," she said. "Not quite yourself."

"I don't know about any dream."

"Whenever I mentioned my work on the tapestry you seemed to retreat," she began. "To go somewhere far from me. You seemed to be in that place when you awoke last night."

Michael shook his head. He was certain he'd hidden his reaction from her, damn it to hell. He turned from her and donned his dressing gown, his eyes fastened on the golden roses which adorned the fine ivory carpet beneath his bare feet.

"You're speaking nonsense."

"Nonsense?" she repeated, taken aback. "You deny it?"

"There is nothing to deny."

She snorted at that and retrieved her wrapper from where he'd dropped it the night before. She belted it tightly about her waist and turned to him once more. She hadn't pressed him about his strangeness regarding the tapestry bearing his crest, since now that it was restored that seemed to be a thing of the past. She must have been mistaken.

She squared her shoulders and forged on ahead. Her hands placed firmly on her hips, she raised her chin to look him in the eye. "You can't possibly deny it, Michael."

"I won't discuss this with you," he said coldly.

Oh, he wouldn't? Well, she wouldn't let him pull away again. She hurried around the bed and came to stand in front of him.

"Why not?" she asked pointedly. "I'm your wife. The woman who lives with you. Who sleeps beside you. I'm the one who heard you muttering incoherently in your sleep as you all but flung yourself out of the bed."

He stared at her blankly. "I spoke?"

"You did," she said. "I couldn't make out the words, really. But you did say something I couldn't misunderstand."

He almost looked frightened. "What was that?"

"You spoke of Coombs." To her surprise he paled. "Does Coombs have something to do with the tapestry, Michael?" she asked in a softer tone of voice.

He shook his head, apparently unable to meet her gaze.

"I don't know."

He shook his head once more. Betsy didn't press him, giving voice instead to another notion.

"Perhaps this has something to do with the mystery," she said.

"What mystery?" His voice was sharp now.

She saw that he too recalled their long-ago confrontation in the stables, when she had broached the subject of his missing fortune. His reaction then had been almost hateful. Still, she continued.

"Perhaps the tapestry is somehow related to your missing fortune," she said. "Perhaps if we speak to Coombs we can get to the truth of the matter."

"Enough!" Michael suddenly shouted. "You would speak of my fortune, or lack of one, to a servant?"

"Michael," she began, her hands spread in front of her. "I think we should find out precisely what happened. You've told me yourself that Coombs has worked at the manor for a very long time. When we return to Cornwall, we should speak to him."

"You would do best to keep yourself out of my business, as I have told you before," he said in a low voice.

"But perhaps if we were to get to the bottom of matters, this could be resolved."

A sneer curled his lips and her belly twisted.

"Did Templeton's visit put you in mind of your husband's failings, Betsy?"

Her mouth dropped open in shock. "How dare you speak to me so?" she asked, her voice shaking.

"I'm certain you found his concern for your well-being quite touching. Surely you wouldn't suffer so under his care?"

Betsy breathed in sharply. "I won't speak to you when you're being so unreasonable," she said through clenched teeth.

She turned swiftly on her heel, coming to an abrupt halt

when he grabbed her arm tightly. She faced him, glaring up at him.

"I'm speaking to you, wife," he ground out.

"Take your hand from me," she returned, tugging on her arm in a futile attempt to free herself.

"You're mine, Betsy," he said, tightening his grip. "You would do well to remember that when you think of another man."

His outrageous statement brought her anger to its fullest. With a firm tug she freed her arm and slapped him hard across his face. She dimly realized she would have found the surprise evident on his face comical were she in a different frame of mind.

"I was merely thinking of you, you bloody fool." She turned her back on him again and took quick strides into the dressing room. "Happy Christmas, Michael," she said over her shoulder.

Chapter 21

The remainder of their visit at Bridgewater Park passed with much discomfort for Betsy. She couldn't bear to be in her husband's company for more than a few minutes at a time. His unreasonable response to her concerns caused extreme irritation whenever she gave it thought. How dare he speak to her so?

She went through the mere motions of enjoying the holiday with her family. Today she sipped at the tea in her cup, not listening to the conversation her mother and Maggie were having as they sat on the settee across from her. Why, didn't he realize she had only his interests at heart?

She didn't care one whit about his fortune but for the injustice of his being deprived of what was his by birth. There was also his strange reaction to the tapestry. She'd never seen her strong, capable husband so vulnerable, and it scared her witless.

But she said nothing of this, priding herself on her success at presenting the façade of a happily married woman sharing the holiday with her family. She nodded and smiled at her husband's comments as she saw fit, and treated him with politeness whenever any of the others were near.

More than once Maggie raised a brow in her direction,

261

questions in her eyes and obviously on the tip of her tongue, but Betsy managed to smile despite the tension knotting her stomach. However would she bear the shame of it should her family learn of her marital strife?

Tension escalated each evening as the hour grew later. She dreaded sharing the beautiful golden bed with her husband, knowing his big strong body would be pressed against hers despite the distance she sought to keep between them. After shrugging off his tentative touch Christmas night, she'd maintained her emotional distance as best she could manage. After mumbling a few choice curses, Michael had left her to her thoughts, giving her his broad back. The next few nights he didn't even attempt to touch her.

When at last they took their leave of Bridgewater Park, she couldn't help but compare their return trip to their ride into Somersetshire just one week past. Michael leaned back against the cushioned seat and slapped his gloves against his thigh as he regarded her through hooded eyes. She sat across from him in the carriage, her back ramrod straight. She was all but pressed against the wall, as far away as she could manage in such close quarters. There were no pleasant words, no sweet kisses, as the carriage rolled over the slight bumps in the road. And no questions from her regarding the carriage's rocking on this day. That was certain.

An exasperated sigh escaped his lips. At the sound, Betsy reluctantly turned her gaze from the window.

"Do you wish to say something, Michael?"

He slanted her a look that spoke of his simmering anger.

"Speaking to me now, are you?" he said in a clipped tone. "With none of your family present? That is surely a marvel."

She shrugged and turned her face away from him. He muttered a curse and threw his gloves on the seat.

"This must end, Betsy," he said at last.

She said nothing, merely gazed outside the window with as much absorption as if the royal caravan was passing alongside of them.

"When we return matters will be quite different, my lady."

"Think that if you will," she returned.

The carriage rolled on, its occupants sharing a very uncomfortable silence.

They stopped at an inn at Devonshire for luncheon, and she couldn't ignore that the large-breasted serving girl seemed very familiar with him.

The truth struck her in an instant. He'd taken his pleasure

with this girl. This meal, which was hearty but unremarkable as far as she was concerned, passed in the now-familiar quiet manner. As they boarded the carriage and settled for the remainder of their ride home, she had to break her silence at last.

"I didn't want to think it," she said softly. "I sensed something, but I did not want to imagine it was so."

"Betsy, please."

She impatiently waved away his words.

"You dallied with that... Oh, I can't think of a fitting word at this moment."

"That was a long time ago," he stated. "Before I ever laid eyes on you."

She studied him for a long moment, and perceived nothing but sincerity in his manner. She nodded and faced the window again.

She hadn't missed the easy smiles exchanged between them, however. It was quite simple for her to imagine them together. Michael was a lusty man. Surely he'd shared with that serving maid what he had with her. True, Michael had been decidedly unattached when last he had been with Molly, or so he'd assured her. But after his concealment of late, after his refusal to open his mind to her concerns about the mystery, she couldn't help but harbor the smallest doubt in her breast.

They did not speak of Molly, or of anything else, for the remainder of their journey into Cornwall. When the carriage at last rolled to a stop in front of Balsam Manor, Betsy alighted the carriage without her husband's assistance and hurried up the wide stone steps to the heavy wooden door. The door was soon opened before her and she breezed into the entryway, her husband in her wake.

"My lady," Coombs said in greeting, bowing low.

Betsy smiled brightly at the servant, allowing him to assist her with her cloak. She brushed her hair back from her cheeks and turned as her husband joined them. Michael took long strides into the entryway, nodding in greeting to the butler. Coombs's eyes went from one to the other.

"My lord," the man said with a trace of uncertainty.

Betsy ignored her husband's demeanor and faced the butler.

"I'm very happy to see you, Coombs," she said. "There's a matter we must discuss directly."

"Her ladyship is mistaken," Michael ground out, sweeping his great coat from his shoulders.

Betsy waved her hand. "Oh, I'm not mistaken, husband."

265

"Betsy."

"Now, Coombs," she went on. "Our visit to Bridgewater Park put me in mind of some wonderful recipes. You and I must put our heads together and bring some of the delectable treats to our cook's attention here. I know Mrs. Rollins isn't very open to change."

Coombs looked nervously at his master and swiftly returned his attention to the mistress of the manor.

"True, the housekeeper might need some convincing," Coombs said with a smile. "It will be my pleasure, my lady."

Michael grunted and grasped Betsy's arm. "A word, wife," he said, leading her away from the butler's speculative gaze.

Betsy had to hurry to keep up with Michael's long, purposeful strides. He directed her into the great hall, and didn't stop until they stood beneath the tapestry. Abruptly, he released her. She clicked her tongue at him as she rubbed her arm. He ignored her show of discomfort and pique.

"I would have believed it beneath you to play such games," he said, his eye dark.

"I was truthful in my exchange with Coombs."

"You won't speak of your mystery," he said. "Nor will you approach Coombs with your ridiculous notions. You will yield to me on this matter."

Betsy looked up at him. Yield to him? Not likely. She nodded in acquiescence, keeping her thoughts to herself. Michael apparently took her silence as acceptance and nodded curtly. He turned to mount the staircase.

"Let's ready for dinner, then," he said.

Betsy followed him up the stairs, her mind working. She fully intended to see his birthright restored. But how?

Surely Coombs would have some useful information to impart. She turned her attentions from Michael's absurd command to the coming evening. She also chose not to ponder at the present time the prospect of another long night spent like strangers forced to share sleeping accommodations.

***

Well, dinner was delightful. Michael drank down his second glass of brandy. He'd closeted himself in his study directly after the meal was concluded, unable to bear his wife's coldness any longer. Her beautiful eyes remained focused on the succulent roast beef on her plate, instead of gazing lovingly into his. Her delicate fingers stroked the stem of her wine glass instead of reaching out to touch his hand as she happily conversed with him. My God, had it only been one week since their argument? He drained the glass and set it down on his desk. He dragged himself from the study, bound for the master's chambers.

As he mounted the stairs, he imagined his wife tucked cozily into their huge bed, her glorious hair fanned out around her face. No doubt she was all but clutching her side of the bed, seeking to maintain as much distance from him despite the large expanse of bed that would already separate them. And so began another night of misery, her body so tantalizingly close yet her heart so far from his.

He opened the door leading to their chambers and stalked into the sitting room, scanning for the sight of his lovely wife. She couldn't prevent his gaze from touching her at least. He removed his jacket and untied his cravat.

"Bloody hell," he muttered as he walked further into the room and found it vacant. He knew just where he could find her. The nearest guest chamber.

"Betsy!" he shouted.

Michael burst into the guest chamber, his hands in fists. One quick glance around the room showed him she was prepared to settle there for the night.

"Tell me you don't plan to sleep in this chamber," he

growled.

She swallowed audibly and raised her chin. "Yes, I do."

He stared at her for a full minute. "Have you lost whatever sense was in that head of yours?"

Her brow furrowed as she placed her hands on her hips. "That was uncalled-for. I merely thought we would both sleep more peacefully if we remained apart."

"Does my presence pain you so?" he asked her sharply. "Perhaps you would have preferred to remain at Bridgewater Park?"

When she shook her head in answer he sighed with irritation. "Then tell me, wife. Do you find me so repulsive you cannot bear to be in the same room with me?"

She gave a shake of her head "Hardly."

Michael stepped forward and took her arm. "You're returning to our chamber this instant," he told her. "You are my wife, damn it to Hell. You sleep with me."

Betsy dug in her heels, shaking her head. "But surely you don't mean to take me."

He dropped his hand as if burned by her. "Do you truly believe I would force you?"

Her eyes widened.

269

"Certainly not," she said. "But would you attempt to seduce me? Most definitely."

"Come then," he said, turning toward the door.

She shook her head in lingering defiance.

He swore softly in response. "Do you wish the servants to become aware of our estrangement?"

"No." She righted the coverlet on the bed. "No. I'll sleep in our chamber, Michael."

He took her acceptance and returned to their chamber. She followed on her own. Without another word, he left her beside the bed and went into his dressing room.

Chapter 22

Michael watched as Betsy removed her dressing gown, desire flaring through him as her nightgown-clad form was backlit by the fire burning in the hearth. His mouth went dry as he gazed hungrily at her body through the thin material. When she climbed into the bed, perilously close to the edge, he did the same. He longed to pull her into his arms, to set aside this ridiculous separation. He squeezed his eyes shut and prayed for sleep to take him.

He awoke several hours later to a strange sensation. Something was tickling his nose. Something soft and incredibly silky. He opened his eyes in the gloom of the chamber and discovered to his dismay Betsy was curled tightly against him, her bottom pressed against his groin, her head tucked beneath his chin. Her sweetly-scented hair had been the culprit. Apparently she was unable to sustain their separation in her sleep.

He dropped a kiss on her silken hair and draped his arm about her waist. Lord, she felt wonderful in his arms.

When she sighed in return and pressed against him more closely, his body reacted in sharp wanting. Unable to resist the notion, he eased his hand beneath her gown to gently cup her breast. Betsy arched slightly, rubbing her bottom against his

271

growing arousal. He groaned softly and kissed the shell of her ear. When she sighed again, his hand went lower to caress her. She moaned as soft as a whisper. He'd never heard such a marvelous sound in his life.

"Oh," she sighed, turning her head a bit. "Michael, what are you doing?"

"Shh, love," Michael breathed in answer. "Please, darling. Don't deny me. Don't deny yourself."

Betsy closed her eyes and slowly nodded. Michael eased himself between her legs, groaning softly as she pressed herself back against him. His fingers caressed her even as he moved within her, bringing her closer to her release. She reached up to grasp his head, her fingers caressing his hair, his cheek. When her climax took her she shook with it, sobbing his name.

Michael held her tightly against him as he poured himself into her, his eyes closed in splendor. He withdrew and turned her in his arms, kissing her lips gently.

She gazed up at him, her eyes a dark violet. "Michael," she began softly, "that was so…"

"Wonderful?" he offered with a grin.

"Unusual," she countered softly. "And wonderful," she amended with a shy smile.

He chuckled. "There are many ways for a man to love a woman."

A shadow crossed her face for a moment. He grasped her chin and looked deeply into her eyes. The uncertainty was there, and he wouldn't let her withdraw from him again.

"Betsy, I can't bear this separation," he told her. "And I don't mean solely in our bed. In the great hall, at the dining table, passing each other on the stairs. It won't do."

"Can't we set aside this estrangement?" he went on. "Pray, tell me you forgive me for my hateful words?"

Betsy studied him, and then wrapped her arms around his neck, sending him onto his back.

"Oh, Michael!" she cried. "Oh, I've missed you."

He smiled his relief and hugged her tightly. "You forgive me, then?"

She rained kisses on his face. "Oh yes." She leaned away from him. "But what of the mystery?"

He pushed aside his uneasiness and let out a breath. "I'll deal with the matter in my own time, Betsy," he said. "In my own way. I promise."

She appeared to yield to him in this, and hugged him again.

"I've missed having your arms around me," she sighed,

dropping kisses on his chest.

"And they have sorely missed you."

He loved her again before dawn and the two of them slept late into the morning hours. When at last they rose and dressed for the day, they took their breakfast in a most leisurely fashion. Michael consumed his hearty meal of ham and bacon and eggs and watched her as she daintily ate her meal of poached eggs, her eyes downcast.

She'd been as passionate, as demanding, as he'd been that last time in their bed and he couldn't have been more pleased. But he was no fool. He knew his wife's mind nearly as well as he knew his own. She had a stubborn streak as wide as the Thames. It was that trait which first attracted him to her at the Derby, along with her lovely face and figure. She wouldn't rest until she knew the truth about her bloody mystery.

As if sensing his close regard she looked up at him at last, smiling shyly. He bit back a laugh, amazed as always at how she could be a wanton in their bed at one moment and as shy as a girl fresh out of the school room in the next.

Silently praying she would postpone any further investigating for at least a fortnight, Michael left her after breakfast to see to his duties regarding the estate. His step felt much lighter than it had the last few days, and he couldn't keep from whistling as he strode into his study.

***

Betsy sipped at her tea after Michael left the breakfast room, her mind running in circles. She vowed anew to make whatever discoveries she could manage. But what of her promise to Michael? She sighed in irritation. She wouldn't permit his reluctance, his inflexibility, to keep the truth from its inevitable disclosure. After all, she hadn't precisely given him her word she would set the matter aside. It was of no consequence.

She set down her tea cup and took herself up to their chamber before going in search of Coombs and of any information he could give on the destruction of the tapestry. She was certain Michael's nightmare of Christmas Eve was related to the tapestry. The fear she'd heard in Michael's voice as he'd uttered the butler's name was chilling. Surely Coombs would be able to illuminate the subject.

After retrieving the recipes she had persuaded the cook at Bridgewater Park to relinquish, they were not merely a means to an interview with Coombs, she went to the kitchens and found the housekeeper just outside.

"Good morning, Mrs. Rollins."

The stout, gray-haired woman's eyes rounded. "My lady?"

Betsy held the recipes out in front of her, causing Mrs. Rollins to look on in curiosity as she read the first few lines.

"These are a few of my and Lord Balsam's favorite dishes from Bridgewater Park, Mrs. Rollins. I had thought to have Coombs speak to Cook regarding these dishes," Betsy said. "However, I believe you would have more sway with her than he might."

The housekeeper gave Betsy a surprisingly-pretty smile. "I'd be happy to take these to Cook." She folded the papers and tucked them in her pocket beside her ring of keys. "Was there anything else you needed this morning?"

"Yes. Can you tell me where Coombs might be at this hour?"

"In his office, my lady. Go along to the parlor and I'll send him to you directly."

Thanking the woman, Betsy returned to the front of the manor.

She spent a few nervous minutes before the butler arrived.

"My lady, Mrs. Rollins said you are you in need of something?"

Betsy smiled brightly at him. "Yes, but I've seen to the

recipes myself."

Coombs nodded. "As Mrs. Rollins advised me." He smiled. "She is quite determined. Well done."

Betsy basked in his praise for a moment. "Mrs. Rollins was most attentive to me, actually. I have been remiss in not taking over the running of the manor sooner."

"You will do well, my lady. Of that, I have no doubt."

"Thank you." She paused, and then forged ahead. "Coombs, how long have you been in service to the Reed family?"

Coombs smiled widely, his narrow chest puffed with pride.

"Many years, my lady," he said. "I came to work for his lordship's grandfather when I was a very young man."

"Then you also worked for the previous Lord Balsam?"

"Yes. When he married and brought his bride here, I became the head of the household staff. She was a wonderful woman, the master's mother. You remind me a bit of her. She liked to ride as well."

Betsy nodded at the compliment, and guilt threatened to assail her. She looked down at her hands. There was nothing for it.

"Coombs, what do you know of the tapestry in the great

hall?"

The man blinked rapidly, and the proof of his recognition wasn't lost on her.

"I do not know what you mean, my lady.

"The destruction to the tapestry, Coombs," she went on. "Surely you saw it was deliberate. What can you tell me of it?"

He reddened and stood, his gaze on the floor. "I cannot speak of any such occurrence."

Betsy stood behind the desk, certain her only chance of learning the truth was rapidly slipping through her fingers.

"Coombs, please," she said. "Lord Balsam seems quite troubled by the memory of it. He must have been quite young. I simply wish to learn the particulars. I believe it will serve to rid him of the discomfort."

The butler's eyes softened for a moment, giving her a bit of hope. That hope was dashed by the man's next words.

"I will not speak of it, my lady," he told her firmly. "I will not be disloyal to the late viscount."

"Disloyal? Oh, please don't think I would ever seek to bring you to such a circumstance. Lord Balsam finds you a most loyal attendant, I assure you."

She then dismissed Coombs, certain she could never

broach the subject again. There had to be another way. She would learn the truth but not at the expense of the butler's comfort.

When Michael joined her for tea in the great hall that afternoon, she had all but decided she would have no one's help in her quest. She made no mention of the tapestry, despite its place of prominence above the hearth.

She did noticed that Michael's eyes were drawn to it again and again, however. She nearly bit her tongue to keep any comments to herself.

Chapter 23

Betsy and Michael decided they would go to London toward the end of February, which was just a few days away. This would allow some time for the to socialize before Michael had to take up his springtime residence at Bridgewater Park. He left it to Betsy's preference if she wished to follow him there in late March or remain in town with Maggie and Philip. Eager as he was to begin the horses' training in earnest, he looked forward with pleasure to squiring Betsy to the various functions in town.

He hadn't been to London for the Season since three years earlier, and that experience hadn't been one he would have wished to soon repeat. The cold women of society, and the deceptive manner in which the majority of the gentry presented themselves, were things to be avoided. But with the prospect of his having his sweet and lovely wife on his arm, he could contemplate without distaste the social intercourse open to them.

It had been several weeks since their reconciliation after Christmas, and the two of them had been immersed in their respective pursuits regarding the estate's return to its former grandeur. Betsy saw to the placement of the previous Lady Balsam's needlework about the manor, along with several of her

most favorite pieces of her own work. With every new addition
Michael was prevailed upon to give his approval, which he did
with little reluctance.

He encouraged her in all her decorating endeavors, and
was pleased that the subject of the ruined tapestry was never
mentioned. As Coombs placed a tray of delectable lemon tarts
before them, one of the favored recipes taken from the cook at
Bridgewater Park, Michael knew with certainty she still
harbored hopes of using the butler's recollections to her own
design. He followed her gaze to the servant's retreating back and
arched a dark brow in her direction. She quickly averted her
eyes. Didn't she know he could nearly read her quick and
beautiful mind?

He refrained from pointing this out to her as he handed her
a glass of sherry.

"I quite approve of your additions to the hall, love." He
nodded toward the largest piece of needlework, one embellished
with morning glories and small birds. "You've succeeded in
warming the castle."

She smiled at his words. "Your mother was quite gifted
with the needle. I believe she too wished to adorn the stone walls
with very large pieces of her handiwork."

Michael looked toward the gallery visible at the opposite end of the hall. "I'd thought you would have seen the portraits in place by now. Have you changed your mind on that?"

"Not at all. The storage room was quite damp and the portraits need a bit of restoration. Coombs has assured me that he will see them restored and hanging in the gallery upon our return to the manor."

"Coombs bows to your bidding now?" he teased.

She dimpled a smile at him.

"I'm eager to see the image of my mother," he admitted. "I'm afraid she is merely a collection of memories to me."

"What memories, Michael?"

He took in a breath. "Sweet scents, I suppose. Warm hugs."

He hadn't seen her portrait for longer than he could remember. Why, the family portraits had disappeared from the gallery around the same time the tapestry had. The unbidden thought sent an icy cold shiver down his spine.

"Michael?" he heard Betsy ask as if from far away.

"Hmm?"

She stared at him and he sensed she could read his distress. Although she must certainly long to press him about it, she said

282

nothing. Her smile seemed forced as she sweetly offered him the last remaining lemon tart on the tray.

He ate the tart and brought her fingers to his lips, kissing away the crumbs. Relief flooded him as the moment of unease was broken. He pulled her out of her seat and into his arms, grinning as he strode through the great hall and up the staircase to their chambers.

It came back to him in his sleep that night, however. He could hear his father's broken voice, his tormentor's laughter. Thrashing about in the big bed, Michael unconsciously sought to remember more. To put a face to that horrible mocking laughter.

Coombs made his appearance in his mind's eye, calming him. At the abrupt conclusion to his dreams he jerked awake, the bedclothes twisted about his legs. A quick glance at his wife showed she still slept. He breathed a ragged sigh and straightened the covers, settling back down beside her.

What the devil had happened all those years ago? Were his horrid hazy memories indeed tied to the tapestry? To his father's missing fortune? Lord, was he soon to be as dogged as his wife?

He closed his eyes and awaited for sleep to finally claim him.

***

Betsy, too, was awake. She'd heard him call out in his sleep, and had felt his thrashing about in the bed. How could she not, his being such a large man? Those troublesome dreams assailed him. The dreams he wouldn't share with her.

His breathing soon grew even and she knew he slept once more. Why was he so stubborn? Didn't he see that all was not well? Both his sleep and his mind would not be easy until he learned what happened to his birthright. Her resolve on this was as strong as it ever was. Tonight, however? Tonight she turned in his arms and kissed his closed eyelids. When the shadow of a smile touched his lips, she closed her own eyes and burrowed closer still.

They left for London on a sparkling morning a few days later. Although it was still chilly, there was a unmistakable hint in the air of the spring to come. Michael settled himself beside Betsy within the carriage, the two of them on the seat facing forward as the vehicle began to roll away from Cornwall. He wore impeccable traveling clothes and his black greatcoat draped over his shoulders. She wore one of her new dresses, this one of sunny yellow despite the date on the calendar. She paired it with a cloak of gold velvet knotted tightly beneath her chin, however.

"Tell me of our townhouse, Michael."

Michael crossed his legs and shrugged. He'd arranged for comfortable accommodations in town, leasing a townhouse for as long as they had need of one.

"It's not far from Wilton's, love," he told her. "My solicitors assured me we'll find it suitably furnished."

"I'll enjoy being close to Maggie," she allowed. "And how long will you remain there with me?"

"A little over a month."

"I know you're needed at Bridgewater Park, but you're leaving your helpless wife to attend the functions unchaperoned?"

"Lady Balsam, I don't believe you have a helpless bone in that lovely little body of yours."

"I'll come with you to Bridgewater Park to train the horses."

"You change your mind each morning," he said without anger. "You'll drive me daft, woman."

Betsy simply grinned at him. He reached over and brushed aside a curl at the side of her face.

"And I suppose after we stop for luncheon you'll inform me that you intend to remain in town with your sister after I make my exit?"

Betsy began to shake her head and then shrugged, holding back her laughter. He chuckled and leaned back against the cushions, leaving her to her thoughts. His mention of the nooning meal put her in mind of that inn with the very familiar serving girl. nervously fingered the velvet cording of her cloak.

"Do you wish to stop at that inn today, Michael?" she asked, keeping her tone light. When he did not answer she glanced over at him. At his obvious bemusement, she quietly added, "in Devonshire?"

He draped his arm over her shoulders. "Surely you weren't troubled by Molly's attentions, were you?"

"You dallied with her."

"And I told you as much, love. The chit means nothing to me, you know that."

"I do," she said quickly.

"Molly saw that we were happily married, Betsy. If she could see that when you were barely speaking to me? That fact is clear as crystal."

Betsy breathed a bit easier then. When they arrived in Devonshire she was put further at ease to see it was indeed as Michael said. While the serving girl's dark eyes continually ran over Michael in appreciation, she served them their meal as she would any other patrons.

When their meal was concluded, they once more boarded their carriage and set out for London.

"I take it you quite enjoyed our luncheon?" Michael asked.

"Oh yes."

She gazed out the window at the passing countryside. The sun still shone and the afternoon was proving to be quite temperate. It grew warm in the carriage, so she removed her bonnet and cloak and set them both beside her on the seat.

"I believe we are coming to a stretch of bumpy road, love," Michael said with a crooked grin.

Her gaze fell to his mouth, which he soon brought to hers. She returned his kisses, sighing as he tightened his hold on her. A gasp escaped her as he suddenly shifted, settling her on the seat opposite.

"Michael, what are you doing?"

He didn't give an answer, but fell to his knees before her and lifted her skirts. She watched him, her heart racing as he slowly removed her drawers. He gently grasped her ankles and placed one foot on each of his thighs. He lifted her skirts higher still until they were nearly to her waist. His eyes sparkling up at her, he lowered his head.

"Oh!" she cried as his mouth began to tease her.

"Shh, love," he chuckled, dropping little kisses on her inner thighs. "You'll spook the horses."

Betsy placed one gloved fist in her mouth, her head lolling back on the cushions as his mouth claimed her once more. The rocking of the carriage moved her incessantly against his mouth. He braced his hands on the seat on either side of her, apparently taking care not to steady her. The motion of the carriage drive her closer to her release, and she couldn't keep soft moans from escaping from behind her fisted hand. Her body began to tremble from within, and the tremors were due to sheer pleasure and not the vehicle's motion.

Unable to stop herself she cried out, clutching his head to her as her climax took her.

He came up and kissed her then, letting her taste herself on his tongue. Before she could catch her breath he twisted in the seat, bringing her on top of him. He ran his hands over her back, up under her skirts. Betsy reached between them and ran her fingers over him, finding him hard to her touch.

"You want me, Michael," she breathed.

"God, yes," he ground out, quickly unbuttoning his breeches.

He freed himself and brought her down upon him, hard. Betsy cried out again and clutched his shoulders, burying her face in the crook of his neck as she rode him. She found her second release only moments before he climaxed, barely feeling his grip tighten on her hips as he exploded within her.

When she came back to herself, she lifted her head to find her husband as affected as she. His head was resting on the cushions, his lips curved in a smile as he sought to catch his breath. She kissed his mouth and sighed, settling her head against him once more.

"You were right about the rocking, Michael."

He made a strangled sound like laughter and held her closer as the carriage rolled on toward town.

Chapter 24

The townhouse Michael had secured was in a fashionable section of London. The house was of gray stone and had several long windows on its façade. They alighted the carriage and Michael escorted Betsy up the wide steps to the glossy blue front door. The two of them handed their wraps to the waiting servant and walked about the house. They located a sitting room in the front, a lovely parlor with a fire burning brightly in the hearth toward the back of the house, and a study which seemed adequate for Michael's needs. The breakfast room was small but bright and the dining room was very elegant. Betsy was certain that the rooms abovestairs would be as comfortably furnished.

"Do you approve of the accommodations?" Michael asked her as they stood once more in the entryway.

"It's lovely, Michael," she assured him. "And I daresay that pretty writing desk in the front sitting room will prove very familiar to me."

He nodded with a smile. "Invitations and calls will soon fill your time."

They climbed the stairs and found their chamber pleasantly decorated and furnished with a large bed. Ignoring her husband's knowing glance, and the tingle it invariably sent down her spine,

Betsy took herself into one of the two adjoining dressing rooms to ready for tea.

The following day, their stay in London began in a most pleasant fashion. Michael took Betsy riding through Hyde Park the next morning, and on several calls in the early afternoon. The expected cards and invitations soon arrived, setting them firmly into the social whirl even though the Season wouldn't truly begin until Easter arrived in a fortnight.

One morning, nearly two weeks after their arrival in town, Betsy paid a call at her parents' grand townhouse. While the house Michael had leased was in the fashionable West End, the Earl of Taunton's was placed squarely on Park Lane.

Her mother greeted Betsy with much warmth and more than a bit of disappointment. "Oh, my son-in-law isn't with you?"

Betsy held out her arms. "As you see."

Her mother's brows knit. "I've grown quite fond of him, you know."

This tickled Betsy. "Truly, Mother?"

"Yes, dear. No other lady of my acquaintance can boast of so handsome and accomplished a son-in-law."

They headed into the parlor, and she soon learned that her

mother wasn't finished giving her opinions.

"He is no Lord Templeton to sure," she went on, "but your beautiful smile has never been so bright as when you're in your husband's company."

"He makes me very happy, Mother."

Lady Bridgewater smiled. "You'll scarcely believe who has also paid a call this morning."

"Who, Mother?" She stilled as she spied her mother's favored visitor.

"Hello, Betsy child."

Betsy could only stare at Lady Sarah Addington, the daughter of a long-time friend of her parents. She recovered herself and dropped a curtsy, managing a tight smile.

"Lady Sarah," she returned coolly, perching on the settee opposite.

Betsy had never cared for the woman, and her dislike grew when she was a child and Lady Sarah had attempted to attach herself to Philip. She and Lady Bridgewater had arranged a betrothal of sorts despite Philip's obvious indifference to Lady Sarah and his devotion to Maggie. She was still quite pretty, Betsy allowed, studying the lady's shining black hair and deep blue eyes. But she knew the woman was cold and manipulative.

Oh she had managed to present an affectionate front whenever Philip had been present, she recalled, treating Betsy liked a favored sister. That false warmth was evident this day as well.

"I was quite astonished to hear of your betrothal to Templeton, Betsy dear," Lady Sarah said, sipping delicately at her tea cup. "But my surprise increased tenfold when I learned you had broken your engagement to wed another."

Betsy bit her tongue to keep her comments behind her teeth. If only Lady Sarah would do the same.

"If my memory serves, your husband is a frightfully handsome man." She wore a sly smile. "Although I haven't seen Michael—excuse me, I believe Lord Balsam is his title now—in years."

Betsy's eyes grew round at the woman's familiar use of Michael's name. She set her own cup down and folded her hands in her lap, turning to face Lady Sarah fully.

"I wasn't aware you knew my husband."

Lady Sarah laughed, a sound that rang as false as her smile. "Oh my dear, you'll find there are few people of high birth whose society I discourage. Pity about his fortune, however."

"What would you know of such matters?"

Lady Sarah sneered then, her mouth an ugly slash. She soon smoothed her expression, smiling sweetly now.

"You would be surprised to learn to what knowledge I am privy, my dear Lady Balsam."

"Sarah will be dining with us this evening, Betsy," her mother said. "Perhaps you and your husband will join us?" She looked at Lady Sarah for a moment. "The earl is quite fond of Lord Balsam."

"We are attending a function this evening, Mother." She too returned her gaze to Lady Sarah. "With Maggie and Philip."

The lady blanched visibly, taking a considerable amount of time to recover. But recover she did, Betsy noted with only mild surprise.

"Ah, Lord and Lady Wilton," she stated. "And how is your, um, sister these days?"

Betsy didn't miss the woman's inference, her hesitation an obvious slight at the circumstances regarding Maggie's birth.

"Maggie and Philip are quite wonderful, Lady Sarah," she said. "Most happy."

"Oh yes," Betsy's mother put in. "Margaret is still as beautiful as ever, Sarah dear. And Philip is ever the doting husband."

Lady Sarah managed another of her falsely sweet smile in the older woman's direction.

"Is that not simply wonderful?" she asked. "Oh, to find such a love as theirs. It is my fondest wish."

Betsy was not fooled for a moment. She couldn't withstand Sarah's company for another moment, nor could she quietly endure the woman's thinly veiled barbs at her and Maggie's expense.

"Mother, I'm afraid I have more calls to make."

Her mouther blinked, but stood and gave her a kiss. "Do tell your husband to accompany you on your next visit, dear."

"I will." She turned to Lady Sarah. "A pleasure, Lady Sarah."

The other woman smirked and Betsy took her leave. Dine with her tonight? Not tonight, and not ever.

***

That evening Michael and Betsy readied to attend their first bash as a married couple.

"You look marvelous, husband," she said, coming to stand before him.

He glanced over at her and his breath caught. Her gown was of silver silk, daring in cut. She wore the jewels he'd given her for Christmas, and the sapphire pendant rested nearly between her breasts. Her hair was upswept, and the sapphire earrings sparkled as she smiled up at him.

"And you, Betsy." He took her gloved hands in his. "I'll have to beat the men away from you."

Betsy waved away his words.

"It's quite early in the Season, Michael," she said with a cheeky grin. "I'm certain most of the younger gentleman still reside in the country. You must content yourself with thrashing only one or two very elderly gentlemen."

He chuckled. "Never mind," he said, taking her elbow.

Her smile grew brighter as they descended the stairs to await Maggie and Philip's arrival.

The party was held at the Earl of Winston's, a most fitting location for one of the first bashes of the Season. The home was large, impressive, and beautifully appointed. Many candles lighted the ballroom, their light reflected off the polished floor. Michael and Philip escorted their wives into the room after greeting their hostess, leading them past the orchestra which played tunefully. Without hesitation the four of them took to the dance floor, enjoying several turns before the ladies at last begged a respite.

Betsy and Maggie were then quite content to sit on two of the many gilded chairs which lined the space.

"I'm surprised the place is such a crush," Betsy said.

Maggie clicked her tongue. "Nothing ever surprises me in town, Betsy."

"Would you like some refreshment?" Michael asked.

Both ladies nodded and he and Philip made their way through the crowd of partygoers. They discussed a few of the horses Michael planned to work with when he returned to Bridgewater Park as they approached the refreshment tables.

As they returned with glasses of punch for Betsy and Maggie, Michael caught sight of Lady Sarah Addington. She was still pretty, he allowed. But he knew a vicious heart was hiding beneath that pretty façade. And from the predatory glint in her eyes, she hadn't changed one whit since he'd first made her acquaintance three years ago.

"That cold bitch," he muttered.

Philip arched a brow. "Balsam?"

Michael merely flicked his head in Sarah's direction. Philip's green eyes narrowed as he spied the woman. He looked back at Michael.

"What the devil could you have to do with that witch?"

Michael's lips thinned. Philip laughed without humor, and Michael blinked at him.

"Not you, too?" he asked in a low voice.

Philip laughed loudly then. "No friend, but the chit did make an attempt."

"Unbelievable."

Philip eyed him closely. "Balsam, tell me you didn't dally with her."

"No." Another glance in Sarah's direction showed she still watched them closely. He turned his back on her once more as they came to where their wives sat. "I'm quite certain we can find any number of topics of conversation vastly preferable to this particular one."

"And what topic would that be, Lord Balsam?" Maggie asked.

"Yes," Betsy added. "I am all curiosity over what has you two gentlemen so captivated."

Michael handed her a glass and took her other her hand in his. "I assure you, love. I'm solely captivated at this moment by the prospect of taking supper with my beautiful wife."

Maggie laughed lightly. "Have you been schooling Balsam, Philip?" she teased. "His tongue is nearly as smooth as yours."

Philip swore his innocence, taking her hand. Betsy smiled at them both, turning to gaze up at her husband.

"Supper, then?" she asked him.

All thoughts of Lady Sarah Addington left his mind as he gazed down at his loving wife.

How could he entertain any thoughts of that viper when he had his Betsy in his sights?

Chapter 25

When the marvelous supper was nearly concluded, Michael bent his head to Betsy's.

"Do excuse me, love," he said. "Wilton and Maggie have gone to speak with Lord Tratham. I wish to speak with him, also."

"Lord Tratham," Betsy returned, sipping at her wine. "What care you of him? The man's horse bested you at the Derby."

Michael smiled widely. "I'm well aware of that, wife," he said. "However, Gusty did beat his gelding at Ascot. And if you recall Tratham has several other fine specimens in his possession. Of breeding age."

Recognition swiftly settled on her.

"Oh, Michael!" she said with excitement. "Do go and speak with him directly. Just think of the marvelous horse we could breed off of Gusty."

"I believe I shall," he said, standing. "Although I daresay you would attempt to spoil any foal that would result."

She swatted at his arm and watched him leave to join Philip and Maggie in the ballroom. She dabbed her linen napkin to her lips and rose, adjusting her skirts. As she was leaving the

300

supper room a delicate hand lightly grasped her arm. She turned to find Lady Sarah's intense gaze on her. Not wishing to be prey to more of the woman's veiled insults, she nodded curtly and began to walk past her.

"Your husband is quite delicious, Betsy child," Lady Sarah purred.

Betsy turned to face her, arching a brow and feigning an indifference she couldn't quite feel.

"Passionate as well." Lady Sarah laughed softly. "I would wager, that is."

Betsy's heart pounded at the woman's inference. She squared her shoulders and forced a look of calm on her face.

"Excuse me, Lady Sarah," she said, her voice even. "I must go join my husband."

"I was surprised to find him attached to you," she went on. "Not that you are without your charms. I've heard that your very generous dowry would have secured any man in the country."

Betsy stared at her for a long moment, speechless. Sarah laughed again, this time loudly.

"It's a pity that I didn't know he was for sale," She made a point of searching for Michael. "I would have purchased him for myself."

Betsy gasped at that and all but ran from her. Hateful woman. Her fingers itched to wring Sarah's lovely white neck. Her mind spun with the woman's words. She would have purchased Michael? How dare she! Betsy rushed headlong into a man standing in the ballroom and mumbled her apologies as he steadied her.

"It is quite all right, Elizabeth," a familiar voice said.

Betsy looked up, startled to find it was Lord Templeton gripping her arms. He didn't seem ready to release her either, running his fingers slowly over her skin.

"Lord Templeton," she said, taking a step back from him. "I didn't see you earlier."

"And had you, would you have danced with me as you did with your husband?" he asked with a sly smile.

"No."

Templeton laughed easily. "I am jesting with you, my dear."

She smiled shakily up at him, still feeling a bit befuddled from her confrontation with Lady Sarah.

"How are you, Lord Templeton?"

"Very well, Elizabeth. Pray tell me what had you in such a hurry just then? You seemed eager to rid yourself of something."

"I was merely eager to join my husband. He's speaking to Lord Tratham regarding our horses."

"Horses," Templeton muttered. "Your husband will never get out of the stables, will he?"

Betsy bristled. "I'm quite fond of the noble animals myself," she said with a tilt of her chin. "And we'll raise the fastest in the country."

He smiled in benevolence again, taking her hand and lifting it to his lips. "I certainly meant no offense, my dear," he said smoothly. "Do remember my offer to you, however."

"Your offer?"

Templeton nodded as Betsy withdrew her hand from his.

"Do contact me should you ever be in need for anything," he said. "Promise me."

Before Betsy could offer any sort of response she felt a presence behind her. She turned to find Michael standing behind her, his eyes sharp. She looked back at Lord Templeton, catching an answering animosity in the man's eyes. A look of kindness soon covered the older gentleman's visage once again as a smile curved his lips.

"And what, pray tell, would my wife ever need from you?" Michael asked.

Templeton sniffed and held himself straight. "It was merely the extension of a kindness, Balsam," he said. "I meant no disrespect."

Michael continued to glare at the earl until the man finally grasped his meaning. With a bow to Betsy, the man took his leave. Betsy watched him as he crossed the ball room. While he had seemed his usual self, gracious and condescending, his face had shown with sharp distaste toward her husband. Surely Lord Templeton would feel some resentment toward the man his former intended married. But why the hateful comments regarding Michael's affinity for horses? And just what was it he thought she would ever need from him?

"Are you giving his gracious offer serious consideration, Betsy?" Michael asked.

Betsy started and saw Michael's features were set.

"Never."

Michael glanced once more at the earl and faced her.

"You weren't laying your troubles at the man's feet?"

"I don't understand you," she said. When he didn't lose his rigid stance she felt her own anger rise. "You don't believe I welcomed his attentions, do you?"

"I said nothing of the sort."

Betsy studied him for a long moment. Her mind suddenly changed its direction from his ridiculous accusations to Sarah's maddening statements. Was Betsy's dowry his incentive to wed? And just what, precisely, did the woman know of Michael's passion?

Suddenly the woman was beside them, her blue eyes fastened on Michael as if Betsy were invisible.

"Why Balsam," she enthused, gripping his arm. "How wonderful to see you again."

Betsy didn't miss Michael's reaction. His face reddened as he moved away from the woman. What on earth was going on here?

Lady Sarah laughed, the sound grating. "I should call you Lord Balsam now, should I not?" She favored Betsy with a smug look and grabbed Michael once more. "It has been too long since last we were in the same company."

"Lady Sarah," he said stiffly, unable to meet the woman's gaze.

It was too much in Betsy's considered opinion. First, his hurtful comments regarding Lord Templeton and now, his odd behavior with this hateful woman. Without a word to either of them she turned on her heel and strode out of the ball room.

***

"Why, Balsam," Lady Sarah went on, stroking her fingers over his arm. "You've certainly changed since last we were together. Matured rather nicely, I would say."

Michael's eyes had been on his wife's retreating back, Sarah's words a meaningless buzz in his ears.

"You will take your hand from me, my lady," he said between clenched teeth.

Sarah giggled and pressed against him. "Oh, but you much enjoyed my touch at one time, my lord."

Michael thought back to that ill-advised near-tryst in a darkened garden three years ago. He deliberately removed her hand from his arm and bent his head to hers.

"You will not speak so to me again." He pulled back to rake his eyes over her. "Is it truly wise to show your true nature when you have gone to such lengths to create the illusion of a woman of breeding?"

He didn't wait for her answer, but turned swiftly to search for his wife. He spied Betsy standing beside her sister, looking alternately miserable and quite put-out. He wouldn't feel guilty about Sarah's insinuations. Instead he would press Betsy to explain her warm welcome to the esteemed earl's magnanimous offer.

He crossed to them and bowed to Maggie, reaching out to grasping Betsy's elbow.

"Have you had enough frivolity, Betsy?"

Betsy made him no verbal answer, simply inclined her head. Bidding Maggie good night, she took Michael's arm and silently accompanied him to give their regards to their hostess before departing.

The carriage ride home was profoundly silent, each of them apparently lost in their own thoughts. Michael fumed as Betsy stared out the small window. What was it that held her attention? Or was she merely working her mind around the pompous Templeton's gracious offer? Bloody hell.

The carriage soon stopped in front of their townhouse and the two of them entered and climbed the stairs to their chamber. Michael entered the dressing room, leaving Betsy to ring for her maid. When he emerged, he found Betsy standing in front of the cheval glass wearing only her chemise and petticoat.

She started as he wrapped his arms around her, but she soon relaxed against him.

"Do you find her pretty?" she asked him softly.

"Who?" he countered, nibbling on her ear.

Betsy turned in his arms, looking up at him.

"Lady Sarah Addington."

Michael pulled back. "I suppose she's pretty on the outside." He stroked her cheek. "But her insides are as black as her hair."

Betsy blinked up at him. "How well did you know her?"

"Fleetingly, I assure you," he said. "We met a few years ago."

Michael didn't want to speak of Sarah at the moment. His ire over Templeton fled his mind as well when he caught his wife's tempting mouth in a kiss. He let the love he felt for her, and the passion he so easily aroused in her lovely body, overtake him as they fell upon the bed.

After spending a good part of the morning seeing to a few errands, Michael returned to the townhouse in a dark mood. He walked into the entryway and glanced at the salver tray used to hold cards from callers. Templeton's card caught his eye. He snatched it up and quickly read it. He hadn't stopped by, to Michael's great relief. He'd added a note, however. Giving his regards and saying how much he enjoyed seeing her last evening.

"Why that pompous ass." he muttered.

Clutching the note he stormed into the parlor, intent on learning the particulars from his wife. When he found her absent from that room he searched the ground floor of the house, his anger mounting. When he finally located her at the small writing desk in the front sitting room, he took great offense at what he assumed she was about.

"What the devil is the meaning of this?" he asked without preamble.

Betsy looked up in surprise.

"Michael," she began, her eyes falling on the crumpled paper in his hand. "Oh, I see you—"

"Are you now penning your suitor a note of your own, wife?" he cut in, walking swiftly to the desk. "Surely you're expressing your own great delight in seeing him last evening?"

Betsy placed her pen on the desk and frowned at him.

"I was writing a letter to my sister Mary," Betsy snapped. "How dare you make such an accusation."

Michael had no real answer to her pique. He raked his fingers through his hair. His mind had been full of Templeton that day; of his pomposity, of his blatant pursuit of Betsy. He'd had the great misfortune of running into the man that very morning, and had found his demeanor unchanged from the previous evening's.

The earl had assumed an arrogant pose and inquired after Betsy's well-being as if he were genuinely concerned about her. And to find a note from the distasteful gentleman in his own salver upon his homecoming? He glanced once more at Betsy. She looked furious, and he was in no mood for a verbal sparring match at the moment.

Without another word to her, he stalked out of the room.

Chapter 26

"Maggie!" Betsy greeted her sister with a warm hug.

"Hello, sweetheart." Maggie kissed Betsy on the cheek. "How are you?"

Betsy sensed something in Maggie's tone and felt a prick of unease. "What do you mean?"

Maggie smiled at her, took off her gloves, and sat down. "You can't fool me."

Betsy sat down to face her. "Not much escapes your notice."

"I saw Balsam's demeanor two nights past, if that is to what you are referring," Maggie said. "And yours."

"He's so unreasonable about Lord Templeton," she told Maggie. "I can't believe he would think I would ever encourage that ridiculous man."

"How is Templeton coming between you now?"

Betsy huffed a breath. "Templeton sent a note yesterday."

"A note?"

"It was nothing, but Michael was quite put out."

"Balsam loves you, sister," Maggie said. "And with that, comes a touch of possessiveness. Also, you *were* once engaged to that ridiculous man."

"But that was in the past, Maggie. And I never felt any real attachment to Lord Templeton. No true affection."

"The past sometimes has great bearing on the present," Maggie said. "What of your own reaction to the lovely Lady Sarah Addington, that viper?"

Betsy felt a flash of pique. "She claims some sort of attachment to Michael."

"And you would believe anything that came out of that perfectly-rouged mouth?"

"She seemed so certain, Maggie. So…knowledgeable."

Maggie waved a hand dismissively. "Surely you haven't forgotten her machinations at Bridgewater Park, have you?"

"Hardly," Betsy said. "But what of Michael's words?"

"What words, precisely?"

"I asked him if he thought her pretty."

"You didn't!"

"I did," Betsy said quickly. "And he said she was pretty but had ugly insides, or something to that effect."

"Well, there you have it."

"But how well does he know her?"

"Sweetheart," Maggie laughed. "Precisely how long did it take you to see through Sarah's pretty façade?"

"Not very long."

"And you were but a child," Maggie said. "Balsam is an intelligent man. He no doubt saw through to Sarah's true personality within moments of making her acquaintance."

"I suppose you're right."

"I know I'm right." Maggie stood and pulled on her gloves, a satisfied expression on her face. "Tell me you won't let Sarah, or Templeton for that matter, cause a rift between you and you husband."

"I won't."

She came to her feet and hugged Maggie again. They walked together to the entry and one of the maids Michael's solicitor had retained stood there.

"My lady," she said with a curtsey.

"Yes?"

She indicated a box resting on the hall table. "A package was delivered for you, my lady."

Betsy thanked the girl, who retreated to the back of the house. Betsy opened the package, a box of beautifully decorated sweets, and removed the card tucked within.

Maggie reached into the box and withdrew a sweet. "Apparently Balsam is feeling remorseful for his response to the esteemed earl," she observed as she nibbled at the confection.

Betsy froze. "This isn't from Michael." She held the card out to her sister. "It's from Lord Templeton."

"What?" Maggie said, taking the card from Betsy's limp fingers. "'My dearest Elizabeth,'" she read aloud. "'It was divine to see you at the Winston's bash. I flatter myself you were as pleased to make my acquaintance anew.'" She blinked at her sister. "What a pompous ass."

"Unbelievable," Betsy said. "Do read on."

"All right. 'I hope your husband has not misconstrued my offer. I would do nothing to diminish your happiness. I hope to see you soon, perhaps when I dine with your parents two days hence.'" Maggie clicked her tongue and handed it back to Betsy. "Can he be serious?"

Betsy closed the box of sweets and took the card from Maggie.

"I must get rid of this," she said nearly to herself.

"Are you not going to tell Balsam?" Maggie asked, her hands on her hips.

"What would he think, Maggie?" Betsy countered. "He was furious to read Templeton's note yesterday. What would think of this?"

"As you will," Maggie said finally. "But your husband won't be put off for long."

Maggie took her leave and Betsy stared at the box for a long moment, finally call out to the maid.

The girl swiftly returned. "Yes, my lady?"

"Please take these back to the servants' quarters," Betsy said. "Do enjoy them."

***

Betsy and Michael were both quiet that evening as they sat in the carriage, bound for the Bridgewaters' townhouse. They found Maggie and Philip in the parlor awaiting the dinner bell, along with Lady Bridgewater.

"Children," Lady Bridgewater said, embracing her daughter and squeezing Michael's hand. "We have a slight change of plans for this evening's dinner."

"Oh?" Michael asked.

Philip shrugged his shoulders when Michael glanced in his direction.

"Yes," Lady Bridgewater went on. "Lord Templeton called on your father this afternoon and I happily extended him a dinner invitation."

Michael's belly clenched.

"Oh, Mother," Betsy said. "How could you?"

"Do not worry about the table's being uneven," Betsy's mother said with a wave of her hand. "I invited another to round out our table."

Michael was stunned to see the lady in question breeze into the parlor, all false smiles and tinny laughter.

"Hello, Lady Sarah," Betsy said.

"Hello, Lady Balsam," Sarah returned. "Imagine seeing you again so soon after our lovely conversation of two nights past."

"Good evening, Lady Sarah," Maggie said. "How are you?"

"I am quite well, thank you. And quite delighted to be included in the party."

A servant announced the arrival of Lord Templeton. Michael turned from her and bent his head to Philip's.

"I can scarcely believe he's here."

Betsy's father smiled sheepishly. "I'm afraid Lady Bridgewater extended the invitation, Philip. Believe me, if I could have retracted it I most happily would have."

"Don't trouble yourself, sir," Michael said, feigning an easiness he didn't feel.

Relief showed in Lord Bridgewater's eyes and Michael at last felt a bit of ease himself. He fixed his gaze on Betsy from across the parlor as Templeton merely nodded in the three gentlemen's direction and went immediately to her side.

"I'm most pleased to see you, Elizabeth," Templeton said.

The dinner was served directly and the room was soon filled with the sounds of shining silver softly clinking against fine china. Betsy appeared pale for a moment as she stared down at the roast beef smothered in rich gravy. Michael was certain it couldn't be the fine fare. Surely she was as uncomfortable in Sarah and Templeton's company as he was.

"I trust you enjoyed my gift, Elizabeth," Lord Templeton said.

Michael's ears perked. What was this? Before he could ask about the man's statement he felt a small hand grip his thigh, quite near his groin. He reached beneath the table and gripped Sarah's fingers. His grasp was not tender as he smiled around clenched teeth.

"You will take your hand from me," he said in a low voice.

Sarah smiled as she sought to find him again, stroking his thigh. She bit her lip as his grip tightened. After a beat, she released her hold and he did likewise. He consumed the remainder of the wonderful meal on his plate, tasting nothing of the tender beef and perfectly roasted vegetables. First to see Betsy conversing so comfortably with that pompous old man, and then to feel Sarah's unwanted touch upon him! Bloody rotten evening.

After dinner the sexes separated. When the gentlemen returned to the parlor, he was confounded to find Betsy absent. He made his way toward Maggie but was waylaid by Lady Sarah.

"Balsam," she purred, running her fingers over his arm.

"Where is my wife?" he asked, barely sparing her a glance.

Sarah dropped her hand. "She took herself out of the room just as we were preparing to welcome you gentlemen. Apparently she couldn't bear to be in Lord Templeton's company."

Michael stared hard at her. "What?"

Sarah smiled up at him, leaning close.

"Perhaps she finds his attentions unsettling in these surroundings."

Michael turned from her to glance at Templeton where he stood talking to Betsy's mother.

"Why would that be?" he asked himself aloud.

318

"He's a formidable man, Balsam," she said, tossing her head. "Very handsome and powerful. But this is her parents' home, after all."

Michael could feel his pulse pounding in his ears as the girl's words penetrated. Was Betsy indeed having trouble maintaining her distance from the esteemed earl? She'd seemed attentive during their dinner conversation, and there was the mention of a gift. Just what had Templeton sent and why hadn't he heard of it before now?

He glanced over at Maggie, confounded by the expression on her face. Was that concern evident in her eyes? Or guilt at what she knew of her sister's fickle heart? He crossed to window and stared out at the garden beyond. He wouldn't seek her out. The last thing he wanted was to argue with her in her parents' home.

The conversation in the parlor was merely a buzz in his ears as he tried to reign in his anger and growing feeling of impotence. That was when he took note of Lord Templeton's departure from the room. Without a care to who might notice, he followed him and found both him and Betsy in the sitting room.

She was crying, and his stomach clenched. Templeton

spoke to her before Michael could even enter the room.

"Come now, Elizabeth," Lord Templeton said, causing her to start. "Such tears can only serve to redden your eyes."

Betsy sniffled and dashed her hands over her eyes. "If you will excuse me," she said softly, coming to her feet.

He caught her by her arms, his grip most familiar in Michael's estimation.

"There, there, my dear." He cupped her chin. "Surely Balsam hasn't brought you to such depths."

Michael stepped into the room.

"Betsy, we're leaving." He arched a brow in Templeton's direction. "Unless you wish to remain here in my absence?"

Betsy's eyes grew round. She shook her head and hurried from the room to bid her family good night. Michael watched her go, and then stepped closer to Templeton.

"You'll keep your distance from my wife, Templeton."

To his dismay the earl grinned. "If you cannot keep your wife in comfort, perhaps you can urge her to maintain her distance from me."

Michael reached out and grabbed the man's lapels. To his satisfaction Templeton finally showed a bit of humility, gripping his wrists in an attempt to free himself.

"You permit your emotions to overtake you, Balsam."

Michael released him with a shove, breathing in deeply to cool his ire. "Get out of my sight."

"You're just like your father, that fool," he said. "His thoughts, too, were always clouded with useless emotions."

Michael was astonished at Templeton's words but somehow managed to maintain the tenuous hold on his anger. He squeezed his eyes shut as the man carried himself regally out of the room to rejoin the others in the parlor.

Much later, Michael stood in his study, pouring an overgenerous amount of brandy into a glass. The anger he'd felt at Lady Sarah's blatant overtures faded to nothing when compared to the emotion that overtook him when he'd found Betsy alone with Templeton. Had she been crying on that man's shoulder?

He refilled his glass. He wouldn't tolerate this behavior. He shakily set his glass down and left the study, bound for his chamber. She would prove to him on this night that she was his and his alone.

No talking, no arguing. Only her beneath him, welcoming him and showing him he was the one she chose despite another more affluent suitor.

Chapter 27

In the solitude of their bed chamber, Betsy sat at the vanity. As she pulled her brush through her hair, she reluctantly permitted her mind to continue in its maddening circles. Lady Sarah had whispered in her ear yet again. Michael didn't marry her for her dowry! He couldn't be so cold and calculating. He loved her. He'd told her so, and had even made such a declaration to her father. Did he welcome Lady Sarah's attentions?

She suspected they'd been together before. The woman had all but stated as much. Was he once more willing to bestow more than his dazzling smile upon her? Cursing her retched thoughts, she placed her brush on the vanity and hung her head.

Michael entered the room some time later.

"Come to bed, wife," he ordered thickly, shrugging off his dinner clothes.

Betsy shook her head in answer, finally lifting her gaze. He appeared rumpled and more than a little intoxicated. She shook her head at him as he continued to remove his clothing. When he had stripped to his breeches, he strode to where she still sat and gripped her arm.

"Come to bed," he said again.

She jerked free of his hold. "No."

She stood and glared at him, tightening the belt of her wrapper. Michael swayed a bit where he stood, no doubt from the brandy she could smell on him.

"What did you say?" he asked in a deceptively calm voice.

"I said, 'no,'" Betsy said, holding her hands in fists. "I'll ask something of you, however."

Michael shook his head in confusion, and then swore as he plowed his fingers through his hair.

"Enough of this nonsense," he muttered, grabbing her arm again. "Come to bed."

Betsy stood firm. "When did you know of my dowry?"

"What?"

"When did you know how rich you would become if you took me as your wife?"

"Why do you ask this now?" he countered. "You didn't seem adverse to gifting me with your dowry." He raked his eyes over her. "Or your luscious little body, if my memory serves."

Betsy saw red.

"When did you know of it?" she shouted. "Was it before that afternoon in the stables?"

Michael just stared at her.

"It was, wasn't it?" Betsy sucked in a breath. "You knew of my fortune before you took my virginity."

"Took your virginity?" He laughed harshly. "As I recall you begged me to rid you of it."

Betsy waved that comment aside. "Did you know of my very generous dowry before we made love in the stables?"

They stared at each other for a long moment.

"Yes."

Betsy's throat tightened. "You don't love me, Michael. You lied to me."

"No."

"You lied to my father," she went on. "And all to get your hands on my fortune!"

His eyes flashed dangerously. "How could I ever love a spoiled little girl like you?"

That was all she would endure. It was as if their weeks of tentative peace since Christmas had never happened as she slapped him across the face.

"Bastard!"

Michael recovered swiftly from her blow and reached out, grabbing her to him. "Not again, my love," he sneered. "You unmanned me this evening with your disgraceful behavior with

Templeton. I won't permit you to do so again, here in our bed chamber."

"What?"

"Pouring out your great misfortunes to the man while your family, your husband, was in the same house."

"I did no such thing."

"And what of his gift? When were you going to tell me of it?"

She pulled in a breath and slowly let it out. "It was a box of sweets, Michael. Unasked for and unwanted. I gave it to the servants."

"Sweets." The expression on his face was blatantly carnal now "Don't you want me, wife?"

"I do not."

He grabbed her chin and held his face close to hers.

"You bought and paid for me, didn't you?" he rasped. "Surely you want me now."

She shook her head.

"Your body tells the truth. Your breath is fast. Your eyes hot on mine." he said. "Even if your lovely, lying mouth doesn't."

She balled up her fist and hit him in the face before leaving their room. She huddled under the covers in the guest chamber, her tears flowing unchecked down her cheeks. Would they never get past the disparity in their finances? It was a long time before she found sleep that night.

When she awoke the next morning the nausea she'd felt over the sumptuous dinner at her parents' house revisited her. Struggling to a sitting position on the small guest room bed, she closed her eyes until the upset in her stomach subsided. There was no great wonder at its cause. Michael's harsh, hurtful words. She ran her fingers through her sleep-tousled hair and let out a groan of frustration. She rose and reluctantly returned to the room she shared with her husband.

Michael was still asleep. He was flat on his stomach, his arms and legs spread out toward the edges of the bed. He snored softly as she crept past him on her way into her dressing room. Unwilling to wait for a servant to bring warm water, she made do with the chilled water in her basin. The soap was slow to lather in the water. She stripped off her nightgown and began to wash herself. When she touched the cloth to her breasts she flinched. Her breasts were tender and aching. She stood before the mirror atop the washstand and ran her gaze down the front of her body. Her breasts appeared larger as well. A thought occurred to her. She'd gone without her monthly bleeding since well before Christmas!

Suddenly the queasiness and tenderness in her breasts came to have new meaning. Could she be expecting Michael's child? She would speak with Maggie. She wouldn't speak of it to Michael today. Not after all he'd said last evening.

When she was at last ready for the day she left the dressing room. A quick glance toward the bed showed Michael had not moved one inch since she entered the chamber. Mumbling a few unladylike curses, she crossed to the vanity and hastily ran her brush through her hair. Gathering some of her things, she returned to the guest room and rang for Ann.

***

Michael awoke late in the morning. He rolled over in the bed and stretched, slowly becoming aware of a dull pounding in his head. Groaning, he rubbed his hands over his face. He froze as a sharp pain assailed him when he touched the left side of his face. Rising, he crossed to Betsy's vanity and peered bleary-eyed into the mirror. His left eye was a bit swollen but that wasn't what caused a string of curses to escape him. The skin surrounding his eye was dark purple and tender to the touch.

He leaned closer to the glass. "What the devil?"

The foggy memory of last evening came back to him. Betsy struck him!. The recollection of their argument followed swiftly on the heels of that memory. He could remember few details in the light of day, save for several harsh words. She'd given no answer to him regarding her behavior with Templeton, aside from something about sweets or some such. No matter. He would have his answers today.

He went into his dressing room and saw to his dress and toilette as swiftly as his aching head allowed. He didn't bother calling for a valet. Dressed for the day at last, he once more peered into the vanity mirror.

"Ghastly." He traced his fingers lightly over the purple flesh. "Perhaps Betsy has something to cover it."

He opened the drawers of her vanity. not really surprised to find no cosmetics within. His wife's flawless skin had little use for such items. It was with much interest he came upon a small stack of letters in the bottom drawer. A quick perusal showed him that several were from himself, written during the separation prior to their nuptials. He cursed as he found Templeton's letter tucked within. The date written upon it caused his anger to surge anew. It was written on the day of their bloody wedding!

He read it quickly and cursed again. How dare Templeton

make an offer of assistance to her on the very day she was to marry him, Michael? And why did Betsy save it? To beseech the man at some future date to make good on his generous offer?

He crumpled the letter in one hand and stuffed it into his pocket. He went downstairs to the breakfast room to learn at last what were her dealings with the esteemed earl.

Betsy wasn't in the breakfast room when Michael arrived, much to his chagrin. He thought for a moment to seek her out directly, but the inviting aroma of strong tea beckoned. Foregoing his usual breakfast of eggs and meat, he selected a few sweet rolls and set his plate on the table. He sat and poured a cup of tea, drinking deeply of the steaming liquid. Closing his eyes, he willed the pounding in his head to subside even as the action caused his left eye to pain him.

After eating his meager breakfast, he located his wife at last. She sat in the parlor, a piece of needlework laying as if forgotten in her lap. Her face seemed pale to him, and a twinge of guilt tugged at the back of his mind. He cleared his throat to gain her attention. Betsy looked up at him, her eyes widening as she glimpsed his blackened eye.

"Oh!" she gasped, coming to her feet. The handkerchief she was embroidering fell to the floor. She crossed to him and

329

reached up to lightly touch her fingers to the injury. "Did I do that?"

Michael smiled ruefully as he grasped her hand. The shock and regret that was clear in her demeanor sent all thoughts of brandishing Templeton's letter from his mind.

"I deserved it."

At his smile Betsy dropped her hand and turned away. She bent to retrieve the piece of needlework.

"I've given some thought to the events of last evening and I feel I must say something," he said.

Betsy let out a breath and straightened to face him again. "Oh?".

He nodded. "I forgive you."

"You forgive me?"

"I don't blame you for being alone with Templeton, Betsy," he went on. "The fact you did so in your parents' home vexed me, however."

"You forgive me?" she cried.

"Now see here," he began. "I realize our argument last night was unpleasant."

"Unpleasant?" she repeated in shock.

Michael's anger made its inevitable reappearance. He

chose not to hear what she was saying, only that she was not accepting his very generous offer of forgiveness.

"You're my wife," he snarled. "I come to you on this day to set aside our disagreement, and you attack me yet again?"

"Disagreement? Unreasonable accusations, you must mean. Get out of my sight. And quickly, before I blacken your other eye!"

"Fine!" He reached into his pocket and withdrew Templeton's letter. "But know this, wife," he went on, waving the paper in her face before throwing it to the floor. "You will not contact this old fool and tell him of our difficulties."

He turned on his heel and stormed from the room.

The next day he learned that Betsy settled her belongings into the guest room. She must give little care to the servants' knowledge of the rift between husband and wife, and he supposed it was because his solicitors had only secured their services for the short period of time they would have need of them in town. He would take a page from her book and ignore the entirety of the situation himself.

A servant came to the study and announced that Philip and Maggie had arrived. He headed to the parlor with little enthusiasm. Philip let out a low whistle as he entered.

"Balsam!" Philip exclaimed. "Tell me you didn't go brawling without me."

Michael scowled at his friend. Betsy spared a glance at him, and unless he missed his guess she was quite pleased to see his injury was still so visible.

"What is it you want, Wilton?" Michael asked coolly.

Philip was visibly taken aback at Michael's demeanor.

"I was in contact with Tratham," he said. "He wishes to forge ahead with our discussions regarding breeding Gusty to a stallion from his stables."

Michael nodded and turned to leave the room. "Come into my study."

He left Philip to follow him and fled. He wouldn't let his wife revel in his discomfort. Not to his face and not to his mood.

In Michael's study, Philip regarded him closely.

"Are you going to tell me who made that colorful addition to your handsome face?"

Michael narrowed his eyes at Philip. "Leave it alone, Wilton," he muttered.

Philip disregarded his words and walked around the desk, leaning closer to Michael's blackened eye.

"It's not overlarge," he mused aloud. "It almost looks as if a small fist... No! Your delicate wife could not have marked you so."

"Enough!" Michael said in exasperation. "I won't discuss this with you."

Philip held his hands in front of himself. "It's not my place to advise you on your marriage, Balsam," he said. "Although I can't imagine what would anger Betsy to the point of violence."

"It's none of your concern," he said firmly. "I will set matters to rights, do not worry."

Michael withstood Philip's close scrutiny for several moments. To his relief Philip nodded at last and turned his inquisitions to the subject of horseflesh.

Chapter 28

"Much is not well, Maggie," Betsy said.

"Did you do that to his face?"

Betsy nodded.

"Why would you do such a thing?" Maggie asked.

"The hateful words he threw at me caused far worse discomfort, though I don't sport any visible evidence."

"Oh, sweetheart," Maggie soothed, taking her hand. "Do tell me. All of it."

Betsy sniffled and shook her head firmly. "No. It doesn't matter at present. But I'm afraid there is yet another complication."

"What, pray?"

"I believe I'm with child." At Maggie's stunned silence she elaborated. "I've been feeling ill," she said. "And I haven't had my monthly since before Christmas."

Betsy was unprepared for Maggie's shining smile.

"A baby!" she said, hugging Betsy close. "That's wonderful news."

Betsy shook her head and slowly pulled out of her embrace.

"How can I take pleasure in this, Maggie?" she asked. "I'm

334

not even speaking to my husband."

"That won't continue for long, I'm certain," Maggie assured her. "You can't harbor animosity toward your husband, Betsy. You love him."

"I do," Betsy said. "But that can't change all that he said."

"But sweetheart, Balsam will surely see the changes your body is undergoing. You can't hide that from him."

Betsy shook her head. "Believe me, Maggie," she said. "I have no intention of letting my husband close enough to see any changes."

Michael's notice of any changes proved immaterial as the following two weeks passed without any sort of reconciliation. They shared no further meals together and made no calls upon friends or relatives. Michael took to frequenting the pubs, apparently having little taste for drinking himself into a stupor within his study. Just this very evening he'd taken himself away from the townhouse for what? She could scarcely imagine.

The next morning, Betsy rose leisurely as had become her norm of late. She'd discovered over the very recent past that by taking her time in rising, her morning nausea was greatly reduced. Stretching languorously, she laid her hand on her belly. A slight roundness met her touch and she smiled. The baby made its presence known at last. Smiling, she rose and set about readying herself for her day.

When she entered the breakfast room she was surprised to find Michael sitting within. The hour was late for him to still be taking his meal. She'd come to relish the solitude of her late morning meal, sipping slowly at her tea and nibbling on whatever caught her fancy at the sideboard. Her good mood greatly diminished, she chose a small portion of eggs and a roll. She sat and picked up her fork, keeping her eyes focused on her plate. Michael's voice stilled her.

"Betsy, this cannot go on. Tell me what you want."

Betsy wanted to shout out to him to tell her he loved her. To tell her that he wanted her despite his knowledge of her dowry. But the distance was still very much evident in his dark and beautiful eyes. She felt her heart sink to her toes.

"I want to go home," she said, the words surprising her even as they left her mouth.

Michael winced visibly at her words. She watched in dismay as his expression became even more remote. He gave a short nod of acceptance.

"We'll leave for Bridgewater Park on the morrow," he said, coming to his feet. "I suppose it's not too early for me to begin the horses' training."

Betsy just stared at him. Bridgewater Park? Didn't he realize that Balsam Manor was her home? Didn't he know her heart belonged within those rough stone walls situated near the cliffs in Cornwall?

She said nothing of this, merely inclined her head in answer. Without another word between them, Michael left the breakfast room and Betsy made a half-hearted attempt to eat the eggs on her plate.

When they arrived in Somersetshire the next afternoon Betsy saw their belongings settled into the large guest chamber they'd shared at Christmastime. As much as she disliked the idea of sharing the lovely space with her husband, she was loath for the Bridgewater servants to learn of their estrangement. And knowing her mother as she did, she was certain the woman would inevitably learn of the division and pester Betsy until she learned all the particulars. Then there was the matter of Maggie and Philip's catching wind of it. She would be mortified.

Thankfully Michael said nothing of their sleeping arrangements that evening as they readied for bed. He didn't abandon his habit of sleeping in all his naked glory, she noted with reluctant admiration. She was well aware of his presence all through the night. His sleeping form occupied a large portion of the bed, seeming even larger as she'd grown accustomed to sleeping in blessed solitude.

She awoke sometime in the middle of the night to find herself pressed against him. Quickly scooting away from him, she squeezed her eyes shut and willed his presence from her mind. She couldn't banish his spiced scent however, or the warmth of his body she could still feel. Letting out a soft moan of frustration, she prayed for sleep.

After breakfast the next day, thankfully taken without Michael's presence, she received a missive from her mother. Sitting in the parlor she opened the letter. Lord and Lady Bridgewater would soon be coming into Somersetshire. Betsy let out a soft groan. The Easter holiday was nearly upon them and she knew she should have realized her parents wouldn't stay in town. Her mother disliked the crowds that descended upon London directly after that holiday's passing, as she'd always professed.

Mary would be pleased. When Betsy spoke with her the previous afternoon she'd been almost surly to be languishing "all alone" at the park. She had the company of Maggie and Philip's children, but they were poor companions according to Mary.

Betsy allowed a smile to curve her lips at the thought of the little angels residing abovestairs in the nursery. That thought brought with it the notion of her own little angel growing inside of her. She once more let her fingers touch her slightly rounded belly. Soon. Soon she wouldn't be able to hide the coming child's existence, not with its father sharing her bed.

Her mother's arrival several days later brought with it a bit of bad news. Lady Sarah accompanied them from town and would be staying at Bridgewater Park for an undetermined length of time. Betsy expressed her concern over the situation when next she found her mother alone.

"Nonsense, Betsy dear," her mother said as they stood in the gardens behind the manor. "You aren't worried about any awkwardness, are you?"

Betsy blinked. Did her mother know about Sarah's comments regarding some sort of past connection with Michael?

"Now, do not fret about an uneven table," Betsy's mother said.

"Oh no," Betsy said softly. "Tell me you didn't invite Lord Templeton."

Lady Bridgewater gave Betsy an expression of dismay. "Whyever would I invite him here?" she asked Betsy. "I do not worry about matters such as the proper number of guests at a table when we're here in the country."

Betsy took a deep breath of relief. When the less-than-welcome visitor joined them in the gardens Betsy gave a her the smallest nod and took herself back into the house, much preferring Maggie's company to passing forced civilities with the loathsome Lady Sarah.

The next morning Betsy woke to an odd feeling within her body. Her stomach felt heavy. Strange. She dressed a bit slower than usual and took herself downstairs to breakfast. Only the ladies were present. Lady Sarah was wearing a pretty riding habit and a hat perched jauntily atop her black braids.

"Are you going riding this morning, Lady Sarah?" Betsy asked, not giving much care to the lady's activities.

"Why yes," Sarah answered. "Oh, you enjoy riding, do you not?"

Betsy nodded.

"Then perhaps you would like to accompany me?"

"I cannot go riding," Betsy said without thinking.

"Whyever not?" Betsy's mother asked.

Betsy's head snapped up in surprise. Maggie met her gaze and raised her eyebrows.

"I don't feel much up to riding this morning," she said in vague answer.

Betsy knew her sister wouldn't be put off for long. As she had fully expected, Maggie remained after Lady Bridgewater and Sarah left the breakfast room.

"Are you all right, Betsy?"

"I'm a bit uncomfortable this morning."

Maggie's eyes widened. "Is it the baby?"

"I'm not sure."

"You'll rest today."

Betsy laughed lightly. "That's all I've been doing."

"Have you told Balsam yet?"

"No."

Maggie did not lose her look of worry as she accompanied her sister into the parlor.

***

Later that morning Michael sat at his desk in the office behind the stables, his mind far from the numbers on the papers spread before him. Betsy was in his thoughts, as always. He'd slept fitfully the night before, fighting the urge to take his wife into his arms as she slept so peacefully beside him. He'd come awake and studied her closely as she slept, trying in vain to imagine what she was thinking, dreaming. He had no notion of what was in her mind.

She was still angry at him. That was certain. But more than once, when she was unaware of his observance, he found her expression soft and affectionate in his direction. He'd been wrong to say such things to her. But she was wrong to keep herself from him since that night, and in more ways than physical. She didn't spare him a single word whenever they were in the same room. It galled him to sit across from her at the dinner table and hear nothing from her. She spoke to everyone present, except for Lady Sarah of course. If only he himself could manage to ignore that woman as easily.

Sarah seemed to attach herself to him at every opportunity. Last evening she'd once more pressed herself close to him and all but offered herself. How could she think he would serve his wife such a betrayal?

"May I ask what it is that has you so intense?" a shrill voice asked from the doorway of the office.

Michael was flabbergasted to see Lady Sarah standing there, a slender hand placed on one hip. He returned his gaze to the papers littering his desk.

"I thought you could accompany me on my ride this

morning," she said with a pout.

"I'm very busy, Sarah," he said curtly. "I have no time for more of your nonsense."

Sarah walked further into the room.

"Time can be a concern," she said, closing the door. "Perhaps you can teach me to ride as vigorously as you did yesterday. I watched you. You looked magnificent."

He didn't merit that comment with an answer. Sarah stepped closer and perched herself on the edge of his desk.

"I know full well why you are so agitated." At Michael's noncommittal shrug she continued. "You've gone too long without a woman's touch."

Michael's head snapped up, his eyes narrowed.

"Are you a witch?" he asked. "How could you know such a thing?"

Sarah leaned closer. "I've seen you with that child," she said. "It is obvious she's kept you from her bed, the silly chit."

Michael said nothing, stunned as Sarah put herself on his lap. Her fingers traced over him and his body reacted immediately from its long denial. Sarah threw her head back and laughed, a smug look clear on her face as she began to work the buttons of his breeches free.

"You want me, Balsam," Sarah said in triumph.

"I'm a man, Sarah," Michael answered, his voice harsh. "That's all."

Michael firmly shook his head and placed his hands on her shoulders to push her from him.

"Take your hands from my husband," Betsy said, her voice shaking.

Michael's gaze found Betsy where she stood in the doorway. The hurt and anger in her blue eyes struck him to the core and he promptly lost any trace of the physical desire that had briefly flickered through his body.

He finally succeeded in pushing Sarah from his lap. "Betsy, this isn't what you presume."

"How could you do this to me?" Betsy asked.

Sarah hurried from the room and Michael came to his feet, his hands spread in front of him. When Betsy ran her widening gaze over the front of his breeches his own eyes followed. Two buttons, he thought with dismay as he fumbled to close them. Undone by two bloody buttons!

Betsy ran at him, pummeling her fists against his chest until he grabbed her wrists.

"Betsy, stop this!" he shouted, giving her a shake. "You

will stop this now."

She pulled back, her cheeks wet with tears. He watched in disbelief as she ran from the office. Cursing fluently, he slammed his fist against the wall.

Chapter 29

"I always thought her such a silly child," Sarah said as she walked into the office once more.

"Leave me, Sarah," Michael growled, not turning to face her. "Leave me unless you wish to feel my hands upon you."

"Oh, I believe I would much enjoy your hands upon me," she answered.

He turned flashing eyes on her, his hands in fists. He dropped his dark gaze to her slender white neck.

"Not where I wish to put them."

Sarah's hands flew to her throat as her eyes grew wide with alarm. Before Michael could feel a glimmer of satisfaction at her reaction, a groom ran into the office.

"My lord!" the young man shouted. "Come quickly!"

"What is it, man?"

"My mistress, my lord," the groom said quickly. "Lady Betsy."

Michael's heart pounded in fear, harsh and stomach-clenching.

"What about Lady Betsy?" He latched onto the man's lapels. "What happened?"

"She took Gusty, Lord Balsam," the man said. "I'd just

placed the saddle on the mare's back when she ran out of your office. I hadn't yet fastened it."

"Where did she go?"

"Over the east pasture." The groom sucked in a breath. "She went in that direction."

Michael had scarcely left the room when another groom rushed into the stables.

"Lady Betsy has fallen!" he cried out.

At the young man's words Michael's heart stopped. Without another thought he ran from the stables. He found her quickly enough, spying Gusty standing beside her as if keeping watch.

Betsy was lying flat on the ground, unmoving. He ran to her, sick with worry as he stared down at her pale face. Her eyes were closed and her breathing shallow. He fell to his knees beside her, cradling her in his arms.

"Ah God, Betsy," he urged, his throat tight. "Please don't leave me. I can't live without you. I love you." He swallowed thickly. "Please don't leave me."

Betsy's eyes fluttered open. She gazed at him in confusion for a moment, then reached up to touch his face lightly.

"Oh Michael," she breathed.

"Betsy, love." He grabbed her hand and placed a kiss on her palm. "I love you. I haven't betrayed you, sweetheart. I would never betray you."

Betsy's gaze warmed and he could see that she believed him. Suddenly she grimaced in pain, wrapping her arms around her middle.

"Oh God, no," she whispered. "The baby."

Michael straightened. "Baby?"

"I'm so sorry, Michael." She squeezed her eyes shut once more. "Oh Lord, no…"

Michael looked on, helplessness filling him. He saw it moments later, blood dark and red staining her skirt. He scooped her up in his arms and stood.

"Fetch the doctor!" he called out to the grooms. "Go. Now!"

With Betsy cradled securely in his arms, he ran to the main house and up the grand staircase to the guest chamber. Her skirts were sodden with blood now, blood that covered him as well although he was scarcely aware of it.

"I'm so sorry, Michael." She sobbed brokenly. "Forgive me."

"Hush, love." He kissed her wet cheek. "Hush."

He settled her on the bed and took her hands in his. Her eyes had closed again and he said a silent prayer for her. So much blood, he thought with growing horror. How could she lose so much blood?

The doctor came quite quickly but not quick enough in Michael's estimation. He refused to leave the guest room despite the doctor's continued insistence that his being present during so intimate an examination was highly improper. He held Betsy's hand in his as she continued to cry softly, her eyes closed and her face pale.

When at last Michael quit the chamber he found most of Betsy's family standing in the hallway. Maggie and Lady Bridgewater wore identical looks of worry, wringing their hands. He glanced down at himself and saw he was covered with Betsy's blood. His baby's blood.

"Balsam," Philip said, grasping Michael's shoulder. "How is she?"

"She'll be all right," Michael said flatly.

"And the baby?" Maggie asked.

Michael stared at her. "You knew of it?"

Maggie nodded. Michael raked his fingers through his hair and sighed, shaking his head sadly.

"The doctor assured me she'll be able to carry another child in the future," he said. "He expects her to recover fully."

He happened a glance at Lady Bridgewater and was struck by the shock and sorrow on the woman's face.

"Why don't you go to her, Madam?" he said. "I'm certain she would much like to see you and her sister."

Both ladies nodded and hurried into the chamber, leaving Michael standing with Philip and Lord Bridgewater in the hall.

"I'm sorry, Balsam," Philip said softly. "Go clean yourself up in our rooms, man." He gave Michael a slight smile. "I imagine your wife would not wish to receive you in such condition."

Michael couldn't smile at his friend's well-meaning attempt at a bit of levity.

"I can clean myself thoroughly, Wilton," he said. "But I'll never be able to wash my child's blood from my hands."

He walked slowly toward Philip and Maggie's chambers, his head low.

***

Betsy sat up in the bed, clean now and clothed in a snowy white nightgown. Her mother and Maggie fussed over her as much as did Betsy's maid, seeing to her hair, her pillows, and her every comfort. Mary sat on the bed, chattering on about anything and everything. Betsy felt a small smile curve her lips at her little sister's chirpy voice, happy to focus on something other than the gnawing emptiness she felt at the loss of her baby.

What would Michael say? First to keep the child's existence from him and then to carelessly risk its life? She closed her eyes and said a silent prayer for her baby's soul, asking for God to grant her forgiveness even if her husband would not.

"Lady Sarah is leaving the park on the morrow," her mother said, drawing Betsy's interest at last.

"Why, Mother?" Betsy had to know.

"It seems she was incapable of sustaining her feigned compassion for any length of time," her mother said. "And I believe she harbored some sort of design toward my son-in-law."

"Lord Balsam would never spare that lady a second glance," Mary said with a nod of her little chin. "He loves Betsy, doesn't he Mother?"

"Indeed, child," her mother said.

Michael quietly entered the chamber and stood well away from the bed, uncertainty in his stance. Betsy stared up at him, her smile fading. Maggie and her mother sensed the change in

351

her and turned in his direction. Wearing looks of gentle understanding, Maggie and Lady Bridgewater arose. Mary gave Betsy's hand a squeeze and hopped off of the bed. Before following Maggie and her mother out of the room, Mary stared up at Michael.

"I'm so sorry about the baby, Lord Balsam," she said.

When the three had quit the chamber, Michael came to stand close to the bed.

"How are you feeling, love?" he asked.

Betsy stared up at him for a moment, trying in vain to think of something to wipe the worry from his beloved face. She soon crumpled in spite of herself.

"Oh Michael, can you ever forgive me?"

Michael came down swiftly upon the bed beside her, wrapping her in his arms.

"Hush, sweetheart," he cooed, kissing her brow. "You've done nothing wrong. I blame myself."

Betsy sniffled and shook her head.

"I felt strange this morning," she went on. "I shouldn't have attempted to ride Gusty."

Michael grasped her chin and brought his face close to hers. "Losing the child wasn't your fault, Betsy," he said firmly.

"If I hadn't upset you, you wouldn't have ridden."

"I should have known you would never dally with another. I let my temper get the better of me." She broke into fresh sobs.

Michael kissed her tears away and smiled.

"Our child wasn't ready to be born, love," he said gently. "She'll come to us, I promise you. When the time is right, she'll come to us."

Betsy pulled back. "She?"

Michael nodded. "I can picture our little love. She'll have the most beautiful blue eyes, just like her mother."

Betsy's spirits lifted. "And hair shiny and black like her father."

"She'll come when she's good and ready, Betsy. I imagine she'll have her mother's stubborn streak as well."

Betsy pinched him lightly on his arm.

"I do wish she were here with us now, Michael," she said as she cuddled closer to him.

"As do I, darling," he said. "But we have each other. Don't we?"

"We do."

She kissed his mouth and settled down comfortably into his strong arms once more.

"Betsy, love," he began, dropping kisses on her hair. "That night when I said those horrid things. You said you would never forgive me." His voice cracked. "Does that still hold true? Or can you set my behavior aside?"

"I forgive you, Michael," she said. "I love you."

Michael let out a sigh of relief.

"I deserve your anger for that night," he said. "I was afraid you would never want me to touch you again."

Betsy recalled the many times he had loved her before that night. He was tender and urgent. Passionate and loving. Not let him touch her again?

"The devil you say," she told him.

He barked out a short laugh and hugged her tight. They spoke of the doctor's visit then, of his words of reassurance. The man was due to visit her in a few days, to make certain all was well.

"Michael," Betsy began, trailing her fingers over his arm. "If the doctor says I am fit for travel, may we return home?"

"I thought you considered Bridgewater Park your home," he said. "That's why I brought you here from London."

Betsy shook her head firmly. "No. Balsam Manor is my home. That's where I wanted you to bring me then, and it's where I want to be now."

He smiled at her and cupped her cheek with his hand.

"Then we'll return to Cornwall as soon as we're able."

Betsy bit her lip as she contemplated another issue, one she hadn't given much thought since that night in London.

"What is it?" he asked. "Are you feeling any pain?"

She shook her head. "Michael, please say we can at last uncover the secret of your lost fortune?" She braced herself for a reemergence of his anger. "Together?"

"I realize you have a sharp mind and only have my best interests at heart."

"Of course."

He smiled. "I was a stubborn fool to resist the inevitable all this time."

"Yes, you were." She gave a nod. "I believe our child will inherit a good dose of stubbornness from her father as well."

"I love you, Betsy," he said, drawing her closer still. "I've always loved you."

Chapter 30

After nearly a month had passed, Michael at last took Betsy home to Balsam Manor. That evening they found themselves settled comfortably before a brightly burning fire in the great hall. Betsy was pleased to see a dish of marvelous fruit tarts accompanied the sherry they drank after dinner.

"What of the horses, Michael?" Betsy asked. "Who will see to their training?"

Michael smiled crookedly at her.

"Your cousin isn't totally bereft of skills, Betsy," he teased. "I'm confident that Wilton and the grooms can put Gusty and the others through their paces until I can return to the park."

"Philip is an excellent rider." Betsy eyes sparkled at him. "Not nearly as skilled as you are, I daresay."

"You, love, are biased," he said. "Perhaps before the end of the month we can revisit Bridgewater Park together? And then you can see to the matter yourself?"

Betsy nodded vigorously. "Gusty will miss you sorely until then."

When Betsy suddenly grew quiet he regarded her closely. Her eyes had darkened to violet and he felt a tremor of desire course through his body.

"Betsy."

She came to her feet. "I've missed you sorely, Michael."

"But your health, love. I won't do anything to jeopardize your recovery."

"I'm well. The doctor assured you as well as myself of that blessed fact."

"Yes, but still."

"I'm not made of glass." She took his hand. "I'm a flesh and blood woman who has been without her husband's touch for far too long."

Michael cursed softly and stood to take her up in his arms. "You are certain, love?" He rained kisses on her face, her neck. "You wouldn't mislead me?"

"Never."

His courage promptly deserted him as he watched her undress in their chambers. She unpinned her glorious hair and let it fall in shining waves down her slender back. She unfastened her petticoats and let them fall to the floor, turning to face him in her chemise which only came to mid-thigh.

"Michael," she said, her tone once more holding an inexplicable note of wanting.

Michael took two steps back from her, his back nearly

pressed against the closed door. He'd thought himself a man in control of his desires. One who could take his wife tenderly, ever mindful of her recent injuries. But now with her so tantalizingly close he felt his blood pound thickly through his body as flames of desire threatened to consume him.

"Sweetheart," he said, shaking his head.

"I want you, Michael." She stepped out of her fallen petticoats and walking toward him. "I want to feel your hands on me. Your lips on mine. We can put the unpleasantness of the past weeks behind us. Perhaps we'll even be so lucky as to create our child this night. Don't you want me?"

"Yes." He groaned. "I want you so badly I fear I might hurt you."

Betsy smiled softly and shook her head at him. She reached up and unbuttoned his jacket and waistcoat, running her fingers over his fine linen shirt. He swallowed thickly as she worked the buttons of his shirt free, dropping it to join the jacket and waistcoat on the floor.

"I've missed you, Michael," she said again, her lips placing teasing kisses on his chest. "So much."

She stroked him through his breeches, smiling up at him as he moaned softly. When she freed him he filled her hands, more aroused than he had ever been in his life. She stroked him again, with nothing between her fingers and his flesh.

"Ah, love," he rasped, closing his eyes.

Betsy placed her lips on him and he thought he'd died and crossed over into paradise. The tip of her tongue flicked over him again and again, burning him like candle flames. When she closed her mouth around him he groaned again, his shoulders striking the door as he arched toward her. His climax tore through him like a thunderbolt, ground-shaking in its intensity.

When he regained his senses he gazed down at his wife through hooded eyes. The apology that had formed on his lips died a swift death as he glimpsed the triumph in her beautiful eyes. She smiled up at him and sat back on her heels.

"I've never made you lose your control before, husband," she said, her head cocked to one side. "It makes me feel powerful."

Michael managed a weak smile at her words.

"Truly?" He straightened from the door. "You fancy yourself powerful, do you?"

She grasped his meaning and came swiftly to her feet, giggling. He caught her easily and brought her to their magnificent bed, coming down on top of her.

"Perhaps we'll see if I can make you lose your control, wife?" he teased, ridding her of her chemise.

"That would be heavenly," she sighed.

He made good on his promise, devouring her lips, her tongue. He brought his mouth to her breast and she delighted in the sensation. When he brought his mouth to her center she thought she would expire.

"Lose your control, love," he urged softly, stroking her with his strong fingers. "Come to me."

He lowered his head again and she did, shouting his name as she came to stunning release. Thankful for his earlier lack of control, he entered her slowly. Stroking deeply and gently, he brought her to her second release before permitting his own.

"I love you," he said, coming down beside her in the big bed. "I'll always love you."

Betsy took a deep breath and turned to him, unable to rid her face of its brightest smile. Without another word they held each other closely and fell asleep, deeply content.

***

Sometime later, Betsy awoke with a start. Michael trashed about beside her, the sheets in a tangle around his long legs.

"No, Papa," he mumbled, his voice high and small.

"Michael," Betsy said, shaking his gently. "Wake up, Michael."

Michael sat up in the bed abruptly, nearly toppling Betsy. His eyes were vague as he stared at her.

"What?" he muttered, shaking his head. "What's going on?"

Betsy placed her hand on his cheek to soothe him. "I believe you had that nightmare again, Michael."

His eyes focused on hers at last. He nodded and laid back down, letting out a loud sigh. Betsy followed, placing her hand on his chest.

"Can you tell me about it?" she asked gently. "Does it have anything to do with the night the tapestry was destroyed?"

"Yes." Michael rubbed his hands over his face. "Does anything escape your notice?"

She gave a stubborn shake of her head. "Tell me of it."

He did, beginning with his memory of the argument between his father and his unknown tormentor and ending with his father's angrily tearing the tapestry off of the wall before falling into heartrending sobs.

"He seemed so helpless, Betsy," he said. "It scared me witless."

361

"You were but a child, Michael," she gently pointed out. "Of course you were frightened. What of Coombs?"

"What?" he asked. "Oh, yes. Coombs didn't make his appearance in this particular dream, as you blessedly woke me from it before that point. That night I must have fallen asleep in the hallway abovestairs, because Coombs woke me and took me to the nursery."

"He knows something of that night, Michael," Betsy offered. "He must."

"We'll question him tomorrow, love," he said. "I should have bent to your wishes before."

Betsy quickly lowered her eyes. "I admit I questioned Coombs, Michael," she said. "After you had instructed me not to."

"Why am I not surprised?" There was no anger in his voice, she was pleased to notice. "And were you able to discover anything?"

"No, I'm afraid not. Coombs grew disturbed when I merely broached the subject. I believe he fears dishonoring your father's memory."

Michael nodded sagely. "I'll assure him that disclosing any information which could assist in the search for my fortune would in no way compromise his years of faithful service to the Reed family."

"He's ever-faithful," Betsy said, settling her head on her husband's chest.

Upon first light Michael gently shook Betsy awake. "Come, slugabed."

"What?"

He kissed her and sat up. "I'm most eager to question Coombs about the quarrel between my father and the stranger on that long-ago night."

"All right." She yawned. "I'll ring for Ann."

Ann came, and in less time than she would have otherwise imagined, Betsy was dressed and ready for breakfast. Michael nodded absently at her when she joined him in the breakfast room.

"Good morning, husband," she said lightly, serving herself from the sideboard. "I daresay you were a blur this morning."

Michael smiled as he poured her a cup of tea.

"I admit I'm not much looking forward to our interrogations, love," he told her. "But I do wish to see it through. I'm sorry if I was less than gallant this morning."

She smiled cheekily as she settled herself across from him.

"After last evening, I would be hard-pressed to hold it against you."

Michael chuckled at that. When they had finished breakfast he escorted her from the room.

"Coombs is usually with the kitchen staff at this hour, Michael," Betsy told him. "Why don't we leave him to the task and see about the family portraits in the gallery?"

He concurred and the two of them crossed through the great hall enroute to the gallery. They walked through the archway, silent. The sheer number of portraits hanging there took even Michael aback. There were frames of varying finishes, all quite large and imposing. His eyes immediately settled on an early portrait of his father.

"You are the very image of your father," Betsy said in awe. "My, he was frightfully handsome."

"You'll find all the Reed men to your liking, I daresay," he teased. "We're all very dark and large."

"Oh, there's the portrait of you mother I mentioned." She crossed the space to stare up at the likeness restored and set in the magnificent gilded frame. "My, how your eyes are so very like hers."

When Michael didn't add his agreement to her statement,

Betsy looked closely at him. He was gazing hungrily at the picture, looking very much like a lost little boy desperate for his mother.

"You miss her."

"I couldn't picture her face before now," he said, his eyes still riveted to the portrait.

Betsy gave him a few quiet moments to drink in the woman's likeness. Her eyes fell to the rendering of the lady's necklace and she let out a gasp.

Michael looked at her with worry. "What is it?"

"The necklace, Michael," she said softly. "Look at her necklace."

It was the very same onyx pendant Templeton had given Betsy when they were betrothed.

"Bloody hell," he began. "That's why it seemed so familiar to me."

"But how did Lord Templeton come to have your mother's necklace?"

"He took it," Coombs said from the archway. "That's the truth of it."

Michael and Betsy both turned sharply at the butler's voice.

"Coombs," Michael began, walking swiftly to stand before the older man. "You must tell me what you know."

Coombs sighed wearily and nodded. Betsy saw the obvious discomfiture on the man's face as they urged him into Michael's office. She sent a maid for tea and settled him comfortably into one of the leather chairs facing Michael's desk.

"You have no fear of dishonoring my father's name, Coombs," Michael told him. "You served this family well and whatever you tell us this day won't change that."

"Thank you, my lord," Coombs said. "But I fear what I have to tell you could be most distressing."

"To speak frankly, I nearly lost my wife not a month ago." He took Betsy's hand in his. "We lost our child. Whatever you have to tell me will surely pale by comparison."

Coombs gazed tenderly in Betsy's direction for a moment before nodding sagely. He took a long sip of his tea and set down the cup, obviously intent on finally beginning his tale.

"It began long before the night of their altercation, my lord," he told them. "Lord Templeton ingratiated himself upon my master's good graces in the guise of friendship."

"But he was much younger than the former Lord Balsam, wasn't he?"

"A bit, my lady," Coombs allowed. "Much closer in age to Lady Balsam, I'd imagine. I hope I'm not overstepping my bounds in telling you the young man much fancied your father's wife."

"She was a beautiful woman," Michael said. "But surely she didn't encourage him?"

"Never," Coombs said firmly. "Your mother was devoted to her husband. She was much like you, my lady."

Betsy flushed lightly as she nodded her agreement.

"But how did Templeton come to take the family jewels, Coombs?" Michael asked. "And what did he have to do with my father's fortune?"

"I don't know the particulars of their dealings, my lord," Coombs answered. "But I do know your father much liked to gamble. I believe he was very responsible, but you may ask his solicitors about that. Then your mother passed on and, well. He changed."

"I can scarcely remember her," Michael said softly. "I do recall my father keeping himself from the manor for a time."

"He was hardly ever in Cornwall," Coombs concurred. "I believe his gaming must have become a refuge of sorts."

"That's so sad," Betsy put in. "But what of that night,

Coombs? Michael remembers only bits and pieces of it."

Coombs took another long sip of his tea as if to steel himself. He looked Michael squarely in the eye.

"Apparently Lord Templeton had managed to rid your father of most of his holdings. The jewelry was the last to go, and it was with much hesitation I saw it packed for the man to take from the manor. Your father was distraught. He and the earl argued heatedly."

"I remember," Michael said in a small voice.

Coombs tilted his gray head to one side. "I was never certain of how much you had heard that night," he said "I'd hoped you'd fallen asleep before their argument."

"It's all right, Coombs," Michael said. "I remember my father's anger. And then his anguish."

"He was a broken man after that night. He instructed me to remove the torn tapestry from the great room and to see all the family portraits place in the storage room in the tower."

"I would wager he couldn't bear to gaze upon his ancestors," Betsy said. "He surely must have been devastated to banish his beloved wife's portrait."

"I appreciate your candor, Coombs." Michael shook the butler's hand firmly. "You've given us much to consider."

Coombs stood and bowed his head. "I'm sorry you had to learn of it, my lord. But perhaps now you can set matters to rights?"

"Depend upon it," Michael said.

After the butler left them Michael sat and drew Betsy down into his lap.

"How could Templeton manage such a feat?"

"I don't know," Betsy said. "What is our course of action, husband?"

Michael looked sharply at her. "You'll keep yourself out of it," he said. "I'm bringing you to Bridgewater Park and will continue on to London my myself."

"I'm going with you," she insisted. "You can't shut me out of this."

Michael sighed in apparent defeat. "No doubt your parents and the Wiltons have all left the park for town by now in any event," he said. "Wilton informed me of their plans before we departed yesterday."

"Then it's settled," Betsy said with a smile.

"Yes, but know this. You're to keep to the townhouse. Oh, damn. We're no longer leasing it. You'll stay with your parents while I see to Templeton. Perhaps I'll bring Wilton into it. He's quite sharp."

Betsy nodded, her mind already formulating a plan to make Templeton admit his heinous deeds. Perhaps Lord Templeton had heard of their previous estrangement? It would be quite simple to perpetuate such a rumor if she were residing with her parents in town.

"Betsy," Michael said, breaking through her reverie. "What are you thinking?"

Betsy feigned innocence and shrugged.

"I must see to the packing of our belongings, Michael," she said, hopping off of his lap. "If we're to leave for London on the morrow there's much that must be done."

Chapter 31

Michael paced within Philip's office, his mind working furiously.

"We must get the bastard to admit to his cheating, Wilton," he said.

"But, how?" Philip countered. "Surely you don't believe he would divulge such information to us, not after holding so tightly to his secret all these years."

"Hardly," Michael agreed. "What of your contacts? Do you believe they have learned anything as yet?"

"Really, Balsam," Philip chuckled. "I wrote to Rawlings only this morning. By the time the devil extricates himself from his lovely new mistress it will be well into the evening."

It was as Philip said, much to Michael's chagrin. The two gentlemen left to rendezvous at a gentlemen's club with Rawlings at the start of the dinner hour. Michael stopped at Betsy's parents' townhouse to tell her of his plans as she herself was readying for dinner. She seemed a bit distracted to him but he attributed her demeanor to fatigue from travel. After all, he reasoned as he climbed into Philip's waiting carriage, they'd spent quite a bit of time riding over the rutted country roads over the last few days.

Rawlings, a man with hair as dark as Michael's, greeted them warmly as they entered White's.

"Wilton! How are you, old boy?"

"Quite well, thank you," Philip said. "Though I'm surprised to see you about so early in the evening."

"Yes," Rawlings chuckled. "My fair Monique was quite put out. Perhaps a trip to the jewelry store is in the offing for tomorrow."

Rawlings turned to Michael and offered his belated congratulations on his wedding to Betsy.

"Ah, the Bridgewater women," Rawlings mused aloud, his eyes holding a faraway look. "One would be hard-pressed to find beauty of equal outside that circle."

Michael watched as Philip's brow furrowed. When Rawlings left them to secure a gaming table, Michael leaned toward Philip.

"Was it something the rake said?"

Philip shrugged his shoulders, his frown easing. "Rawlings met Maggie soon after our marriage, Balsam," he began. "He fancied her for himself and attempted a seduction."

"What?" Michael asked in amazement. "And still he lives?"

Philip chuckled at that. "Suffice it to say the man earned his way back into my good graces by aiding in Maggie's rescue from a far more dangerous man than himself."

"You must tell me all of it, Wilton. And soon."

Philip nodded. "At another time. One evening far in the future, when this matter is set aside and we're well into our cups."

Rawlings beckoned them to a table and they joined an elderly man sitting there.

"Lord Pombrey," Philip said with a bow. "How gracious of you to permit such unseasoned gentlemen as ourselves to intrude upon you."

The thin old man laughed easily. He studied Michael for a long moment, finally motioning for him to sit.

"My, but you are the very picture of your father," he said.

"I've often been told so, sir," Michael returned pleasantly.

"I believe you don't share his attachment to the gaming tables, however," the man went on. "Most fortunate, that."

Michael merely inclined his head in answer. They shared some excellent brandy as they played half-heartedly at a game of Commerce. Michael tamped down his desire to question the man directly about precisely what he knew of his father's past difficulties, permitting Philip and Rawlings's easy banter to carry the early portion of the evening. It was Lord Pombrey who finally broached the subject which was so plaguing Michael's mind.

"Your father was most fortunate in his choice of a wife, Balsam," he said. "Pity in other matters his luck deserted him."

"Do you speak of cards, sir?" Michael asked carefully.

"Among other things," Lord Pombrey said.

"I only discovered as much quite recently, I'm afraid," Michael said. "I knew nothing of it."

"You wouldn't have, my boy," the old man said. "You were but a babe when your father lost it all."

Michael looked quickly at Philip, who gave a small nod of encouragement. Taking a deep breath, Michael leaned toward the old gentleman.

"Sir," he began, clearing his throat. "What do you know of my father's dealings with Lord Templeton?"

The old man's sharp eyes widened. "My boy, Templeton fleeced your father of all his worldly belongings, save for his manor house."

Michael bit back the anger he felt at the confirmation of all his suspicions. He must know it all.

374

"Lord Pombrey, what can you tell me of that time?"

Lord Pombrey shook his gray head sadly. "Templeton was quite a rake in those days," he said. "He worked his way through most of the young ladies of society and possessed the luck of the devil when it came to cards."

"Pity your father didn't share such luck, eh Balsam?" Philip offered in comfort.

"It wasn't always so," Pombrey quickly added. "Your father merely gambled for recreation until after your mother passed on. He missed her sorely, I believe."

"But how did Templeton wrest his fortune from him?" Michael asked.

"That scoundrel took advantage of your father when his spirits were at their lowest ebb," Pombrey said.

"Templeton used his skill to cheat my father out of all due him," Michael stated. "Out of all due me."

"True enough," the old man said. "Only Templeton cannot boast of such skill now. You won't see his face in this nor any other respectably establishment."

"What?" Philip asked in surprise.

"What do you mean, sir?" Michael asked.

"Why it's very simple, my boy," Pombrey replied with a

wry smile. "He owes nearly every gentlemen in this room a sizable sum and has absolutely no hope of making good on his debts."

The three young gentlemen shared a look of surprise at the man's astounding disclosure.

***

Betsy had found it quite simple to draw Templeton's attentions to herself again once they returned to London. She'd invited him to her parents' townhouse and played the role of the downhearted lady. He'd preened and commiserated, and she'd forced herself to express an urge to unburden her poor aching heart. It took little effort on her part to secure an invitation to dine at his London home. Michael was with Philip, so she forged ahead with her own plan.

Betsy sat in Lord Templeton's grand dining room now, holding on to her restraint with an ever-weakening grasp.

"You look absolutely ravishing this evening, my dear Elizabeth," Templeton said with a sly smile. "I believe the past few months have given your beauty a maturity it lacked before. You are utterly breathtaking."

Betsy's lips thinned and she inclined her head. "I'm not the same girl who accepted and then rejected your offer of marriage,

Lord Templeton."

Templeton waved his hand in the air and leaned across the table, his eyes on her bosom.

"You may not be that pure maid," he said, reaching out to stroke her neck. "But the change is far from unpleasant, I assure you."

Betsy took a breath to calm her ire. They soon retired to the parlor to partake of their after dinner sherry. The time had come. Templeton sat close to her on the settee and boldly placed his hand on her knee. Even beneath her many skirts Betsy could feel his fingers digging into her soft flesh.

"I still want you, Elizabeth," he said, bringing his face to hers. "I would wager Balsam taught you well, given his tendency toward the common."

"That's enough," she said, her voice soft yet firm. "I won't sit here and—"

"And what, my darling?" he countered, grabbing her to him. "I was so close to possessing your favors, Elizabeth."

"And my dowry?" she said, leaning back from him.

His eyes narrowed. "Yes," he said bitterly. "I would have been well set had we seen our betrothal through."

"What is your meaning, sir?"

"Your dowry would have secured my standing, my dear," he said. "I needed your money, and came away from my negotiations with your father empty handed."

"But when you took the Balsam fortune," she began before she could stop herself.

Templeton caught her blunder. He came to his feet, anger twisting his aristocratic features.

"What do you know of my dealings with Balsam?" he demanded to know. "Tell me this instant!"

Betsy's own anger flowed freely now. "You cheated Michael's father out of his fortune!"

He raised a hand as if to strike her. "How dare you speak so to me?" When she shrank from him he lowered his hand. He straightened his jacket and smoothed his brow. "Balsam was so heartsick after losing his wife, I couldn't help but take what the man offered."

"You lie," Betsy said, sitting straighter. "Michael's father was heartbroken, that's true. But you used that to cheat him out of everything. You even took the family jewels."

To her amazement Templeton threw his head back and laughed.

"You figured that out, did you? Pity that's all I have left."

"But, how can that be?"

"If I was in possession of my own fortune, my dear," he began, "would I have gone through the trouble of trying to secure such an insolent chit to wife?" He grabbed her to him once more. "Although I admit I did look forward to breaking you of that stubbornness. Perhaps I shall this night, for you are a most succulent little piece."

Betsy froze as he pressed himself against her, her heart pounding as she tried to think her way out the deplorable position.

"Yes," Templeton crowed. "The sacrifice of my manly self would have been well served to gain both your dowry and your favors."

He gave a wicked laugh that chilled Betsy to the bone.

"It *was* him," Michael said from the doorway.

Templeton glanced over at Michael and Philip in obvious shock. Betsy took the opportunity to kick him in the shins to make him release her.

She stood toe to toe with him now, staring up into his ruddy face.

"How dare you think to perpetrate such a ruse?" she cried. "You cheated Michael's father and very nearly cheated my

379

own!"

Templeton drew up to his full height, his eyes narrowed to slits.

"Why you insolent little harridan!"

He raised a hand and Michael came forward.

"Lay one finger on my wife and I'll kill you with my bare hands, Templeton."

Betsy crossed her arms and gave a nod of approval. Michael gave her a look that promised a scolding later, but she merely smiled. He looked at Templeton again.

"Balsam," Templeton muttered. "And Wilton, another lucky bastard."

"I would guard my words if I were you," Philip said in a low voice. "I believe more than one gentleman would be pleased to see you gone from Society."

"What?" Templeton asked in confusion.

"Your debts are legendary," Michael said. "Far exceeding my father's, I believe."

"You'll never see a shilling of your father's fortune, Balsam," Templeton sneered. "Although I must say it brought me quite a bit of amusement before it was gone."

"It's not all gone," Betsy said.

Templeton waved his hand at her dismissively but Michael caught her meaning.

"The jewels, Templeton," Michael said. "You will return my family's jewels."

"I don't have the jewels."

"Spare us all the inconvenience of another deception," Philip said.

"You're in possession of them," Michael went on. "I will have what is due me."

"You'll never be able to prove they are yours, Balsam," Templeton said. "Your worthless sod of a father is dead, as is that temptress of a mother of yours."

Betsy's breath caught at the man's words. To her amazement her husband smiled, but it was not a smile she ever wished to have bestowed in her direction.

"You wanted her, didn't you Templeton?" Michael said. "But she loved my father as my own wife loves me. Why, the very necklace you gave Betsy was my mother's own, was it not?"

Templeton snorted. "You have no proof," he stated again.

"Oh but we do," Betsy put in. "One particular portrait hanging in Balsam Manor will easily prove our claim."

Templeton knew it then and Betsy saw it in his eyes. He took a step back from them, looking very much like a cornered animal.

"Think hard on it, Templeton," Philip said. "You certainly wouldn't wish to see this story circulated amongst the *ton*, would you? How would you be able to lure another unsuspecting heiress to use her dowry to pay for your amusements?"

Templeton cursed again, loud and long.

Much later, Betsy laid across the big bed in the guest chamber at her parents' townhouse, several lovely necklaces and bracelets dressing her otherwise naked form. Michael stood beside the bed with masculine appreciation in his gaze.

"My God," he mused aloud. "I didn't think it was possible to improve upon your beauty."

Betsy laughed, her voice husky as she ran her own eyes over her husband's fit body. She brushed her hair back over one shoulder and smiled.

"Shall I remove them, husband?" she asked coyly, coming up on one elbow.

He shook his head and stripped out of his clothes. He joined her in the bed, turning to hold her above him. She was ready for him, and took him high and deep into herself.

"Ah, Betsy love," he ground out, holding tightly to her hips. "Come to me."

She did, sobbing as she declared her love for him. He let go, exploding high inside of her. He held her then, professing his love over and over as he rained kisses on her flushed skin. When their senses were more or less returned to them he helped her remove the pieces of jewelry, setting them carefully aside. When she was no longer adorned so regally he grasped her shoulders and held her away from him.

"You're even more beautiful without them," he said, bemused.

"You, my lord, sound like a man much in love with his wife."

"Guilty as charged," he returned.

They settled down in the bed, wrapped in each other's arms.

"I'm sorry about your father's fortune, Michael," Betsy said after a bit of silence. "I know what it meant to you to recover it."

Michael shrugged and held her closer. "I thought I was nothing without it." A frown marred his brow. "That I had nothing to offer of myself." He lost his frown and smiled at her.

"But with my wife's fortune, I believe I'm well set."

"Never mind," she laughed.

"I'm sorry I wouldn't let you investigate into the entire mess sooner, Betsy." He chuckled. "Not that my words could stop you. You're quite dogged, do you know that?"

She arched a brow. "I'm a dog, am I?"

He shook his head. "No? How about a fox, then? You're quick and cunning. A vixen."

She considered his suggestion for a moment, and then nodded. "That, I'll allow."

He kissed her laughing mouth. "I love you, Betsy," he said.

Betsy touched her hand to his cheek. "And that's all I've ever needed," she said, cuddling closer.

Epilogue
Spring 1828

A fire burned brightly in the great hall of Balsam Manor, adding its warmth to the room. Its walls were no longer damp, and its space was no longer empty. Its master was no longer solemn, either.

Michael had only just returned from Bridgewater Park that very day, seeing to the horses' training at the stables there. The breeding and raising of the horses was at last settled in Cornwall as well, making good use of as well as building upon his wife's fortune. He gazed at the burning logs, marveling again at the changes made to his life since permitting a certain stubborn beauty into his heart. That thought led to the other female in his life, a joy who would no doubt prove as delightfully unsettling as his wife.

"Papa!" a high voice shouted.

He turned toward the sound, not at all surprised the mere thought of his little love sent her to him. She ran toward him with her arms outstretched, her black curls flying out behind her.

"Missy," he said, scooping her up in his arms. "Whyever are you in such a hurry?"

Michelle Elizabeth Reed, named for both his mother and hers, stared up at him with big blue eyes.

"I missed you, Papa," the little girl replied, her tiny brow furrowed. "Didn't you miss me?"

"I wasn't gone for very long, sweet," he teased. "Surely you haven't driven your mother mad in my absence?"

"Very nearly," Betsy replied, trailing in the child's wake. "One would think you were gone for a year rather than a fortnight, the way she's been carrying on."

Michael ran his gaze over his wife, finding her still as beautiful as the first time he'd seen her in the stables at the Derby.

"And what of you, wife?" he asked. "Did you miss your husband?"

Betsy came up to him, placing her hand on his cheek.

"Sorely," she returned, brushing his lips with hers.

"We have to see the little horses, Papa," Missy said. "They've missed you too, I think."

Michael chuckled. They did indeed have quite a few foals to see to, a fact that promised an excellent return in a few years should the offspring prove as fast and strong as their sires. Betsy updated him on the horses' fine condition and the two of them began discussing the strengths and weaknesses of the one-year-olds in their possession.

"Mama said you would take me riding when you returned, Papa," Missy cut in. "Will you take me riding, Papa? Right now?"

Michael laughed. "All right, Missy." He set her down on her feet. He and Betsy shared a look. He fixed his eyes on his daughter once more. "Can your mother come along?"

"Oh yes!" Missy giggled. "I do so love to watch Mama ride."

The three of them walked toward the stables, hands clasped. Betsy mounted first, soon riding over the grounds in her usual manner. Her long, thick chestnut braid, bounced and soared behind her as her mount fairly ate up the ground. Michael lifted Missy up and placed her on his shoulders as the two of them watched her.

His mind went back to that dark time before she came into his life, a time when regaining his fortune and holding stubbornly to his self-reliance was of the utmost importance. Betsy had changed all that for him. He'd once likened her to a breath of fresh air, one that brought new life to him. He now knew she had come into his life with much more force than that.

"Ooh, look at Mama ride!" Missy said, breaking through his reverie. "What's a lady fox called again?"

Michael knew where this was headed. Since before Missy was born, he'd teased Betsy with the nickname, but he hadn't thought Missy aware of it.

"It's called a vixen, sweetheart."

Missy nodded. "Right. Fixin."

"Vixen."

She nodded again. "Uncle Philip showed me the fox at the hunt last week, Papa. Mama's as fast as that fox."

"That's very true, sweet," Michael said with a grin.

Betsy was as quick as a fox, and she certainly was a vixen. His vixen. She was sharp and determined and the very best woman he knew.

Betsy reined in her horse and gracefully dismounted. He took her hand and said a silent prayer of thanks as he kissed her. She was his vixen and his love. She was his everything.

And he was ever grateful that she'd been determined to have him.

About the Author

JoMarie DeGioia is a bestselling author of Historical and Contemporary Romance. She's known Mickey Mouse from the "inside," has been a copyeditor for her tiny town's newspaper, and a bookseller. A hybrid author, she also writes Young Adult Fantasy/Adventure stories, New Adult Romance and Paranormal Romance. She gets lost in DIY projects around the house and works out plot ideas during long runs. She divides her time between Central Florida and New England.

Discover other books by JoMarie DeGioia

The Bridgewater Brides series, including

The Heir's Treasure

The Viscount's Vixen

The Earl's Beauty

The Gentlemen Undercover series, including

A Hero and a Gentleman

The Shopgirls of Bond Street series, including

That Determined Mister Latham

The Dashing Nobles series, including

More Than Passion

Pride and Fire

Just Perfect

More Than Charming

The Gentlemen Undercover series, including

A Hero and a Gentleman

The Cypress Corners series, including

Finding Harmony

Taming Jake

Loving Cassie

Winning Ben

Showing Jessie

Seeing Shannon (Barefoot Bay Kindle Worlds Novella)

Dreaming Eli

Giving Chase (Barefoot Bay Kindle Worlds Novella)

Kissing Bree

The Gifted YA Fantasy/Adventure Trilogy, including

Gifted

Braunachs of the Dell series, including

Luke's Gold

Patrick's Promise

Connect with me online

Twitter: https://twitter.com/JoMarieDeGioia

Facebook: https://www.facebook.com/JoMarie.DeGioia.Author

Website: www.jomariedegioia.com